HIS MASTER'S DAUGHTER

Christina Rich

Published by Forget Me Not Romances, a division of Winged Publications, previously published by Heartsong Presents

Copyright © 2019 by Christina Rich

All rights reserved. No part of this publication may be resold, reproduced, stored in a retrieval system, or transmitted in any form or by any means, electronic, mechanical, recording, or otherwise, without the prior written permission of the author. Piracy is illegal. Thank you for respecting the hard work of this author.

This is a work of fiction. All characters, names, dialogue, incidents, and places either are the product of the author's imagination or are used fictitiously. Any resemblance to actual events, locales, or people, living or dead, is entirely coincidental.

ISBN-13: **979-8-8689-8420-4**

Chapter One

Near En Gedi, Judah
835 BC

Ari's heart hammered in his chest as the horses thundered toward the groves. Instinct had him reaching for where his sword should have been, a sword he had discarded years ago when he'd traded his life of a warrior for that of a bond servant. He'd been a fool to leave his weapons hidden away when danger lurked close at hand, but he could not very well play the servant dressed as a soldier.

It would do no good to dwell on this lack of foresight, even if it had almost got him killed years ago. Instead, he picked up a curved lava stone and prepared for battle.

He peered around the corner. The queen's soldiers brought their mounts to a halt on the dusty pathway, their eyes trained in the distance. Ari followed their line of sight and inhaled a sharp breath.

Sh'mira, his master's daughter, stood at the edge of the grove. She cradled a white flower in her palm, her nose mere inches from the petals with her eyes closed. He knew she was lost in the fragrance as she was wont to do and completely unaware of her audience.

Hefting an empty pot onto his shoulders, he straightened to his full height. With the lava stone firm in his palm, he stepped out of the shadows and made as if he were about his everyday chores.

Perhaps his presence would discourage the warriors from their wicked intent, for their arrival could result in nothing but evil. Ever since Queen Athaliah had killed most of the royal family near seven years ago—her sons, daughters and grandchildren—the royal guards had terrorized all of Judah. Stories of their infamous conquests had reached even this remote village, putting a fear into the hearts and minds of all. A fear that rivaled the fear of the fabled Leviathan and other sea monsters.

A horse snorted. Ari's feet wobbled on the pebbles as he worked his way toward the grove. He'd never feared a battle before and although his warrior instincts thrummed through his veins, his years out of service shook his confidence. Perhaps, it was the crude scar on his thigh, a reminder of his last encounter with the queen's men.

"You should not be here alone."

Mira turned, her lips tight, gaze guarded. "Who are you to tell me such?"

He sat the clay pot to the ground and broke off a dying branch. "A servant looking after his master's interest."

"I am a grown woman, able to care for myself." She jerked a withered limb from its mooring. "Just because I am *maimed*," she bit, "does not mean I'm helpless."

He dropped his hands to his sides. Her gaze a pool of desert water after a heavy rain. "I did not mean—"

This woman was far from helpless, he knew that.

"Did you not?" She tossed the branch into the pot. "You are forever following me around tending *my* duties. You would think Father bonded you to be my nurse."

"I only think to repay your kindness for tending my wounds when I first arrived."

"For seven years?" She let out a disgruntled sigh and walked further down the lane.

Ari grabbed her arm, turning her back to him. Her cheeks flushed and his warmed at the contact. He released her. Crossing his arms over his chest, he stepped back. "If not for you, I would have died. I would not have you meet the same fate." He tilted his head toward the guards high on their mounts.

She leaned forward, peering around one of the trees and then straightened. The length of her tresses brushed over his forearm like a feather. The flowery fragrance of henna blossoms tickled his nose. How had he not noticed this about her? Odd, one touch after all these years, and he was suddenly aware of how she smelled.

A whinny from the horse brought his head back to reality. He glanced over his shoulder and bit down on his tongue. The devastation left in the guards' wake, remained fresh in his mind even after all these years. The young king's mother had been badly used before they slit her throat. Fortunately, Jehosheba, the boy's aunt and Tama, Mira's cousin, who had been serving as a nurse in the palace, had the wits about them to take the babe from his dying mother, giving Judah hope for the future. A truth Mira did not know. "In their eyes, all women, young and old, are helpless."

Mira's gaze shifted toward the riders once again. "I will not cower before them."

Her lack of cowardice was worthy of any warrior. However, it was not courage that fueled her attitude. "Would your pride see your father brokenhearted?"

She sucked in a sharp breath. "I wonder how a man of your wisdom became destitute enough to become a servant."

The horses' hooves came closer. "As you know, I repay a debt of kindness. Your father offered me refuge when I was wounded. Come," he extended his hand toward the small village. "We must get you back within the walls of your home."

The sound of the muffled clops halted, replaced by the creaking of leather as the men dismounted. Ari's muscles tensed. He faced the pair of guards and forced his life's blood to an even rhythm. The men standing before him were the queen's own personal guards which meant they were on a mission much higher than destroying altars to God and keeping peace. Had they discovered the child survived?

"Looks like we've interrupted two lovers."

She squeaked. "You dare—"

Ari pierced her with a dark look and shoved her behind his back. He bowed his head. "Forgive my mistress."

*

Words clung to the tip of her tongue. Self-control had never been one of her gifts. The blame could be tossed at Ari's feet for causing her lack of speech. His humility had been replaced with an uncharacteristic bold protectiveness leaving her confused. Not to mention the touch on her arm had caused her knees to turn to honey and her toes to curl. Something Esha, the man seeking her hand in marriage, had never caused.

Who was this man who often offended her with his kindness? This man who insisted she was weak and helpless by his actions?

"She's distraught over the immature crop." Ari picked a budding green fruit from the tree as if to prove his statement.

"Your mistress, you say?" The taller of the two soldiers stepped forward and pushed Ari aside. He lifted his fingers and touched her hair.

Bile churned in her stomach. It was squashed when Ari grasped the guard's wrist and stepped back in front of her. Protecting her like a shield. The shorter of the two soldiers placed his hand on the hilt of his sword even as he took a step back.

The man laughed. "You are bold, slave."

"Servant. I am a servant." He dropped the soldier's wrist. "It is my duty to protect my master's property. Including his daughter's virtue." Ari seemed to grow ten feet taller and two feet wider. His bronzed skin gleamed in the hot sun. His stance and bearing caused both guards to shrink. How had she not noticed how strong and handsome he was? *Because he treats you like a crippled beggar.*

"If this woman's virtue is a matter of importance to her father, why does he allow her to venture away from her home alone and without covering her head?"

Mira bit down on her tongue. Her virtue was hers alone, not her father's. Not any man's. However, the law said otherwise. A law the guard did not recognize. She arched onto her toes and tried to peer over Ari's shoulder. His silky black hair lifted on a breeze, tickling her nose and forcing her back to her feet.

Ari shifted, blocking more of her view. "Forgive me, we were under the belief God's Law no longer mattered."

Laughter erupted from both the guards. "You are correct, slave. God is dead. The queen's law rules this land, along with the wooden idols she worships."

Hidden behind his back she couldn't see much, but she could see the tick in Ari's jaw, feel the heat emanating from his skin, the controlled anger exuding with each of his measured breaths. She knew he did not approve of Queen Athaliah's worship of idols made by men, knew he continued to worship God and keep His commands.

A low rumble vibrated from Ari. "Her—"

She fisted Ari's tunic in her hands, halting his words.

"Her father, my master is expecting us."

Mira relaxed her hold on his garment but kept her fingers pressed against his back. His solid presence brought her comfort in the midst of danger, and for once she was thankful for his interference.

"Your master can wait." The guard reached around Ari and grabbed a hold of her wrist.

Chapter Two

The soldier yanked on Mira's arm, pulling her from behind Ari's back. Ari bit down on the inside of his cheek. He would not allow this man to harm her. However, if he fought the men with the training he'd received among the temple guards, they'd know he was not who he seemed to be. They'd wonder why a warrior priest pretended to be a servant among a simple farmer and his family and Athaliah's entire army would descend upon this tiny village with destruction. The past seven years of servitude would be for naught if the rightful king of Judah met his death because Ari could not maintain control.

When the guard grabbed a handful of Mira's hair and buried his nose in the locks, every muscle in Ari's body vibrated with the need to kill him. He palmed the lava stone and shifted forward ready to die protecting his mistress as she had done for him when she'd fought off a pack of dogs ready to devour his battered body. That night, long ago, burned in his memory. The way she had fended off the dogs with no more than a firebrand. He had been beaten by men such as these, left barely alive only to be ravaged by wild animals. If it had not been for her and her courage, he would have died at the jaws of the hungry beasts. He would not allow her to be treated harshly by these men.

Lord, I need your help.

The wail of a ram's horn echoed across the rocky desert. A call Ari loved from his days as temple guard. The use of the shofar by the queen's soldiers was one of many abominations marring Judah. It often brought great sorrow to his heart. However, he could not be more thankful for the answer to his hasty prayer.

"I promise to return," the Queen's guard said as he released Mira before he and his companion mounted their horses and cantered away. Praise God the patrol obeyed the command, leaving Mira unharmed.

She touched his arm, rocking him on his feet. Without thinking, he traced his finger along her brow and the curve of her ear, tucking her hair behind her back until his hand rested on her shoulders. "Are you well?"

"I am. Thank you."

Her graciousness proved she'd had a fright. He'd been scared too.

How close she had come to being used. Her chances for a good marriage near lost. He dropped his gaze to the finger imprints on her wrist and shoved his hand through his hair. Stepping away from her sweet innocence, he expelled the breath caught in his lungs. His pulse kicked.

He glanced toward where the soldiers had ridden. He refused to allow his pulse to settle until the dust cloud disappeared into the horizon.

"You should not leave the walls alone." He faced her, arms crossed.

She swallowed. A wounded look fluttered through her eyes as she knotted her hands into her tunic. "I have chores to attend."

Reaching out, he took her fingers in his. The tips warm in his palm. "Even so..."

Mira pulled away from him and released a shuddering breath. All civility between them gone. "Even so I will not live no better than a slave in my father's house, being told when and where I can go." She stalked away.

Her words cut, but he knew she said them out of fear. Fear of what those men could have done to her. What they might do if they returned as promised.

Guilt stabbed him at the thought of the queen's cruel minions destroying the innocence of his master's daughter. The soldiers preyed on the weak, the helpless.

How was he going to keep her safe from another incident if she insisted on being stubborn? For he had no doubt the guards would return.

His first priority was to protect the child king. Just as it had been since he'd followed Tama and the child to this small village that awful night. They'd left Jerusalem because of the danger, and now it seemed to have followed them here.

He scrubbed his palm over his face. Tama, the boy's nurse, would no doubt miss her cousin, and Mira her, but perhaps it was time to take him and leave. But to leave his master's family, defenseless? Leave Mira to the mercy of the soldiers? There had to be a way to protect them all.

He returned to his work, his mind heavy. Why had the soldiers even come? And why now, after six years of absence? He jabbed the lava stone into the basin and scooped out the last bit of mud. He smoothed the clay texture over the stones, filling the gaps in the rock wall.

"Shalom."

Ari spun on his heel, the tool cutting into his palm. His eyes focused on the hunched, graying man before him. Ari bowed low befor his master whom he wanted to please. "Shalom, *adon*."

His master gripped Ari's shoulder. The warmth of the aged hand reminded him of the man's waning strength.

"Come now, my son. There is no need to be startled. It is I, Caleb, your friend. Rise."

Ari scraped the lava rock clean before balancing it on the edge of the earthen bowl. He dipped his hands into a small basin of water, scrubbed away the clinging plaster, and dried them on a cloth.

Straightening to his full height, he scanned the area for a sign of the queen's soldiers. "My forgiveness, Master Caleb. I had just seen the queen's soldiers."

"No forgiveness need, Ariel. I saw them ride away in haste and wondered at their presence. Perhaps, they are keeping peace."

Peace, when they inflicted so much violence? Ari shifted his gaze beyond the rugged hills toward Jerusalem. When would Jehoiada, the high priest, send for them? Perhaps he should risk sending a message to the high priest about the increased patrols in the area? It was time to take the boy and leave. "Is that all, Master Caleb?"

"You have done a fine job, Ariel. It is nearly finished, yes?" Caleb ran his fingers over the contours of the piled stones.

"Another layer of plaster and it will be complete." He had labored beneath the hot sun for months over what would be Mira's portion of Caleb's home once she married. He had prayed for her happiness and asked the Lord to bestow upon her great blessings as he had set the stones. It was the closest he would ever come to ministering to God's people since he couldn't perform the temple duties. Not that he bemoaned his fate. Keeping the young king safe was an honor.

Sorrow filled Caleb's eyes. "These walls should have been built by Mira's bridegroom."

A protective instinct gripped Ari. He'd seen the way the men of the village steered clear of his master's daughter. Even the promise of great wealth had not swayed many to seek out her hand and Esha, the one that did, was no more than a drunkard with idle hands refusing to help harvest the crops.

If Ari weren't bound by vows already made before he had come to this village, he would offer his troth to her if only to save her from a cruel marriage to a sluggard. It was the least he owed her and Caleb for saving his life.

Caleb dropped his hands to his sides and sighed. "Alas, I fear she will never marry. I know I should force the issue. It is well past time for her to do so, and my health is waning." He eyed Ari. "But who is worthy of her?"

The urge to respond expanded Ari's chest. From all he'd seen, no man was worthy of Mira, even when she was contentious, a tendency which only seemed to occur with him, but it was not his place to say.

Caleb cocked his head to the side. "Forgive the ramblings of an old man?"

"There is naught to forgive, *adon*."

"Come. Let us sit in the shade." Caleb waved his hand toward the terebinth tree.

Taking his master's arm, Ari helped him walk the short distance to the cut bench beneath the large tree where the thick leaves would shield them from the hot sun. Ari sat beside his master. Looking across the pale rocky desert, he waited for Caleb to speak, wondering if he should tell his master about the guards accosting his daughter.

"The Year of Jubilee is coming. I am certain the queen has sent her soldiers to ensure there will be no uprisings. Yet, that is not what troubles me." Caleb drew in a slow breath. "Your time of servitude is near its end."

Caleb's soft tones skidded over Ari's heart. Caleb had been all that was kind, and Ari would stay if God willed it. However, his life was not his own. Until he was released from his vow, his life belonged only to the Lord and his duty to protect the child.

"I know not whence you came or why or what choice you will make when it is time to release you."

At this moment, Ari himself did not know if he would leave, or choose to remain bound to Caleb. The choice was not up to him, but God.

Caleb wrapped his fingers around Ari's wrist. "I am an old man, Ari. I have come to think of you with great fondness."

"As I you, *adon*," Ari assured. Caleb had been like a father and Leah like a mother. While the affection he felt for them could never compare to his love for his own parents, he had grown to love them deeply. His years spent in the temple had blessed him with discipline, but garnered little, if any, affection outside his family's travels to Jerusalem.

Caleb's dark eyes pierced his. "Please. Allow me to finish. You have worked much harder than all my servants. Yet, I know," he tapped his fist against his chest, "you are no man's servant."

No. Ari belonged to no man, only to the Lord.

"I do not know your quest or what lies ahead. You are a great teacher, Ariel, and should be teaching God's laws."

Ari thrust his fingers through his hair. Had Caleb discovered the truth?

He had never told Caleb about his past or the reasons he had sold himself as a servant. His master had never asked. If he did, Ari would not lie. But he could not, would not, confide in his master about his true mission.

"Do not worry over much, Ari. Perhaps, I assume incorrectly. You have a gift." Caleb paused briefly. "You teach young Joash well the ways of the Lord. Ways not many are blessed with."

Rising from the bench, Ari rolled his shoulders. His years of training for temple guard had never prepared him for the battle waging within his heart. Although Caleb's assumptions were wrong, he was too close to the truth.

"I have taught all who were willing to listen to God's law."

Caleb nodded. "Yes, and as I said, a fine teacher you are, too. However, I cannot help but think your teachings are purely for the boy's benefit."

"You are mistaken. The boy is an eager learner, but" Ari said, shaking his head, "it is for my benefit just as much as any." In this he did not lie. Sharing the law kept him from forgetting the words written on his heart, for when he left Jerusalem, he had left most everything behind. His temple duties, his home…even his ambitions had been left in the tunnels beneath Jerusalem when their queen went on her murdering rampage, seeking to destroy her husband's heirs, King David's descendants.

"I mean no offense." Caleb rose from the cut stone. "Come. It is hot. Let us get a drink from the well."

Ari appreciated the change of subject, but he would rather convince Caleb that he had not singled the child king out when it came to teaching God's laws. However, Ari could tell Caleb was done speaking on the subject. "Sh'mira has just gone that way."

She would not approve of her father walking so far from his bed.

"Has she, now?" Caleb's feet hesitated and then he smiled before resuming. "Let us see what my child has to say, today."

The corners of Ari's mouth lifted. Mira's tongue could be viperous when she was in a good mood. Given the way she had left him only moments before, her mood was far from joyous. He should at least try and deter his master from a confrontation with his daughter.

"You should allow Leah to tend you, *adon*." Ari grasped his master's arm and assisted him along the cobbled pathway. Caleb's tunic dragged along the stones.

"Bah, I may be old, but I can still walk outside of my walls. Even if my daughter thinks otherwise."

Ari halted the chuckle in his chest. His master sounded much like his daughter. "The heat is heavy. Look." He swiped beads of moisture from his forehead.

Caleb laughed. "Then maybe it is you whom Leah should tend to."

Having learned long ago that his master was as stubborn as two oxen with full bellies, Ari chose to keep quiet.

Caleb glanced at Ari, his eyes filled with emotion. "If you choose to stay as my son, you are most welcome."

His heart swelled at Caleb's affection. "I am honored and blessed by your offer."

He gazed toward Jerusalem. His deception made him unworthy of such an honor. Until he received word, he would not be free to make his own decisions. Although, he wouldn't mind staying. Caleb's family had become like his own. But it was not up to him. Resigned to continue his trust in the Lord, he nodded. "If the Lord wills it."

"There are many who would think my daughter cursed because of her maimed fingers and scarred hands and thus wish not to marry her, not even for the price of my land, but you, my friend, you treat her with respect and kindness. You would care for her with or without my legacy."

His heart clogged in his throat. He had only moments before entertained thoughts of a union with Mira, if only to keep her from a wicked marriage with Esha, the drunkard. However, with the words spoken aloud by her father, he knew it impossible. "I treat all the same, *adon*. As God would have it."

Caleb's breathing became labored as they crested the hill. "I understand. You must have family somewhere."

Ari shrugged his shoulders. What was he to say? The truth would bring more questions. Caleb might be aged, but he was not addle minded.

"Abba."

Mira. The sound of her soft lilt rolled along the cobbled stones and banded around his heart. Ari lifted his head and locked his gaze on her. She did not sound, nor look, as if she'd just been accosted by armed men with evil intentions. Instead, she sat on the edge of the well at the bottom of the hill, her posture elegant, graceful. Like the purest of waters cascading over the contours of lifeless rocks, she brightened the mundane and turned the barren landscape around her into a breathtaking oasis.

Had Caleb's offer cemented her into his thoughts and turned him into a poet? Or was it his fear for her life, the need to protect her?

Respect and kindness was not enough to spend an eternity together, not when he wanted the love his parents shared. What Caleb and Leah had, too. Besides, even if he could be swayed to marry Mira, she did not like him much.

"Allow me to give you a piece of wisdom." Caleb chuckled. "Nothing puts the fear of the Lord in a man more than seeing his daughter, whether it is seeing her for the first time upon her birth, or seeing her now, knowing her rebuke, though meant with every breath of her love, will flay my bare flesh like a whip."

His master actually looked as if he had paled at the sight of his daughter. Ari felt pale himself, but it had nothing to do with fear of her tongue and everything to do with how she had begun to make him feel. She made the air seem freer, lighter. She brought out his protective instincts. At the same time, she drove him mad with confusion. And that alone was enough to reject his master's offer, if one were to officially come. However, if Mira showed any amount of willingness…

"Save me, will you?"

Ari laughed. "Of course, Adon." But who was going to save him from being shackled with a contentious wife if he couldn't remove the madness plaguing him where Mira was concerned.

Chapter Three

"You have eyes for the slave, now?" Rubiel said. "He is not for you."

Mira dipped her head to hide the blushing of her cheeks at her sister's words. It had not been the first time she'd watched him over the years, though she had never before been caught. He was a fine man, as handsome as any. His bearing strong and proud, yet humble and diligent. He was unlike any man she had ever known, free or slave. His heart seemed good. Yet, he angered her often.

True, he saw past her imperfections. He never looked at her with disgust. Instead, he coddled her, suffocated her as if she were...*helpless*. Defenseless. Of course, today, she would have been at the mercy of the soldiers if Ari had not intervened. She was thankful, yet angry. Why?

"What authority have you to say such things, Sister?"

Rubiel gripped Mira's chin and looked her in the eyes. "He is a bond servant, Mira. You should seek to marry your equal."

Mira bowed her head releasing her sister's hold. She recalled the way the corded muscles in his shoulders and arms vibrated. The coldness in his eyes as if he could fell the soldiers with one look. Even armed with their swords they had backed away from Ari as if they too thought him deadly.

For a small moment she had glimpsed a different man. A dangerous man, one who was not from humble means. A man far above her status. In that moment he brought to mind the stories of King David's mighty men. Men who singlehandedly defeated great armies. "It does not mean he is any less of a man."

"Oh, dear. Ari is very honorable, but he will soon leave us."

The thought hitched in her throat. What would her father do without him? "Perhaps, he might stay."

"What of his people? Have you thought of them? He might have a wife."

Although she'd often wondered where Ari had come from she never once had imagined he might have a wife. True, he often left their villa with her father's permission, but she never thought it was to visit family. Surely, if he'd had one she would have known.

"You need a local man. What of Esha? He seems to like you well enough. He works hard and is handsome enough." Rubiel raised the jar full of water from the well.

"Esha works hard on drinking Abba's wine."

Rubiel laughed. "What does that matter? He'd be a good husband sleeping all the time as he does."

"Bah, I would rather have no husband than one of Esha's character, even if he is "handsome enough" as you say. I have enough chores to attend. I do not need to take care of a drunkard as well."

"Mira, you must truly consider Esha. My Nathan says he is the one man who does not mind that you are maimed. Besides, if Ari stays, he can help you take care of your husband." Rubiel glanced at the man walking beside her father with appreciation. "He's certainly strong enough to tend to your future husband. Ari does everything else for you."

"Esha is not my betrothed, nor will he ever be." Heat flooded her cheeks. "Besides, if Ari stays it'll be for Abba and no other reason. He only helps me to repay a debt he believes he owes."

"For saving his life?" Rubiel nodded toward Mira's hand. "It is commendable of you, Sister, for saving him from those dogs when he was left for dead, especially with your fear of the beasts. Does the slave know? Does he know why your fingers are scarred and twisted?"

Mira shook her head and curled her mangled fingers into the folds of her tunic. If only she had listened to her father when she was but a girl she never would have wandered off alone and been attacked by a wild dog. Then she could have married long ago. Married for love, not for the price of her father's land, which she had no doubt was all Esha hoped to gain. She closed her eyes and gathered what courage she could find.

"Abba's patience is at an end. I heard him speaking with *Ima*. If you do not find a husband soon, he'll accept Esha's suit."

Esha might be handsome, but she didn't miss the look of revulsion whenever he spied her. No doubt, he would be a cruel husband. Perhaps, not abusive, but he would neglect her. Given the way he reacted whenever he glanced at her hand, there would be no union between them. No children. She was certain he only coveted her father's land and his wine.

"If only there were more men as diligent as Ari. One who has not forsaken God. One who will see Abba's land become even more prosperous." One who made her heart to flutter as Ari had done when he'd smoothed her hair behind her shoulder earlier. If only he felt something besides pity for her, maybe a little respect for her abilities to care for a household.

"Your slave will be free in a few days' time. He'll leave as they all do."

"Ari will stay," Mira predicted. "He has to. Abba depends on him too much." If he didn't, then she would follow him and convince him to return to her father's house.

Mira hefted the yoke upon her shoulders. Rubiel attached the jars of water to their hooks, the weight boring into her neck. Before Mira headed toward her father, Rubiel dipped a cup into the earthen jar and placed it in her good hand draped over the yoke.

"Here, take this to Father. He is weakening." Her sister kissed her cheek. "Mira, I hope for your sake you are right, but please, for me, beware your heart."

Beware her heart? The man may have caused her pulse to beat a little faster, but she did not love him. He was good. Honest. Hardworking, and he cared for her father as a son should. "It is not for my heart, dear Sister, but for Father's that Ari must stay."

She met her father and Ari as they reached the bottom of the hill. She gave Ari an apologetic look when he took the cup from her hand and pressed it to her father's lips. Her father labored to control his breathing.

"You should not be here, Abba," she chastised.

Ari handed the cup back to her and lifted the yoke from her neck.

"You would deny me your beauty, Sh'mira," her father said, a twinkle in his eye.

"Father, do not think you can charm your way out of this. Does Ima know you have left your bed?" She wrapped her arm around her father's frail shoulders and ushered him back toward home.

"It was your mother's idea I get fresh air."

"I do not think she meant for you to walk so far. Are you trying to meet your death?"

Ari raised a dark, winged brow. He must have gained confidence from their earlier encounter with the guards if he dared chastise her, even if it was a silent one. It had not escaped her notice over the years that this man's size could probably command an entire army, especially since he easily managed her father. But now, she had no doubt there was much more to him than servanthood. Knew with certainty he could command respect from his enemies with one look.

"Would it be such a bad thing, Daughter?"

"Abba," she cried.

"*Adon*, you should not speak so carelessly." Ari's words were for her father, but his gaze bored into hers. He seemed to will her strength and understanding. "As much as we would all long to pass from this earth and into the great rest of our God, you would be greatly missed."

"My apologies, Sh'mira. My bones are weary."

"Soon. Soon, Abba, you will rest." She patted his arm. Her father longed for an eternal rest, but a selfish desire to cling to him claimed her. Losing him would break her heart.

Her father halted his steps. The dust covering the pathway swirled over his sandaled feet. "First, I must tend to business in town." He glanced at Ari. "I need the mind of

Solomon and the strength of Samson. I need you to attend me, Ari."

The corners of Ari's mouth curved upward. "Of course, *adon*."

Panic filled her chest, squeezing and tightening. The guards promised to return. Who would protect her? Certainly not Esha. And what if they accosted her father on the road? Would Ari's lone strength be enough to see her father protected? "You cannot, Abba. Not until you are much improved." Mira used her eyes to plead with Ari to not placate her father.

"The matter is of importance. It can wait no longer, Daughter. Besides, Hebron is a day there, a day back. Not much at all, you will see," her father replied.

"But…"

Ari's brow furrowed.

"The queen's—"

"She is right, *adon*. You cannot think to leave your family unprotected."

She silently thanked Ari for not revealing the earlier events to her father. He'd only fret, weakening his health.

"I would send another, but I do not trust…" Her father began to wheeze and cough. She patted him on the back as Ari held on to his arm.

"We will discuss the matter more after you rest," Ari said, shadows evident in his eyes. Grim lines etched his handsome face. It was as if the yoke he bore for her was not the only burden he carried. For the first time, with her sister's words fresh in her mind, she wondered about his days before he arrived on her father's land, lips parched and body battered. Dying.

Footsteps on the path interrupted her musings. Fear pounded in her blood. Had the soldiers returned? She lifted her eyes, shielding them against the sun with her free hand and breathed a sigh of relief at the sight of Joash.

He ran toward them, his dark curls bouncing just above his shoulders. His tunic danced against his thighs, exposing his scarred knees. The scrapes the only evidence that this young boy, six summers old, was but a child. Such a shame he did not laugh and play more. He was too serious, much like the man who diligently taught him God's Law. Ari's arrival had truly been a gift from God, not just to her father, but as a mentor to their people during a time when the leader of Judah had banned God from the land.

Joash stopped. And as if in command of all the world, he lifted his head and looked her father in the eye. "Abba, Leah has sent me to fetch you."

"Is that so?"

"I would not lie," Joash replied as if offended. Mira wanted to smile at the boy who had filled a special place in her heart, who had placated the emptiness of her womb all these years.

"Of course not, my son." Her father extended his hand out for Joash to escort him home. "You should do as you are bid."

"Yes, Abba." Joash placed his small hand into her father's frail palm. "Leah has made challah."

"Has she now?"

Her stomach grumbled at the mention of her mother's fresh-baked bread. Brushing her troublesome veil back over her shoulders, she fell into step beside Ari.

"That one is too serious," she said.

"As he should be," Ari replied.

She tilted her chin and considered the boy. Her cousin had arrived with the boy near six years before, only days after Ari had. She'd claimed the babe's parents had been killed, left an orphan. Her father took him in and began raising him as his own. "How so? He's only a child. He should run and play. He takes his studies too much to heart."

Ari twisted his lips, which she found endearing, although what she really wanted to do was to run her fingers along the seam and smooth them into the heart-warming smile she had found appealing.

"If there were more men such as that child, there would be less horror in the land."

It was the closest she'd ever heard him come to speaking about the terror ruling Judah. "You speak of our queen?"

He looked into her eyes as if searching her soul. "It does not matter of what I speak. But the boy...it is obvious God has destined great things for him."

Mira laughed. "It is not likely Joash will rise one morning from tending sheep and become a king like David."

It was barely perceptible. If she hadn't made it her duty to memorize Ari's every nuance and bearing over the years—not because she fancied herself in love with him but rather so she could find his weaknesses, make him feel helpless as he did her—she never would have known. But she saw. It was almost unbelievable. He stumbled. This sure, strong man tripped over his feet and stumbled.

"Be careful, Mira." Her name, a mere whisper, rolled over his tongue and curled into her heart. Her breath caught in her throat for he had never before addressed her by her name. "Our Lord may decide to prove you wrong."

Chapter Four

"I do not like your leaving, Ari."

He finished rinsing the plaster from the pottery bowl and rose to greet the woman who had risked her life to carry Joash away from Athaliah's clutches. "I do not like it either, Tama. There is naught to be done, unless you wish to tell your uncle the truth about the boy. Would you place your people in more danger than they already are? Would you risk sacrificing Judah's future king?"

"You know I would not." Tama wrapped her arms around her waist. Fine lines crinkled at the corners of her eyes. Her youth had long since vanished. "With the soldiers prowling…" Dropping her hands to her sides, she bowed her head in defeat.

Ari lifted her chin with the tip of his finger. There was no doubt the burden of their secret weighed heavy on her shoulders, as it did his. The soldiers' presence seemed to be weakening her resolve to see their mission through. He stared into her eyes and willed her strength, courage. "Tama, if not for you and Jehosheba, the boy would have perished along with all the others. You've been a dauntless protector, and I believe you will continue to do so in my absence."

"I am not sure I can."

"You have no choice." His voice sounded harsh even to his own ears. Given the widening of her eyes, she heard it, too. He meant to encourage not dishearten her. He scrubbed his palm over his face and released a frustrated sigh. "My apologies, Tama. I did not intend to speak harshly. I will only be gone two days. Three at the most. Be vigilant, as I know you are. If trouble should arise, you know what to do.

All will be well, Tama. You will see. We must place our hope in our God."

Tama nodded. She stiffened and seemed to stand taller. "You are correct, Ari. Our Lord has not hidden us here for all these years only to deliver us into the hands of our enemies." She glanced up to the darkening sky. "I cannot say I look forward to our return to Jerusalem when the time comes, but I'll be happy when Jehoiada sends for us."

Ari understood. The elders had continually praised him for his gift of perseverance, and even though he considered his current duty an honor, he longed for the day when he didn't have to be on guard and ever watchful, the day when the child would become another's responsibility.

Henna lightly danced in the air, and an awareness of her presence pricked his nape. "Hello, Mira."

"Mira," Tama greeted her cousin with a kiss to each cheek. "I was admiring the work Ari has done to your home. Not much longer and it will be complete."

Mira's cheeks reddened, and she dipped her chin, looking to her feet. "That is what I'm told."

His heart saddened at her lack of enthusiasm. Did she not want a home of her own? Did she not want to marry? Given her suitor, he did not blame her.

"I do not mean to interrupt." She glanced at him through hooded eyes. "Abba seeks word with you, Ari."

"Shalom, Ari." Tama bowed.

"Shalom, Tama." She skirted around the corner of what was to be Mira's home.

"I pray our hope is not in vain," he said beneath his breath. As soon as the words were out of his mouth, he regretted speaking them. His lack of faith soured his stomach.

"Not in vain?"

He shook his muddled thoughts. "Pardon?"

"You pray our hope is not in vain for what?" Mira waited for an answer.

He half growled and half laughed at his lack of secrecy. "Given, you do not seem pleased with your home—"

"Oh, it is not that," she said, ducking beneath the doorposts. Her fingers glided along the scrolling. Her eyes filled with delight. She glanced at him. "It is beautiful, Ari.

The time you've taken to build—the artistry—I am very pleased." She twisted her lips. "It is Esha I am displeased with. I had hoped he would find another bride, but I fear my father's land is too much a prize."

He smiled. "In that, I fear you are correct. Have you taken your concerns to God?"

She tilted her head in consideration. "I—I have not thought—that is, no, I have not."

"One thing I know." He paused, glancing through the window he had shaped with the stones so the evening twilight could shine. "God delights in our conversation with Him. He asks we seek His face, even in small matters."

She dipped her chin, kicking the toe of her sandal into the ground. "Even our fears?"

He drew in a shuddering breath. "Even our fears. Did not King David write, 'Bow down thine ear to me; deliver me speedily: be thou my strong rock, for an house of defense to save me'?"

The corners of her mouth turned upward. "'For thou art my rock and my fortress; therefore for thy name's sake lead me, and guide me.'"

"Mira, you must seek God, in times of trouble, and trust He'll be your rock and fortress."

Dropping her hands to her sides, her smile disappeared. "I fear the guards will return while you're gone."

He longed to reach out and hold her hand, to reassure her all would be well. He took a step from her. "I do not like leaving either. Even if I were to stay, I am only one man. A servant. I would not be able to defend your father's village against the queen's men."

She shook her head, the bronze silk veil ornamented with tiny glass beads covering her hair danced at her shoulders. "But I saw you. I saw them tremble before you—"

"Enough. Every day since I have been in your father's house you have scorned my help and now you seek what I cannot give." She crossed her arms over her chest. "I am only a man, unworthy of your faith. Forgive—"

Mira held up her hand and pushed past him, but not before he witnessed a tear sliding down her cheek.

"Wait," he followed behind her. "If we tell your father."

She swiped at her eyes before facing him. "No. I refuse to be the cause of his health failing any further. He'd only worry. You go, as you must. As I said before, I'm neither defenseless nor helpless."

He watched the gentle sway of her hips as she walked away and wondered what had just happened. Her behavior left him confused. Her lack of courage and diminishing pride proved the incident with the soldiers had pierced her sheltered innocence.

*

Clenching her fists, she paced. Why could the man not see reason? Why could he not convince her father to stay? Her father always listened to him. Always. And now that she wanted, no, needed his help, he refused.

"Daughter, why do you fret so?" Her mother entered the courtyard. A basket of linens propped on her hip.

Mira plopped down onto the wooden bench. She could not tell her mother about the soldiers, she'd only tell her father, but was that what really bothered her, or was it something else? She puffed out a breath of air and crossed her arms. "Rubiel told me Abba is going to accept Esha's suit."

"Ahhh," her mother sat beside her, the basket at her feet. "You know your father is ailing. He only wants to see you settled before he weakens."

"I know, Ima, but why can't I find one like Abba?"

Laughing, her mother wrapped her arm around her shoulders. "Things were not always easy between me and your father. I dreamed of living in the palace attending the king's daughters. I did not wish to marry."

"What happened?"

"King Jehoshaphat sent my father to Hebron to teach God's laws. My father continued to visit over the years. When I came of age to marry, he betrothed me to a man I had never met. A year later we were married.

"The first time I set eyes on your father was when he came to claim me as his bride."

Mira laid her hand on her mother's thigh. "I always thought you loved Abba."

"Oh, I do, child, but not at first. At first I was angry. He was gentle and kind." Her mother smiled as if remembering. "Patient. I was prideful, childish. Scared."

"It remains, Ima. I do not wish to marry Esha. I do not wish to speak ill of him either, but even Ari, as angry as he makes me, would be better than a drunkard."

Rising from her seat, her mother laughed again. "In this, child, I am in agreement. Ari is better suited to your spirit and he is handsome, too, yes?"

Heat flooded Mira's cheeks. "Ima!"

Her mother winked. "He reminds me of your father when he was younger. You could do worse."

Mira sighed. "He's my father's servant."

"He will soon be free."

Free to leave. "He'll be free to be the man he once was, Ima."

"Just remember, a contract does not create moral character. Ari is a faithful servant. He has a servant's heart and that cannot be a disguise."

Could it not? Had she not seen glimpses of a different man? One who was not so humble and subservient?

Chapter Five

"Ariel, it is with joy I am to see you." Caleb lay on his mat with his head propped on a bedroll. A wet cloth rested against his brow. Red patches blotted his cheeks and down his neck.

"I see our walk caused you difficulties, *adon*."

"Bah, I am old, nothing more." He rose onto his elbows. The cloth slid to the ground. Ari rushed forward. He picked up the soiled linen and tossed it into a basket outside the doorposts. "My thanks. Now, come, sit beside me. We have matters to discuss."

Ari slid his fingers through is hair before taking a seat beside Caleb. "If this is about Hebron, I do not think your health will sustain the trip."

A spastic cough erupted from Caleb.

Ari patted him on the back, before offering him a drink of water. "Perhaps, you should lie back down."

Caleb shook his head. "No. What I have to say is important. Each day the Lord gives me is a blessing, but I would see matters settled before I die."

His master pulled a rolled parchment from the side of his mat and handed it to him. Ari did not know whose hands shook more, his or Caleb's.

The twine fell to the ground as Ari loosened the knot. Caleb's hand rested on his forearm before Ari could unroll the letter. "Wait. Hear my heart."

An erratic thump beat against the wall of his chest. If he had not already been sitting, he would have collapsed. Whatever Caleb had to tell him would not be easy to accept. Worse, by the knot in his gut, it would be more difficult to reject.

"I have no brothers. Leah a brother who is bound by other duties. I have no sons other than Nathan who will soon take Rubiel as his wife, and although well suited for her, even if he could leave his father's house, I do not trust him to have Mira's best interest." He sucked in a breath.

Ari rested his elbows on his knees, his fingers tented, the parchment resting between his hands. "Caleb—"

"Do not deny me this request, Ariel. It has not gone beyond my notice how you care for my daughter. You are kind and generous with your patience where she is concerned. I know all too well my child can be strong minded."

Caleb's view of his daughter must have been colored with a father's love. She was stubborn and prideful.

"She's much like her mother was when we first married in that regard. You have not allowed her to scare you. You are not wary of her disfigurement."

A thick lump formed in his throat. "Caleb, I must—"

"I realize what I'm about to ask is unusual. My circumstances are unusual. Take time to consider my offer before you deny me." Caleb began to cough, but it subsided before it began. "There is a betrothal contract." He held up his hand. "I do not expect to bind you if that is not your heart. I only wish for her to be watched after. I know you would do so and I've given you the legal means. If you find you cannot marry her...I ask you see that she marries a man of her choosing, one who would care for her. I would not see her married to Esha."

Either would he, but it was not his duty. He glanced at the parchment nestled in his hands.

"There's a marriage contract as well. If you are in agreement, all you need do is sign your name. There is no need for a bride price."

Ari rose from his seat and crossed his arms over his chest. "You must understand, *adon*, I am not free—"

"I concede you may have family, but if that is true why have you not contacted them?"

He had, if only to tell them he was safe. That the child was safe. Before he could respond Caleb continued.

"I have released you, Ariel." Caleb struggled to rise from his mat. He shuffled toward Ari and laid his hand on his arm. "You are free. Free to leave, free to stay. I only ask you seek God's face before you answer."

Caleb's words cut him at the knees and cut him hard. He was unworthy of the man's trust. Unworthy of his daughter. A light tap on the doorjamb kept Ari's lips pressed firm.

"Abba." Mira pushed aside the covering and entered. Her presence a double-edged sword. "Food is ready."

If he were free, he would not hesitate to sign the contracts if she were agreeable. The truth, however, was more like iron shackles than being a bond servant to Caleb had ever been. He wasn't free. Wasn't free to leave. He wasn't free to stay if he chose. He was not free to marry the woman standing before him. He was bound to a child for the good of Judah, bound to God's will.

*

His gaze pressed against her, palpable, boring right through to the center of her being. She did not even have to look. He'd been watching her from the moment he'd left her father's chamber. This time it gave her pause. Had she juices from the roasted meat dripping down her chin?

She swiped at her mouth with the back of her good hand and then as covertly as possible looked for the telltale signs of grease.

The courtyard filled heavily with the scent of roasted meat. The fire snapped and crackled as Rubiel turned the hunk of lamb over the fire. Why did he stare so broodingly?

"You have decided not to go, Abba?" Joash asked from his seat next to Ari.

The juice Mira poured into her father's goblet overflowed onto the table.

"Mira, pay attention, child," her mother said, tossing her a drying cloth.

"Forgive me, Ima." The deep red liquid seeped through the linen, spreading in all directions. Images of bloodied bandages as she'd fought to keep Ari alive sprouted into her mind. She'd fancied herself in love with him then, before he woke and declared her maimed. Before he had treated her as if she could not spread grain onto the fields, tend the sheep, or pick the harvest. Of course, he had been plagued with madness induced from the pain of his wounds and the herbs she and her mother had treated him with. He had spoken of many things that did not make sense as he tried to push himself up from the mat. The only word she truly understood was maimed.

Her anger at his brash observation had led to resentment, but today something had changed. Today, she had needed his help, whether she liked it or not. Today, her heart filled with gratitude at his presence.

All day she had fretted over his departure. Feared he'd leave her to fend off the queen's men when they returned. Had he convinced her father to cancel his plans? Had he told him about the incident? Is that why Ari continued to watch her?

She peeked at him through the drape of her hair in hopes he would not catch her. However, his black eyes caught hers. Startled at the knots forming in her stomach, she gathered up the soiled linen and rose.

"My thanks, Mira." Father lifted his cup to his lips and sipped before answering. "I have decided to stay. Your mother made me realize I did not need to go after all." His gaze slid toward Ari. "It is my hope that my business is complete."

"What business, Father?" She'd bit her tongue too late. The words were out. Ari's eyes grew wide, his skin paled. After his time with her family he should be used to her inability to control the wayward organ. Her question was not cause for the panic creased on Ari's brow. Unless of course the business had something to do with her. Perhaps the earlier incident. She ground her teeth together. Her father needed no other burdens upon his shoulders.

As if reading her mind, Ari shook his head. A silent message loud and clear. He had not betrayed her wishes. Then why would her father's business, which obviously had something to do with her, unnerve Ari?

Chapter Six

"I speak of your marriage."

Mira's bottom jaw dropped. She snapped it closed and then opened it again. A firestorm swirled in her amber liquid eyes. This brash young woman struggled to form words. A first. It did not take long for her to find the iron in her spine.

Like a child, she crossed her arms and stomped her tiny sandaled foot. "I mean no disrespect, Abba. I beg of you, do not make me marry Esha."

Caleb gaped at his daughter as if she'd grown a serpent's head. "This is a family matter, Mira. We will discuss it later."

She scanned the courtyard. Servants, slaves and family members stared at her. Her shoulders hunched. She swiped her hand over her cheeks, first one, then the other. It was strange how her defeated tears were somehow tied to his emotions.

"Please, Abba!"

Caleb shook his head a moment before she ran from the courtyard. The muscles in Ari's legs urged him to run after her, if only to explain the situation. However, the knot in his belly told him she would not think him much of an improvement over the drunkard.

Dark, foreboding clouds should have cut a path over the table. It would have suited his mood. Thoughts crashed around in his head. Something else altogether squeezed tight in his chest at Mira's distress. He'd made a vow to protect Joash, keep him safe until the appointed time when he would claim the throne of Judah. He'd also made a vow to serve Caleb, a vow from which he was now released, with the hope on Caleb's part, that he'd marry his daughter. A marriage that could never occur.

Ari scrubbed his palm over his jaw. The entire situation reeked of fermentation. It left a bitter taste on his tongue and a bag of shekels in his belly. If he were another man...if it were another time...he would honor Caleb's request.

"If it pleases you, *adon*, I would seek the Lord."

The corners of Caleb's mouth lifted. "Of course, Ariel."

He left the courtyard and entered his shared quarters. Four stone walls. Lonely and cold, even in the heat, without all the servant's mats cluttering the floor. Isolation closed in until he could no longer breathe.

A roar thundered in his ears. His heart beat out a tattoo, a tattoo that threatened to increase until he'd collapse from the erratic rhythm. He did not want to be consumed by the loneliness, eaten by the icy hardness forming in his chest. The only way to counter the coldness was to enter into the presence of God. However, the reality piercing his chest told him God may have forgotten him.

He grabbed a rolled mat and climbed the stairs to the flat portion of the roof. He peered across the horizon as the sun began to disappear, leaving indescribable hues stretching from north to south. Here the roaring in his head lessened, here he could almost breathe.

Until the hour reminded him, with a desperate longing, of all the rituals he had performed at the temple. In this place, there was no lighting of ceremonial lamps, no song echoing off the temple walls, no offerings to the Lord, no training his men in the courtyard, only the words of the prophets stamped in his mind, words he often shared after the evening meal.

He raked his fingers through his hair. There would be no words this evening. Not from him.

Releasing the cord from around his bedding, he flung it out before him. The soft fleece called to his knees as he prepared for his prayers. A flicker of light caught his attention. The distant glow faded and breathed to life in rapid succession before slowing and repeating.

He moved closer to the edge of the roof and scanned the horizon for another signal. A small, faint glow, no more than the twinkle of a barely visible star, responded. He crossed his arms over his chest. Athaliah's soldiers remained close, but not close enough for him to ascertain the messages passed between camps.

The muscles running down his neck and across his shoulders tensed. At least Caleb had chosen to stay, which eased the burden somewhat. If his master had decided to leave for Hebron, as a servant, Ari could not defy him. Even as a free man, would Ari have done so? He owed Caleb much, yet his duty was to protect the child. A duty he could not perform while he was miles away.

"Perhaps the soldiers are, in truth, only here to keep the peace." The closing in his throat told him otherwise. Devastation always followed in their wake.

There was no doubt the men would come back for Mira. If he signed the contracts hidden in his bedding, he'd be bound to protect her. How was he to protect her and the child at the same time?

An ache sparked in his chest over the dilemma. He was caught between donkey's teeth. Tama would guard Joash well if needed. They'd formed a plan years before, and she knew it well. She'd also proven herself once before. There was no question that Tama would not fail her duty to the child. But would he fail to protect Mira if the soldiers came back for her?

"Ay!" The contracts were not even signed. It was impossible for him to write his name on the parchment and yet he already considered her his responsibility, especially when he thought of the queen's defiled men touching her.

A rumble vibrated in his chest, and he clenched his fingers into fists until pain sliced across his knuckles. He released the pressure of his nails from the palms of his hands and rolled his shoulders. She was not his to protect. One scrawl of ink and she would be his, but he could not, would not take her as his wife without love, even to save her from an awful marriage to Esha.

He looked toward Jerusalem and knelt on his mat. He gazed across the twilit sky. Shades of blues and grays disappeared into the inky blackness of night, revealing the twinkling of stars placed in the heavens by the hand of God. His chest tightened, expanded, choking off the air in his lungs. Never had he felt so divided. More than anything, he longed to do the will of the Lord. What His will was, Ari no longer knew. And if the Lord did not show him soon, what was Ari to do?

Stay? To be in the continuous presence of Mira without marriage. Watch a man unworthy of Mira's affections, even in her scorn, take her as a helpmate? The thought soured his stomach.

Ari scrubbed his hand down his face. As much as it pained him to never see her again, he knew where his duty lay and it was not to the woman who had captured his protective instincts.

A soft breeze rustled his garments, bringing with it the sweet smell of the henna blossoms hedged around the vineyards. He saw Mira, pure and innocent, in his mind's eye, leaning over one of the small flowers inhaling the scent just as she had earlier in the day. His life's blood quickened with the need to touch her fingertips. To press his lips to her brow. If only for a second.

Ari gripped the neck of his tunic in anguish and threatened to rend the garment in two. Even when Jehoiada sent word of his imminent freedom, Ari knew he could never return to the temple and the duties he'd held before Athaliah's murderous rampage. Life as he had known it had ceased to exist when he had left the gates of Jerusalem. And as hard as it had been to abandon his beloved city with all haste in her time of trouble, it would be even more difficult to leave this village and the friends he'd made.

Blowing out a breath of air, Ari released the fabric and prayed for peace to settle his anxious heart. Although he had not forgotten even one day to meditate on the Lord's law, at times he doubted whether God had remembered him. Had the Lord abandoned him altogether? Had the Lord forgotten Joash? Had the Lord forgotten His covenant with King David?

"Do you remember your promise to David, Lord? 'Your house and your kingship shall ever be secure before you, your throne shall be established for evermore.'" He shook his fist at the heavens before bowing his head in remorse.

Questioning God's faithfulness did not set well in his soul. He knew once the questioning began, it would soon fester and eat away at his heart. Ari fought the urge to bury his face into his hands. Instead, he stared into the great void and waited for some sort of reprimand from God Himself. The quiet was only interrupted by the bleating of a goat. Still, he waited, for God's peace to cloak him. Just as he was about to give up and seek his sleep, a star streaked across his vision and faded into the dark night. He recalled a psalm memorized from childhood.

The Lord doth build up Jerusalem: he gathereth together the outcasts of Israel. He healeth the broken in heart, and bindeth up their wounds. He telleth the number of the stars; he calleth them all by their names. Great is our Lord, and of great power: his understanding is infinite. The Lord lifteth up the meek: he casteth the wicked down to the ground.

If the Most High, in all of His greatness, cared to name even the stars and knew their number, would He not remember Ari?

"Forgive me. The unknown is like torment." He paused. "If You hear me, O Lord," his voice a mere whisper to his own ears, "grant me Thy guidance. Thy wisdom. Courage. I am Your servant, Most High, humbled before You." Whether bound to another man's house or in freedom. He inhaled the warm, henna-scented night air. An ache throbbed in his chest at the fragrance so much a part of Mira. Could he love her? Could she love him? Of course, it did not matter if God did not will it. Closing his eyes, he bowed his head. "I will go where You lead."

Had God heard his prayer? Ari could only hope. For there was a promise in that psalm, one Ari would hold on to until Jerusalem was restored from Athaliah's devastation.

Lying down, Ari laced his fingers to better cushion his head. Seeking to remove Mira from his thoughts, he tried to recall the faces of his brothers, and that of his sister, who had surely grown and married. He recalled the etchings in the stonework of the temple walls, many of which he'd tried to recreate in the bricks he had laid for Mira's bridal house. Ari smiled and shook his head. No matter where his thoughts began, they always seemed to lead him back to her. Thoughts that had occupied his mind ever since his master had suggested a marriage with his beautiful daughter.

The light thrum of strings began to filter into the night. Mira often played the lyre for her father to soothe his ailing health, which always amazed Ari given the condition of her disjointed fingers. He'd never asked what had caused the scarring and curling of her fingers, but he'd heard the servants speak of an accident when she was a child, one where a wild dog had attacked her. If their stories were true, that made her rescue of him all the more courageous.

Tonight it was as if she played for him and him alone. The chords, a soft, yet whimsical tune clashed through his conscience. It spoke to the warring emotions within his soul. When he went home, would he long for this isolated place? Would he long for a glimpse of the beautiful Mira? Would he long for her scorn and her outspoken ways?

Perhaps.

*

Mira uncurled her legs and rose from the woven rug. She leaned her lyre against the stonewall and tiptoed from her father's chamber. His snoring assured her he slept soundly. Entering the courtyard, she massaged the gnarled joints of her fingers on her maimed hand and recalled the incident that had altered her life. She'd been naught but a young girl with the thought to protect her father's sheep from the wild dogs. She'd never forget the vicious attack. The way the dog clamped down on her hand, jerking, twisting all the while clawing at her flesh. How could she, the scars she bore had kept her from an appealing marriage.

"You play with sorrow, my daughter." Her mother sat in the center of the courtyard in front of the hand mill. Several oil lamps illuminated the lines of age around her eyes.

Mira dropped her hands to her sides, hoping she had not been caught massaging her fingers. "Do you ever wonder, Ima, if God truly hears us?" she asked, sitting across from her mother. Mira scooped a handful of corn from the pottery bowl and dropped it into the center of the mill. She gripped the wooden pin extending upward from the round stone just above her mother's hand.

"Of course He does," she replied tilting her head to the side. The little coins, depicting her mother's status as wife, adorned the headdress she wore and jingled with the slight movement. Mira had done away with her own simple veil once the servants had sought their beds, and so her hair hung freely down her back. A light breeze brushed across her cheeks, lifting her hair off her neck. She liked to imagine the wind was the Lord's way of approving her slight rebellion.

"What if we do not know our own hearts?" Using the wooden pin to turn the stone, together, they ground the grain to a fine flour.

"What is it you ask, child?"

"I desire something, here," she said, tapping her heart with her free hand. "What if my desires are selfish? What if they go against God's will? What if He hears my prayers and it causes another's prayers to go unanswered?"

Her mother halted the grinding. She brushed her fingers along Mira's jaw as she smoothed back a lock of hair. "My child, you must trust God and His infinite wisdom. Prayers never go unanswered, but if they are not answered the way we think they should be, it is because God has something better for you."

Mira considered the wisdom of her mother's words. She knew she was right, but at times it was difficult to trust. For years she despised Ari for making her feel weak. But today he made her feel protected, cherished. Not an object to be pitied. She'd found herself daydreaming at the well, daydreaming of a union between her an Ari. The more she considered the idea, the more she longed for a marriage with him. But it was more than just wanting Ari for her husband, and that is what she did not understand. Why would God open her eyes to a glimpse of who Ari was only for her father to demand she marry Esha?

"You should rest, Mira. It is late." Her mother curled her hand around her fingers. The warmth and tenderness of her touch brought momentary relief to her aching joints.

"I should—"

"Rubiel will be here soon to help. Now go on."

"Yes, Ima." Leaning across the mill, Mira pressed her lips to her mother's sun-kissed cheek. She rose and started for her chamber.

"And Mira," her mother called.

"Yes, Ima?" Hope bubbled in her chest. Would her mother tell her she didn't have to marry at all?

"Not all is ever as it seems. That is why you must trust God. If God wills it, then it will be so. Have faith."

"Sleep well, Ima," Mira slipped off her sandals outside her door and entered the women's sleeping chamber with a heavy heart. The urge to fall prostrate overwhelmed her, an urge driven not only by her thoughts of Ari but from some sudden weight of fear that her life was about to change. Soon her father would pass from this life, and it seemed, soon she'd be the wife of a man who could not stand the sight of her.

She unfastened the girdle holding close her outer tunic. She slipped the heavier linen from her shoulders and folded the fabric before laying it on a small wooden stool. Careful not to disturb her cousin Tama, the servants and the young children, she stepped over their sleeping bodies and crawled onto her mat and beneath her blanket. Sleep would elude her, or at least until she worried her mind to exhaustion. "God, bring peace to my heart. Help me to trust in You and Your ways." She knew she could not control the future, but this feeling of foreboding would not release the hold it had on her.

"And, God, protect my family from the queen's men if they choose to return." An image of Ari standing against the guards pressed into her mind. "Give Ari the strength to keep us safe."

Once she spoke her request, the burden on her heart lightened and she breathed a sigh of relief. No matter what occurred on the morrow, the God of Abraham, Isaac and Jacob would be with them.

"And, God," she whispered into the night. "If I've found favor in Your eyes, please keep me from a distasteful marriage."

Chapter Seven

"I do not remember my fields being so vast."

"Do you wish to rest awhile?" Ari tugged on the donkey's lead to slow him down.

"Are you tired, Ari? Do you wish to rest your feet again?" Caleb grinned down at him as if he knew the real reason Ari had earlier claimed aching feet. Ari's feet were used to long walks, but Caleb, even riding a donkey, was not used to long minutes outside of his chamber.

Even though Caleb's mind was that of a young man, his body was far from it. The ashen hue of his master's cheeks proved as much. Ari should have insisted he stay abed, but Caleb had been adamant about seeing his crops. After all, Caleb argued, he may never get another chance to see a harvest.

"We are close to the end, *adon*," Ari encouraged. "Then we can rest before heading back home." Even though they had been gone less than an hour, he knew his master needed the rest. However, Ari could not halt the gnawing in his belly that had existed ever since they had left the walls of the village. A sickening sensation, which grew worse with each passing moment.

"Then we press on, my son."

Ari rolled his shoulders to wear off the uneasiness tensing his muscles and tugged on the donkey's lead. They descended a pass and encountered a few servants tending the crops. The servants watched them, curious as to why their master had traveled so far from his bed. Ari bowed his head and focused on the path. He, too, wondered why Caleb chose this day to see his legacy. Certainly it was more than a dying man's wish to see his fields once more.

"Shalom." Caleb's toothless smile greeted his servants. Each bowed their heads in return.

A sense of foreboding returned with a vengeance as they passed the small group. His nape pricked as if he crawled around in a bush of thorns. Someone watched him. Temptation to investigate further tugged on his innards. But he did not wish to alert whomever it was observing them.

Ari chastised himself for his foolishness. Surely, the heat boring between his shoulders was only his imagination. Caleb was a kind master, his servants loyal. None would dare harm him, would they?

"It is guilty, I am for not allowing the fields the rest required by the law," Caleb said, gripping the donkey's short mane for support. "I do not think it would have gone unnoticed by the queen's spies." He lowered his voice. "I fear I will not see Judah restored…"

The sadness in Caleb's voice choked Ari.

Caleb wiped his brow. "I am glad we did not travel to Hebron. It would have taken us a week there and back at this pace." He coughed. "I fear it is not the same."

The city, once a center of worship, bore the scars of Athaliah's hand. An Asherah pole had even been erected at Abraham's tomb. The queen's faithful often defiled the holy place with sins comparable to Sodom and Gomorrah. "Jerusalem is no different," Ari mused aloud.

"Ah, is that where you are from?" Caleb tilted his white peppery beard and peered down at him. Curiosity was not the only thing that shone in his black eyes. It was as if he asked Ari to have faith in him. To trust him. But Ari's secrets were not his alone to keep. However, admitting he hailed from Jerusalem would harm nobody. At least he hoped not.

"You could say. Yet I've been bedding down in the desert for a few years, now." Ari smiled at his master.

"Yes, so it seems you have." Caleb laughed. His laughter quickly changed to a bout of coughing, and Ari worried if his master would return home to his family, or if he would perish here and now. Ari pulled the stopper from the bladder of water and touched the edge against Caleb's lips.

"Better?" Ari asked once Caleb's chest settled.

"Thank you, my son." Caleb laid his hand against Ari's shoulder. The unspoken meaning went straight to his heart. It was like a searing brand sizzling deep into his being. How could he disappoint this man? Even if his presence here was a lie, he had come to love Caleb and his family. But his duty to God, his duty to his kingdom and his secrets, kept him from staying. Kept him from accepting Mira as his bride.

Ari bowed his head. "I am unworthy, *adon*."

Caleb slid off the donkey's back before Ari could help him. He pressed his hands on either side of Ari's face and looked him in the eye for long moments and then nodded as if pleased with what he saw. "I've never seen a more worthy man than you, Ari."

The searing in his chest returned, thrusting deeper, encompassing the whole of his breast. Caleb's words were like a hammer upon his conscience. Like an earthen jar crushed beneath the weight of a boulder. It was more than he could bear. *Lord, give me strength.*

"I will not press," Caleb said. "Come, sit beneath the shade with me awhile."

Ari looped the donkey's lead around a low branch and eased beside Caleb. High clouds shadowed parts of the rocky outcrops while the sun illuminated others, leaving them more mysterious to the eye. He had no doubt the shadows held many secrets, much like his heart.

"We are far from prying ears, Ariel." He turned his gaze fully on him, piercing Ari to the core.

Ari held his breath. He was not ready—

"I could not be more certain." Hands clenched, Caleb paused. "I am certain...

"Certain about what, *adon*?"

*

Hefting a cruse containing oil from last year's crop of olives, Mira carried it toward the bake oven where she intended to brush a small amount to each cake of bread.

"Why so downcast, Mira?" Rubiel asked as she placed an earthen jar on the ground in front of her.

Mira pressed her lips together. Ari and her father had not been gone long and she missed them. Missed him. Feared his absence if the soldiers should return.

"It is difficult, I know but you must do your duty to Abba and marry Esha." Rubiel leaned close. "I saw the way you watched the slave last eve. I contend he's handsome but he is a slave, Mira. You must remove your heart from him."

The cruse slipped from Mira's hand, shattering on the ground. She thrust her hands on her hips and glared at her sister as oil oozed over her feet. It would do no good to argue the condition of her heart or where it lay. She had watched him with new eyes, and her heart was curious. Perhaps, even interested a little if the increased beat in his presence was any indication. "He is not a slave."

"Servant, slave, they are one in the same."

"And soon he will be a free man. What say you then?" Kneeling, Mira began gathering the shards of pottery. A few small pieces clung to her flesh leaving her blood to intermingle with the thickness of the oil.

"I say he no longer belongs to us. He will most likely sell himself to a higher bidder. I hear there are women among Athaliah's court who would pay a high price for a man as handsome as your slave."

Her sister's mean words pierced her heart. It seemed the more she ignored Esha's marriage pursuit the meaner her sister became. Mira did not like Esha and would not marry him unless she was forced by her father. He was a deceiver and a drunkard, unlike Ari. "Ari's not a slave, mine or anyone else's," Mira argued, knowing it would not matter.

"Daughters!" Her mother clapped her hands together. "There is no need for argument." Her mother pierced Rubiel with her sternest look. "Child, you must learn to speak with caution. Your tongue is like a viper."

"Ima!"

Mother held up her hand. "No, Rubiel, I blame myself for spoiling you as I have done. Now, where is your betrothed?"

He was probably hiding near a camphire hedge with Esha. The two, no doubt, were drunk on wine, after all, one of the pitchers was missing, but she wouldn't speak as harshly as her sister had done. It never did well to give an eye for an eye, although treating her sister with kindness had not gotten her anywhere either. Besides, Ima's question was enough to set Rubiel in a huff. It'd take her a few hours to find her betrothed. When she did, she'd suffer angry embarrassment and would hide until her temper cooled.

"Thank you, Ima." Mira glanced up at her mother.

Her mother pressed her fingers to her temple as if to ward off a head pain. "A blessing it was only a small jar and not a larger one."

"Forgive me, Ima"

"You worry over much, Mira. Of course, I forgive you." Her mother gave her a quick hug, careful not to step in the oil. "Now, go wash your feet. I'll have someone clean this up."

"Yes, Ima."

Mira walked to the cistern. By the time she had reached the well, her feet and sandals were covered in a sticky, dusty mess. Much of the desert clung to her toes. She sat on the rock wall, slipped her sandals off, and placed them in a trough of water, to soak. She plunged her feet into the tepid water next to her sandals and began to scrub them with the linen cloth tucked in her girdle.

Mira tried to calm her anger. She should not find fault with her sister's concern, no matter how misplaced it was. Perhaps Rubiel believed Ari would treat her harshly because of her disfigurement as others had done. Could her sister not see Ari had never done so? He was different?

It angered her that Rubiel thought so little of him. Especially when he was obviously a man of integrity who lived by God's law. He did everything her father had asked of him and more. He held God in the highest reverence, as all men should.

She gasped. All the time he'd offered his help, he had only been doing as God required him and she had treated him with scorn.

"Forgive me, God." She bowed her head in shame.

She had treated him abhorrently. Lashing out with her tongue because she lacked confidence in who she was in the Lord.

How could she have treated such a handsome man with raven-black hair the color of the darkest night, with a silver shine as if the moon had kissed each strand so awfully? A man with a kind and generous heart?

Her pulse quickened even as the space in her chest closed as if to keep an image of Ari tucked within. It had stung when Rubiel suggested Ari would be willing to sell himself to one of Athaliah's court for lustful purposes. She knew he would never do such a thing, still...he had had a life before her father took him in. And there was a possibility that he would return to his former life. Perhaps even to a wife.

The sound of feet pounded on the path. With an urgency that alerted her senses. She pulled her sandals from the water and with haste wiped them clean, before tying them around her ankles. She rose and found Joash in a frantic run.

"M-M-Mira," he said in between harsh breaths.

"What is it? What has happened? Is it Ima? Abba?" The shrill screams of women carried to her ears. The rumble of men's shouts echoed them. All the air left her lungs.

The soldiers had come back. She started running toward her village.

"No!" The fear in Joash's voice stopped her in her tracks. "Come. We must hide. Quickly. I must see you to safety."

Mira was torn between helping her family and hiding like a coward with the boy. Something deep in her belly forced her to grab Joash's hand. He led her along places she had never realized existed. They ran in the heat of the morning through thick brush and over sharp jagged rocks until they came to the edge of a pool so breathtakingly beautiful she nearly forgot they had been running for their lives. Until she heard the thunder of hooves approaching.

"My, Lord, save us," she cried, yesterday's fear revisited her double-fold.

"Come." Joash jumped into the pond and swam toward a wall of falling water. Panic seized her at the threat the water posed. It was one thing to cast out your nets, quite another to step foot in water where you could not see the bottom. Yet, Joash disappeared beyond the falls. Fear for the child's safety left her to follow him.

She waded through the water, constantly looking over her shoulder. Yet, she also sought the boy's every movement. Mira stood in front of the water tumbling from the cliff above, unsure of what to do. The bubbling froth roaring in her ears rocked her back and forth. She thought she'd heard the whinny of a horse, but when she turned to look, Joash grabbed her hand and yanked. Mira lost her balance and fell behind the curtain of water.

Smoothing her wet tresses back from her eyes, she could see large, blurred figures through the cascading water, searching the edge of the pool. She stood there, Joash's hand gripped in hers, veiled by the falling stream, unable to move for fear they'd be discovered. Mira wished for a clearer view of their pursuers, but she could not do so without giving up their hiding place. And the roar of the falls kept her from hearing their words.

After a few moments, when the blurred visions disappeared and all seemed safe, Joash nudged her to follow him as he climbed the rock wall behind the falls. The child slipped into the darkness. She reached up and gripped the rock jutting out from the wall and hefted herself up onto the ledge.

Sitting there, she could see through the waterfall the soldiers had returned. They prowled the edge of the pool. She held her breath when one knelt. But then he rose and left.

A soft glow appeared from behind her. She glanced over her shoulder and gaped. The light illuminated a cave complete with furnishings large enough to hold a small family.

"Who, who showed you this place?"

"Ari."

Puzzled, she looked at the child. Surely he was mistaken. How would Ari know of such a place? She rose, dripping wet from her seat. Her ears pounded with the water crashing to the pool of water below. But she was sure the sound was not what made her feel faint. She noticed many things that would never have belonged to a man desperate enough to sell himself as a servant.

"You must be mistaken," she whispered as she tiptoed farther into the cave toward a wooden chest that had caught her attention. She stared at the cedar box with a lion carved into the top. Scared at what she would find, but unable to halt her movements, she knelt on a thick, plush rug. She unhooked the latch and opened the lid. Handfuls of shekels, golden goblets, ornately engraved short swords and swaths of fabric too rich for a man of Ari's humble standing were nestled within the chest.

Two small black boxes sat on top with leather straps draping down the side. She drew her finger along the beautiful script. The box tumbled and slipped to the bottom of the chest. She reached in to retrieve it. Her fingers brushed against a lumpy leather bag. She removed it from the chest and held it up.

Her heart pounded against her breast bone as she untied the cord. The leather bag opened like a flower. Several stones appeared against royal silk. One of the stones caught her eye and she picked it up with her gnarled fingers. She held it up to the oil lamp nestled into a nook in the wall. The stone lit like fire, flaming to life in her hand.

She glanced down at the other stones. The rushing sound of the falls seemed to grow louder and she swayed. She knew each tribe had their own signet. Her father wore a similar one around his neck. Why would Ari have all of these?

The flaming stone began to warm in the palm of her hand. She laid the pouch down to better examine the fiery stone. She held it closer to the lamp.

"You must be mistaken," she repeated, her voice louder.

"No. It was Ari."

With the stone flickering in the palm of her hand, she knew the boy spoke the truth, a truth she did not have time to question. For the next breath had her looking into the eyes of one of the men who hunted them.

Chapter Eight

Mira didn't think about what she was doing, she only acted. She grabbed one of the weapons lying on one of the benches and jumped in front of Joash. The weight of the weapon wavered in her hands. She braced her feet, lest she fall over. Her heart pounded in her chest. Her breaths were short and quick.

Lord, I am but a woman, and this man is a giant.

Water cascaded over the contours of the giant's bulging shoulders as he scanned the cavern with an assessing eye. His hands hung loose at his sides. He seemed relaxed, which caused fear to pound a little harder in her head.

His right eye twitched as the corner of his mouth curled. His chest expanded and she thought he might charge at her. Instead he nodded, turned around and left.

The sword began to drop from her hands but she stilled the muscles in her arms. She released a breath of air, and sucked another in. Laying the sword back in its place, she picked up a small dagger and looked at Joash. "Stay here."

Mira peered over the edge of the rock just as the warrior dove beneath the falls. She climbed down and slipped into the water. She edged around the rocks until she found an opening in the falls to where she could spy the man.

The warrior rose out of the water. Waves sloshed against his shins, rocking him back and forth with the motion. He swiped his hand across his eyes.

"Praise be to the gods you are alive, Ianatos." A queen's soldier sat with his legs crossed a good distance from the shore.

Mira's footing slipped and she sucked in a sharp breath of air as she grabbed hold of a rock. The warrior tossed a glance toward her before jamming his hands on his hips. He glared at her, rolled his shoulders as if to ease the tension. "Your gods have naught to do with my swimming capabilities, Roab."

Roab's eyes widened. His lips stilled, but his hands fluttered like a griffin ruffling its feathers.

"Your superstitions are no more than a child's imagination."

"The creatures…" Roab crawled forward on his hands and peered into the waters.

Mira dropped her gaze to the water lapping around her waist.

"There are no dangerous creatures in these shallow waters." Ianatos bent down and snatched a small fish in midswim. "Unless of course, you fear this." He held the fish eye level and watched as it puckered its mouth. He glanced at his companion. "Hungry?"

Roab's mouth moved much like their meal, but no sound emitted. Ianatos stepped onto the jagged bank and tucked the flapping fish between the rocks. "Hand me a linen."

His companion stood to his feet, pulled a piece of cloth from one of the sacks and handed it to him. His gaze scanned the pool of water. Mira pressed back into the shadows. "What did you see, my friend? Did you find the rebels?"

Ianatos wiped the droplets of water from his head and then over his shoulders before drying his chest. Mira held her breath. What would this giant warrior tell the Hebrew? Long moments of silence caused her heart to pound in her ears.

"You were under the water a long while. Longer than any man can hold his breath in a bath."

True. However, if the Hebrew discovered the warrior hadn't been in the water the whole time, the queen's guard would descend upon them. She waited, wondering if she'd have to defend Joash against these trained soldiers.

"You forget my upbringing."

"Yes, you Philistines have a way with the deep. It's as if the gods have granted you gills."

Ianatos laid the cloth over a rock. He eased to the ground and reclined in the sun. "Might I ask you a question, Roab?"

Roab squinted. "I'm curious, Ianatos. You are a man of few words."

"Few words are needed for a soldier." He picked up a small stone, glance toward where Mira stood and tossed it into the water.

"Then ask, my friend," Roab said as he formed a ring of stones for a fire.

Ianatos crossed his arms. Deep lines furrowed his brow. Mira bit down on her tongue. What question would this man ask his companion?

"Why is it you Hebrews have turned away from your God?"

Mira clamped her hand over her mouth. How often had she wondered the same thing but dared not ask even those men she knew remained faithful.

A stone tumbled from Roab's hand and rolled down the embankment. "You speak treason. What is it you found in the waters?"

Water lapped around her waist. A chill crept over her arms. She closed her eyes and prayed.

"Nothing."

She snapped her eyes open. "Thank you, Lord."

"I saw nothing." Ianatos sat forward. "I'm only curious as to why you praise bronze idols instead of your true God."

Glancing up at the sky, Roab rocked back on his heels and sat. "Our God has abandoned us. We worship idols because our queen requires it of her people. If she were to demand we bow to the one true God, we would."

Roab's reasoning held no foundation. Mira could tell he was fickle. As were most of the Hebrews who'd turned from God.

Mira began to climb back onto the ledge when Ianatos's voice halted her.

"It grows late. You should build a fire atop that ledge so we might send a message to Suph that all is clear while I finish preparing our meal." Ianatos pointed to a high place above the waterfall.

She watched a few moments as Ianatos cleaned the fish. His gaze darted toward her as his companion left the area. Mira didn't know why this Philistine had chosen to keep her and Joash a secret, but she was thankful for the blessing.

Chapter Nine

"*A*don, adon!"

Ari jumped to his feet and peered down the path. Matthias, one of Caleb's servants, ran wild-eyed looking to and fro. Air whooshed out of Ari's lungs as if he'd been punched. He sucked in hard and forced his muscles to relax when his mind screamed at him to run back to the village.

"Matthias, here!" Ari waved.

Matthias glanced at him, his eyes haggard, bruised. He looked like a man bedeviled. Ari was not alone in his discernment.

"Shalom, Matthias," Caleb called. "What is wrong?"

The man bent over, hands on knees. In between heaving gulps of air, he tossed weary glances over his shoulder as if he expected a great cat to appear. Or worse.

A rock settled in the pit of Ari's stomach. "Matthias, you have naught to fear," Ari offered as he handed him a jug of water.

Matthias uncorked the bottle and sipped from the opening. Tears clung to the rim of his eyelids. He tried to speak. "They have come."

"Who came?" Caleb asked.

But Matthias continued as if Caleb had not spoken. It was not like the man to show disrespect, which could only mean he had been given a great shock.

"I knew they would come and bring fear to this land. And they did."

"Who, Matthias? Who?" Caleb shook his head. His hands trembled.

"Men of war. They came and, do you not smell the burning?"

Ari lifted his nose and caught a faint whiff of charred wood.

"The queen's guard is scouring the village. They were—were asking about the children."

"The children?" Caleb's brow furrowed deep.

Ari bit back the curses on his tongue. Had Athaliah discovered Joash's existence? Ari glanced at Caleb, whose eyes filled with tears. He could tell by the movement of the older man's lips that he lifted up a prayer.

"We—we should return," Caleb choked. "Matthias, if you would carry word to the next village—"

"Of course, *adon*." Matthias bowed and raced away on nothing but his sandaled feet.

Ari bowed his head. "Caleb, I do not wish to leave you, however, I feel helpless. I should have been there." Ari's conscience weighed heavy upon his heart. What evil had he brought on these good people?

"We will go together, pray this beast will make haste and hope the Lord has spared our family."

Our family. Ari's heart swelled even as it broke. He wished for Caleb's confidence, but he could not stop the urgency pushing at his feet and the fear gnawing in his chest.

"If only we had grain to offer up to the Lord," Ari mused aloud thinking it would please the Lord to have a burnt offering.

"Do you think our God cannot see our circumstances?" Caleb asked.

Ari shook his head. "I'm quite certain He does, but the law—"

"Athaliah has banned our altars to God. But that has not stopped those of us who trust in the Lord from lifting up our thanksgiving." Caleb tilted his chin, looking toward the sky. "I believe the Lord to have a compassionate heart toward those who love Him. If He did not, the world would have perished with the flood."

A breeze blew across the rocky desert and encompassed Ari, cooling his skin from the blazing sun. It was as if the Lord had commanded the wind to agree with Caleb. Perhaps, his master was correct. Perhaps, the all-knowing

God, creator of heaven and earth was more concerned with the intent of a man's heart than his actions.

"Help me down, Ari."

"Yes, *adon*."

Caleb wrapped his arm around Ari's shoulders as he helped him off the donkey. "You must quit calling me master, Ari. You are a free man, and soon, I pray, my son."

"Until that day, I will continue to give you the honor due you, *adon*."

"So be it." Caleb wrapped his bony fingers around Ari's arm and shuffled toward a small grove. He knelt and motioned for Ari to do the same. "Let us thank the Lord for safe travels and the protection of our people."

Ari watched as Caleb lifted his tunic off his shoulders and draped it over his head. A pang of longing gripped Ari.

He did not want to take the time to pray. He wanted to run back to the village. To Joash and Mira posthaste. He needed to see with his eyes, not just hope in his heart, that they were well. However, he must trust in the Lord, even blindly. If only it were easier done than said.

After their prayers were finished, Ari helped Caleb back onto the donkey and tugged rider and beast through the fields and between a canopy of branches. It did not take long for the sweet scent of the *afarsemon* to be replaced with the distinct scent of charred wood.

What had only this morning been vibrant greenery with blooms, was now a blackened mess. Their steps slowed as they took in the sight. Ari assumed shock had overtaken Caleb's tongue. For Ari knew he hadn't words for the desolation either. Only disbelief and anger at the needless destruction of Caleb's crops. And a deep concern for what lay ahead of them.

They rounded the corner and Ari halted his footsteps. He reached out and wrapped his arm around Caleb the moment he collapsed to the ground and gaped at what should have been an altar at the edge of the fields. Caleb's shoulders shook with his sobs.

All that remained of the altar was a pile of rubble. Ari dared not inspect the smoldering pile further. Knowing the cruelty of Athaliah's guards, Ari feared the worst. However, all he saw were chopped portions of branches from the surrounding olive trees.

"Who would do such a thing, Ari? Who?"

Ari closed his eyes. There was no need to answer Caleb, for both knew the truth. Besides, he wished not to waste another moment before he set eyes on Mira, and of course, Judah's rightful king. "Let us be done here."

As if realizing he might find the same horror at home, Caleb's eyes widened in fear. "You are correct, Ari."

Lord, what have I done? I never should have left them alone. Even for a short time.

Ari could argue the whys of the matter, but the truth was he was responsible for this tragedy. And he had no doubt Athaliah would have a grand laugh when she realized Ari's part.

His conscience ate at him as they approached the walled village. For he heard nothing but wailing. "Lord, forgive me," he muttered beneath his breath.

"What need of forgiveness do you have, my son?"

It was not the Lord who had asked the question, but Caleb. Ari would much prefer to speak with God on this matter.

"For my iniquities, *adon*," Ari responded, hating his deception.

"I suppose we all have them, do we not?"

Unable to speak, Ari nodded.

Just as they were about to enter through the gate, Ari halted. "I do not think it safe for you to go any closer. Not yet."

"I must," Caleb said.

"I will go." Ari would go and see the destruction. He would—what would he do? Bury the dead to save Caleb from such devastation? Ari drew in a ragged breath.

"We will go together." Caleb laid his palm on Ari's shoulder and searched his eyes.

Ari's shoulders sagged.

"I must know that my family is unharmed."

"But, *adon*—"

"No!" Caleb snapped. In his years of service, Ari had not once heard his master raise his voice.

"Yes, *adon*. I understand, you must do what you must."

Afraid of what they would find, Ari felt the urge to drag his feet. Yet he wanted to drop the donkey's lead and run as fast as he could. He would not breathe easy until his gaze touched Mira and Joash.

A swath of sand blew around them making it difficult to view the cattle enclosures but Ari knew they were close. Close enough to taste the acrid smell of death.

No sooner had they spied the earth-colored structures than Rubiel, with her long black hair streaming down her back, ran to greet them, Nathan fast on her heels.

"Abba! Oh Abba, thank the Lord, all is well with you."

Caleb shifted his weight and struggled to dismount. Ari wrapped his hand around the old man and assisted him.

"Tell me, child?"

She halted in front of them, tears streaked down her swollen cheeks. "Soldiers came and..." she choked.

Her betrothed patted her shoulder. "It is all right, Ruby," he crooned. "There now, you should see to the children." She looked up into his face, her eyes red-rimmed, a mixture of trust and anger marring her features.

"But—"

Nathan stopped her with a finger to her lips. "Allow me, Rubiel."

She stepped forward, pressing a kiss to her father's cheek. "Shalom, Abba." With that she hung her head and walked back to the center of the village.

"I fear she will never forgive me. I was not here when the soldiers came. The women and children were left defenseless."

Caleb pressed his lips together and lifted his hand to Nathan's shoulder, his gaze shifted back and forth as if seeking the truth. Nathan had a tendency to shirk his duties. This, no doubt, was one of those times. By the worry etched on his brow, Ari had no doubt the man was remorseful.

Ari's gaze searched for Joash. Since Rubiel had gone to care for the children, there was hope. But that didn't stop the heavy stone rolling around in his stomach.

He had prayed the Lord would spare them, but with the look of grief in Nathan's eyes, his hope waned.

"My wife?" Caleb asked with choked emotion.

"Leah is fine. Bruised, but fine."

"Thank Ye, God."

"Soldiers came."

A pain so sharp, as if his own sword had severed his arm, pierced his chest. Mira? He dared not ask. "What of Joash?"

Nathan bowed his head. His feet shifted in the sand.

Impatient and out of control, Ari grabbed the front of his tunic and hefted him off the ground. "Where. Is. Joash?" he ground out.

"Ari!"

Ari's heart quit pounding in his chest, but it was only Tama. She ran toward him. Her face swollen and ashen. Her eyes red-rimmed from tears.

"He's gone." She collapsed against him.

Ari gripped her shoulders to keep her from falling to her knees.

"He's gone. I failed him." Her sobs increased. "I—I tried to find him. I went near the cave—b-but soldiers were guarding it."

He understood the pain of failure. It cut him deep. "There is no need to worry, Tama. All will be well. You will see."

If only his words were true. He handed Tama to Nathan and then turned toward his master. "*Adon*." He pierced Caleb's gaze with his eyes. "I am unworthy, but I ask that you trust me."

"You cannot think to trust this bond servant, Father," Nathan interrupted. "It's obvious he brought the soldiers here."

Nathan's words twisted the blade deep into his soul. "Trust me, Caleb. I must go with haste to find the boy." Ari dropped his chin. "When I see him to his rightful place, I will return." He once again lifted his eyes. "I vow it."

"Of course, Ari. You are a free man. You must do what you must."

"My thanks." He turned toward Nathan and Tama. "What of Mira? Is she well?"

Tama's mouth slackened.

Nathan's eyes narrowed before he hung his head in shame. "I did not realize—that is, she has not been seen since the attack." He lifted his eyes. "I'm sorry, Caleb."

Caleb fell to his knees, ripping his tunic at the neck. A cry of anguish on his lips. If Ari had not been so cold, if he had not been as stiff as the stone walls, he too would have fallen to his knees.

"I should have been here," Nathan cried in distress.

Ari did not wish to know where Nathan had been when the soldiers went on their rampage. As much as he wished to fault the man, Ari should have been the one to protect Caleb's family. Especially since he knew the danger. The blame did not lie with Nathan, but with him. Directly at his feet. His iniquities were catching up with his sandals.

Ari laid his hand upon Caleb's head and his other on Nathan's shoulder. "It is no one's fault but my own and on my honor I will find your daughter and bring her back," he assured them. He would locate Mira and return with her unscathed or die trying. "I vow it before God."

Chapter Ten

Light filtered through the curtain of water, waking Sh'mira from a fitful sleep. Nightmares of armed men chasing her through crowded streets continued to haunt her, even after she rubbed the sleep from her eyes. She stretched and realized the small body that should be next to hers was missing. She sat up, curled her legs beneath her and massaged the soreness from her fingers. "Joash," she whispered.

Only the sound of the rushing water and the echo of her own breathing met her ears. "Joash."

Nothing.

How long had she slept? She had only intended to close her eyes a short while. She had not planned on sleeping, especially since she did not know if the soldier watched them.

She slipped her sandals onto her feet and rose from the makeshift bed. A quick look told her Joash was no longer in the cave. Panic seized her. Where could he have gone? Wrapping a tunic around her shoulders, she stepped to the edge of the cave and followed the path of rocks leading to the small pool of water this side of the falls.

She let out a sigh of relief when she spied the child wading in the water. Caution warned her against calling out his name lest she startle him causing him to cry out. It would not do for the soldiers to hear him if they remained camped beside the pool.

She climbed down the stones and sat at the edge and waited for him to acknowledge her presence.

"I must prepare for my journey," he said in a tone that spoke of authority.

She had no idea what he meant by his journey, but she would not question him now. "I was only concerned."

"Of course, Mira. I did not mean to cause you worry."

She wrapped her arms around her knees and watched the wall of water stream into the pool. As beautiful as this place was she wanted to go home. She fought the tears threatening to burst forth. Had her mother and sister been unharmed? What of her father?

And what of Ari? If he knew of this place why had he not come for them yet? Had something happened to him as well?

She swiped her fingers across the corner of her eye. "Do you think they are still out there, waiting for us?"

Thank the Lord the man who'd found them chose to keep their whereabouts hidden.

"I do," he responded.

For some reason Joash understood their precarious situation more than she did. She'd been afraid to ask questions of him. At first, because she did not want to worry him further. But then, after searching the confines of Ari's secret cave she feared the truth. If it was as she suspected, Ari not only lied to her, but he brought trouble to her father's doorstep. And now, with worry heavy on her heart, she needed to know what they were fighting.

"I wonder, what are they after?" she asked.

Joash shrugged in a way that told her he knew.

She slid her hand down her leg and played with the ties on her sandal. "What do they want?"

"I am bound by an oath." He turned to her, his dark eyes filled with apologies. "Soon your questions will be answered."

The child had barely seen six summers, yet he held a bearing fit for a king. Mira blinked. Her thoughts caught in her throat. The conversation with Ari fought to the forefront. Could it be? Could this young child somehow be related to the royal family? Is that why Athaliah's guard had attacked their little village?

"Impossible," she spoke to herself as she rose from her perch and brushed her hands over her tunic. It was more likely he belonged to the priests given some of the items in the cave, but then what did that make Ari? "Come, the day grows late. We must decide what we will do."

Mira climbed back into the hidden cave and waited for Joash. After a few minutes he entered, back stiff, his head held high. He wore a tunic trimmed with a humble weave and a simple turban wrapped around his unruly locks, but one would have thought he was covered in gold.

He bowed to her as he entered. "My apologies, Mira. The wait is long and difficult, but I fear..." His bottom lip began to quiver and for the first time she saw the child he should be.

She stepped to him and enfolded him in her arms. "All will be well, my Brother. You'll see." She rubbed circles upon his back with the tips of her fingers. "God is with us."

He pulled back and looked her in the eye. "You are correct. And soon Ari will come for us, I know it."

"And you know this how, Joash?" It'd been hours and Ari had yet to come.

"Ari promised. If aught happened he would come for me." The child spoke with complete faith.

His faith tore at her heart, made her want to fall to her knees and cry. She had trusted Ari, too. Had trusted him completely, even when she'd been angry with him. But now she knew him for the liar he was. And for all she knew her family had perished because of his lies. How could she tell this child that his faith had been misplaced?

What if Ari never came? What if he broke his promise to Joash? What if he lay injured, or worse, dead?

She pressed a kiss to the top of his head. "We will wait one night. If he does not show, we must return home."

"But what if the guard...what if they are still there?"

She saw the fear and something else she could not ascertain. "I cannot leave you here alone."

"Come," he said, grasping her hand. He led her deep into the cave where natural light filled the entire room. She glanced around and noticed cut windows. Mira gaped in awe. They were slanted in such a way that if any were to come upon them from the outside they would not be seen from above.

"Here," Joash said, unrolling a parchment.

She squinted at the drawing. A picture of a waterfall showed their position, and the large body of water depicted the Sea of Salt. "What is this?" she asked pointing at what looked to be a box on a pyre.

"This is where we must go."

She'd lived in this valley her entire life and had never heard of such a place. But then she'd never known of this cave either. It looked as if they would have to leave the cave after all in order to get Joash to his destination, but she'd heard the terrain was unfriendly. And even if Athaliah's guards were not lying in wait for them there were many other dangers. "I do not understand."

"Ari always said it was a place of safety. If he did not come for me, then I am to follow the signs to make it there." He pointed to the place on the map. "And I am to give them this."

He unfolded his fist. In the palm of his hand he held a gold ring. She touched it with the tip of her finger and turned it over. She inhaled a sharp breath, and looked the child in the eyes. This child was not meant to be a priest at all. Before she could stop herself, she fell to the floor on her knees and bowed at his feet.

*

He waited long, tense moments for the pair of soldiers to leave. He could only pray and trust that the Lord had seen to Mira and Joash's protection, and that any foolishness on his part would be hidden from his enemies.

Wrapping the cloth satchel high on his shoulder, he slipped into the cool spring and waded to the edge of the falls. Ari closed his eyes and breathed deeply. There was no time to waste, but he lifted up another beseeching prayer.

Then with one last look around, ensuring that no one watched, he dove into the water and swam beneath the falls. His gaze gradually followed the stone pathway to the entrance. No evident sign of what he sought.

A boulder slammed against his heart. He chastised his lack of faith in the Lord. Finding an empty cave was near impossible to grasp, yet his feet refused to carry him to the landing. He feared the unknown too much.

"Forgive me, Lord, for my lack of trust." He bowed his head, his wet hair falling over his shoulders. Ari waded to the edge and pulled himself onto the rock. The faint scent of cinnamon wafted in the air, a scent unfamiliar to this place. Hibiscus, rose, lilies but never cinnamon. Mira had been here.

He lifted up a prayer of gratitude. His heart much lighter than moments before, he climbed the steps and entered the cavern. He untied the satchel from his shoulders and allowed it to slip to the rocky floor. He slipped off his sandals.

Ari blinked his eyes and fought to clear his vision. Her warmth and scent infused every orifice of the cave. She had to be here, somewhere. He blinked again. His eyes focused on the rumpled makeshift mat. Then he scanned the corners and hollows.

The things on his wooden chest had been moved around. His heart threatened to rip apart as he eyed the circle pit where no ember of fire flickered.

Had they been discovered? "Oh, Lord," he prayed.

His knees threatened to buckle with grief. He rubbed the back of his neck. Where could they be?

A slight whisper echoed off the walls. The hidden cove. How could he have forgotten? In three long strides he rounded the corner.

"Rise, Mira." Joash's childlike voice was a little shaky as if he were uncomfortable with making demands of those around him.

Chapter Eleven

Instinct told him to rush into the hidden cove and wrap his arms around Mira, to fuse her so deep inside his soul that he'd never have to worry over her well-being again.

Instead, he tamped down his urges with steely self-control. The fear that had prodded him to race the distance from Caleb's house refused to be soothed. He continued to shake. No matter what he'd heard with his very ears, no matter that he'd felt Mira's presence, he still continued to shake.

"They are safe. They are safe," he chanted to himself. "Thank you, Lord."

Ari breathed deeply, and then exhaled. One step. Two. Three, and then four. One long stride and he exited the long pathway and stood inside the entrance to the cove. He gazed with awe at this proud woman prostrate before her young king. No wonder Joash sounded bewildered. Even he had no idea who he really was.

A ray of light filtered through the windows carved hundreds of years ago. The light illuminated her beauty as locks of unveiled burnished gold cloaked her frame and Joash's feet. It reminded him of the first time he'd seen her.

"Mira, I beg of thee, rise," the child's voice quavered, then as if he had just become aware of Ari's presence, Joash turned his dark, frightened gaze to him.

"Ari, you came! I knew you would." Joash ran to him, leaving Mira where she knelt. The child propelled his small body into Ari's thighs and wrapped his arms around his legs. Ari lifted him in his arms and hugged him tight, but not once had he taken his eyes from Mira.

"Did you, now?" Ari asked.

"Yes, of course, Ari. You promised, remember?"

He smiled at the boy and dropped a kiss to his head and then set him on his feet. Joash shifted his gaze between Ari and Mira. He shuffled his feet as if he were about to be chastised. At last, Mira turned her head and peered through the tresses hanging around her. Ari grinned as he ruffled Joash's unruly mop of curls. Mira rose to her knees and pushed back her hair.

"I know I should not have shown Mira the ring, but I wanted to ease her worries."

A hearty laughter burst from Ari's gut as he took in the wariness and shock on her face. "And did you?"

Joash stared at Mira for a few long seconds before he answered. "I do not think so, Ari."

He laughed once again. "No, I do not believe you did either, my young friend."

"Will you forgive me?" Joash said with genuine concern. "I know I was not to show anyone the map or the ring, but—" Joash dropped his gaze to the floor.

Ari hugged him closer. "There is naught to forgive. You did as you thought necessary." His eyes fell upon Mira. "Rise, Mira, before your knees become sore."

*

It took longer than she would have liked for her mind to understand all that had occurred in the past few moments. She offered a puzzled look at Ari who seemed amused at her position on the floor before she glanced over at Joash.

The child's brow furrowed in concern, his eyes held a wealth of worry. Blinking back her bewilderment, she did as commanded and rose.

"I—I…" She wrapped her arms over her stomach.

Ari held up his hand halting further speech from her. "You two must be hungry. I have brought food."

Of course, she was hungry. Hungry for information on her family. Hungry for answers as to why he had hidden among them for so long. Why he chose her family to hide Judah's king. Why he never said a word. She was hungry all right. But since his arm draped over Joash's shoulders in a very protective manner—as if she'd harm the boy—and since he didn't seem to be forthcoming she would hold her tongue and wait.

Ari tugged on one of Joash's curls. "I left my bag by the entrance. You may begin the preparations so we can eat," he said, ruffling the child's hair. Joash hugged Ari's legs, and then rushed to the other room.

Her feet were immovable, like the giant stones. Her knees like olive oil. And when Ari raked his hand through his hair as he did now, her thoughts became muddied. She near forgot she was angry at him.

"He does not know," he said, his deep timbre raked down her spine. She swallowed past the knot in her throat. How could she have ever thought to be mad at him? *Because he endangered your family. Possibly even caused their deaths.*

Mira shook her thoughts. "Who does not know what?"

"Joash." He took one long stride and stood before her. His breath flowed over her like a cool breeze in the hot desert sun. He reached for her hand, the warmth of his touch raced to her toes. "He does not know who he is." He uncurled her fingers and plucked the ring from her palm. A ring she had forgotten she held.

"Oh." A small word, a small useless word. What was she supposed to say? Especially when he stood so close, his cheek so near hers. He moved closer, his lips a hair's breadth from her ear. She closed her eyes and swayed on her feet, swayed toward the strength offered in his arms.

Before she could allow her arms to wrap around his neck, he stepped away.

"And," he hesitated, his black eyes boring into hers, "he will not know. No one can know. Do you understand what that means, Mira?"

If there was one thing she found difficult above all other things, it was concentrating when Ari spoke her name. When his *r*'s rolled over his tongue as if he were vowing his never-ending love. But his voice was flat, emotionless. This was not the Ari she knew. Her anger returned in full. "Of course."

He arched his brow, an action that left her clinching her fists at her sides, causing pain to ripple through her marred hand. She shoved past him. Her feet quickly halted as he grasped her upper arm. Over the last few days she'd dreamed of him reaching for her hand just for the simple pleasure of it, but she never wished to kick him in the shins, until now.

"It is his life," he growled. "A life I am bound by God to protect."

She shook her hair over her shoulder and glared at him. "His life is worth that of my family?"

She knew what it meant to Judah to have King David's line restored. Knew the restoration was worth the lives of many villagers, yet she couldn't help the venom slipping from her tongue. Couldn't help the anger at Ari's betrayal. His lies.

"It is not what you think." Ari released her.

Her heart cried out in rebellion. He crossed his arms over his chest and turned his back on her. The ever-confident bond servant cowered, it was then she noticed the missing band from his arm. It was enough to break her heart. Ari was a free man.

He glanced over his shoulder. "I care very much for your father."

"I will return home."

Ari spun on his heels. "No," he said with an authority that could command an army, and probably had.

A hint of anger flashed into his eyes and she remembered she didn't really know him. Not after all the lies he'd told.

"I will keep your secret."

"It is not safe to take you home."

"I will go alone."

"No."

"Ari, it is not far from here. All will be well with me."

"You need to stay with me until the child is safe."

She could not bear it, even if it were for only another day, she could not bear being in his presence another moment knowing he was a free man. Knowing he would walk away from her family. Her family depended on him too much. She depended on him—whether she liked it or no. "I cannot, Ari."

"You have no choice, Mira. I will return you to your father when Joash is safe." He took a step toward her and enfolded her in his arms. The curve of her cheek pressed against the beating of his heart. The warmth of his breath caressed her brow and she wondered if he was going to kiss her there as her father had done whenever she scraped her knees as a child.

A child she was no more, and the emotions swirling in her chest made her long for more than a touch of his lips to her brow. Her hopes of marriage fizzled and disappeared like a falling star. She could never marry, not with the knots he tied to her heart. Not unless it was to him.

If only he were in truth a man of humble means. A man in need of her father's kindness.

His arms tensed, and he finally pressed his lips to her head. Tears fought their way to her eyes. Why did he have to be an important man from Jerusalem? For he could be nothing but, given the honor he held guarding the king. Why, after all the years of disliking him for following her around and tending her tasks was it now she thought she could possibly share the kind of affection with him as her parents did for each other? She would have been better off had she accepted Esha's suit months ago, even if he did scorn her for her imperfections.

She slid her hands between them and pushed him away. She wouldn't look at him. She couldn't, for there was no doubt he'd see all the anguish warring within.

"If I may, I would like to cleanse." Cleanse the pain tearing her apart.

"Yes, of course, Mira." He released her. "I'll make sure the pool is safe."

Chapter Twelve

Ari couldn't leave Mira's presence fast enough. When he'd seen her, seen that she was unharmed, all he could think about was holding her. But then Joash's words sunk through his fogged brain. And once he'd gotten past the vision of Mira, he understood what had occurred. Her knowledge of Joash's existence could have her killed.

Of course, she could have easily been killed when the soldiers came upon her the other day, and she had not known the secret then. It did not matter, she now knew some of the truth, a truth that could be used against her if she were to be captured by the queen's men. He could not return her to her home. Not until the child was back in Jehoiada's care.

Besides, not knowing if she was safe was like no other anguish he'd ever known. The travel to Jerusalem would take days and he'd prefer not to have Mira out of his sight for that long.

But now he was unsure if he had made the right decision. Something had shifted in the alcove. Something in Mira. As if she were a part of his sword arm, yet veiled behind a stone wall. And that alone scared him more than the idea of facing Athaliah's guards. At least with them he could fight with his sword. He knew the kinks in their armor.

He halted in the tunnel leading to the outer cave and leaned against the cool rough rock. How was he supposed to breach Mira's defenses?

With patience. He nodded, agreeing with the voice in his mind. Ari pushed away from the wall and rounded the corner.

"You are doing good, my friend," he said.

Joash sat in front of the fireless pit, mixing dough. "I like adding the honey. It makes it sticky."

"And it makes it taste good."

Joash giggled.

"When I return I'll begin the fire, and then we can make cakes."

Ari stepped out onto the ledge, the bright sun streamed through the curtain of water. The magnificence of God's artistry left him in awe. Even with all the chaotic emotions ambushing him he felt the peace of the Lord raining down upon him. He must remember the Lord's will was at work. He must trust that, in the end, all would be well.

There really was no need to check the pool. Unless someone had seen him slip beneath the water no one would know of the hidden cove. But he'd needed time to gain his composure after his encounter with Mira. Which shouldn't have bothered him considering he wasn't free to take her as his wife. At least until his duties to the king were fulfilled.

He raked his hand through his hair. Somewhere between the time Nathan had announced Mira's disappearance and the moment he'd laid eyes on her, he knew she belonged to him. Only to him. He had within his possession the contracts to prove it, all they needed was his mark.

He only hoped she would warm to him before he told her about her father's offer. Perhaps there would be time during their travels to Jerusalem.

He knew the moment she stood on the ledge. Knew because his heart began to beat faster.

Mira moved to stand beside him, her shoulder only inches away. Not for the first time had he noticed that her hair flowed freely. He clenched his hands to keep from touching the silk-like layers gracing her shoulder.

"Have you lost your veil?" He shouldn't take her to his parents unveiled. Not that they would mind, but he didn't want his brothers to see the treasure he chose to take as his wife, lest they try to steal her from him.

"No. Although it is quite filthy." She wrinkled her nose.

He loosened his fingers and gave in to his desire to touch her hair. He rubbed a few wayward strands between his thumb and index finger. Her breath hitched as if she felt his touch. She turned her eyes toward him with wide innocence. Her perfect bow-shaped lips offered a gift he could not take until he pledged his troth. "I will purchase you a new one."

Shadows crossed into her eyes. "I cannot go with you, Ari."

He grasped her arms and stared down into her eyes the color of polished Lebanon cedar.

"You have no choice, Mira." He wanted to force the issue, to claim her as his wife at this very moment if only to gain her obedience. Her life depended on her coming with him.

She released a breath of air and pulled from him before burying her disjointed fingers in her tunic. It was a gesture she often performed when nervous. "If you will leave, I will bathe now."

"Of course." He relented, although, he was reluctant to let things stand as they were.

She maneuvered the natural rock stairway until she sat with her arms wrapped around her legs on the last stone. She glanced at him. His heart swelled with an emotion unknown to him. An emotion he'd seen in his father's eyes when he looked upon his mother. An emotion that left him feeling vulnerable.

Ari sighed. Their travels would be long. If they could not find any common ground, their time together would be torment. However, it would give him time to convince her she could trust him again. And maybe, just maybe that she'd be happier married to him than to the likes of Esha.

Ari closed his eyes for a mere second, branding the image of her into his mind.

*

How could her stomach flop around like a fish just at the sight of him, not to mention the joy that filled her heart when he touched her hand or how her breath hitched when he tucked a strand of hair behind her ear. Ay, he was perfectly made with the Lord's own hand.

However, she could not trust him, which meant she couldn't trust her reaction to him. She wriggled her nose. If she held onto his deception, it would not hurt as much when it was time for them to part.

Of course, she understood the need for secrecy where Joash was concerned. However, it did not make her feel any better about their situation. It did not make her feel any better that her village had been attacked.

Thoughts of her family crashed down upon her head. Not one word of good news passed Ari's lips. But then she had not asked either. Did that mean they had perished under the guards' assault? What of her father and her mother? Had they survived? Ari had promised to return her to Abba, but what of her mother?

She hiccupped, choking back the torrent. It would do her no good to dwell on what she had no control over. She may not trust Ari, but her hope was in the Lord and his infinite wisdom.

She swiped the tears from her eyes and untied the sash holding her tunic in place. She shrugged the tunic off, allowing it to drape on the rock. With only her loincloth and linen around her breasts, she slipped into the water.

She stayed close to the edge. Close enough to keep her hand firm on the rock. Since the water reached her shoulders, she didn't have to arch her neck too far to soak her hair. Thick, long strands tangled around her limbs. It was as if she were cloaked in an ornately decorated robe. She closed her eyes, luxuriating in the cool spring and the silky caress of her own hair.

The power of the crashing water from the falls into the pool sent a thrill of excitement to her toes. To be caught, hidden within nature's womb, soothed her heartache a little.

If courage belonged to her, she'd take up her *tunic* and swim from this hidden oasis. Knowing Ari would catch her before she made it past the palms kept her feet planted on her slippery perch. If only she could just slip beneath the wall of water, if she could quickly swim to the edge, if she could...

Foolish, foolish woman. Ari had ever been perceptive. Often, even finishing her sentences before she could form a complete thought. Besides, he'd find her at her father's house. And he'd sure enough come for her. Wouldn't he?

She recalled the fierceness in his gaze when she said she was going home. As if she'd pained him. Although she couldn't pretend to know why. He was leaving. The lack of his band around his upper arm proved such. He'd chosen freedom. And she was certain her father would have asked him to stay.

She skimmed a hand over her wet hair, until she reached the ends, and then twisted, wringing out the excess water. Her thoughts stirred into a sandstorm.

If Ari had chosen freedom, he more than likely would not come after her. No, much to her distress, he'd continue on his journey to wherever he intended to travel. She glanced up to the ledge. He had not returned.

Before her courage abandoned her, she grabbed her tunic, slipped it over her body and dove beneath the water.

With escape firmly in her mind, not once had it dawned on her that danger would exist on the other side of the waterfall when she resurfaced. But when she cleared her hair from her eyes she blinked, once, and then twice, the bare bronzed backs of Athaliah's soldiers gleamed in the hot afternoon sun.

*

"It looks as if we are about ready to start a fire," Ari sat next to the boy.

Joash smiled while he patted the last of the cakes into a disk. "Ari, may I ask you a question?"

Ari stretched out his legs and reclined onto his forearms. "Of course. You know you can ask me anything?"

"Why is it Mira bowed at my feet? That is an honor only given to the one true God."

"You are correct, my friend."

"Then why would Mira do such a thing? I am not the Almighty."

Ari laughed before plucking a piece of dough from the bowl. "No, that you are not. Were you scared when the soldiers came?"

The child tilted his chin as if to contemplate the question. "At first I was confused, and then I ran. That's when I found Mira. She was at the well when the soldiers came."

Closing his eyes, Ari lifted a prayer of thanksgiving to the Lord for protecting her.

"At first she wouldn't listen to me, but we heard the screams and then horses as the soldiers came after us. I could not leave her there. I had to protect her."

He cringed at the story. He could only imagine the horror Joash and Mira had felt at the sounds. She must be worried about her family, and in his relief at finding them safe, he'd forgotten to give her word. "You did well, Joash. You have much courage for one so young."

He'd have to wait until she returned to give her news of her family.

"Ari?"

"Yes, Joash?"

"You once said that most men were afraid of what lurks in the water."

The corner of his lip curved upward. "Yes, I did." He recalled the very moment he'd told him of the myths believed by men. The boy had been more interested in pictures of such creatures than feared by the possibility of their existence. Of course, he'd only told the boy the stories in order to reassure him that the cave was a place of safety.

"A soldier was here," Joash said as if he were talking about lacing his sandals.

Ari rose to his feet. "Here?"

"Yes. He stood right there." Joash pointed to a spot on the ledge.

"When?" The air caught in Ari's lungs.

"Not long after we came here. He stood there staring at us. Mira grabbed your sword and swung it at him. He left and hasn't returned."

*

Afraid to release the air filling her lungs, Mira allowed it to ease out of her nostrils as she looked for a nook to hide.

Lord, hide your servants from our enemies.

"I've searched the crags and nothing," the Philistine spoke with frustration to his comrades.

"The boy is not a rumor. One of the servants told me of the child's arrival when he was a babe. A royal nurse brought him to that village." Another soldier crossed his arms over his chest. "I want him found. I want him killed."

Fear for Joash raced down her back.

"And the girl?"

Mira blinked. Her heart raced frantically.

"I want her brought to me. Unharmed."

She inhaled sharply. A hand covered her mouth and before she knew what was happening she was pulled beneath the surface. She fought against the arm banded around her waist, clawed at the hand clasped over her mouth.

She twisted and turned in her assailant's arms. Water stung her eyes, open wide with fear. Before it all began they surfaced. Mira blinked her eyes to clear the water. Her exhausted body sighed in relief at the sight of Ari, but her mind wanted to rail at him for scaring her. However, his hand remained tight against her lips.

"Shh," he whispered near her ear. "Come, very quickly and do not make a sound."

She nodded and followed close behind up the steps and into the cave. She stood there, her wet tunic clinging to her as it dripped on the floor and watched as Ari made hand gestures to Joash. She watched in silent shock as Joash carried out Ari's bidding. Ari shoved foodstuff into sacks, and then shoved it into her arms. He lifted one of her feet and tied a sandal to it, then the other.

Her thoughts were in turmoil. Guilt assailed her. Because of her anger, because of her selfish desire to thwart Ari, she had endangered Joash.

She tried to read Ari's brisk movements, the darkening of his cheeks and the fierce tick in his clenching jaw. Did he blame her? It was his right.

He shoved his sword into its sheath and tied it to his belt. How would they leave? There were many of them and only one Ari.

Oh, Lord, forgive me!

Mira wanted to ask Ari where they were going. But Ari seemed hesitant to speak, which left her question unasked.

Unanswered.

Chapter Thirteen

The self-control that had earned him his position as Joash's personal guard was threatening to fray. It should have been obvious when he told her she had no choice but to stay with him that it was dangerous for her to leave. He didn't think she'd disregard his warning. Not in this.

The high color in Mira's cheeks and her downcast eyes as he tied her sandals onto her feet proved she'd realized the consequences of her actions. She would not try another escape.

He laid his short swords onto the crumpled mat and rolled it tight before tying it with a cord. He'd no doubt they'd need all the weapons they could carry. He never thought another man would enter the water out of fear of what lurked in the depths. But one had. A Philistine mercenary if the bronze helm and armor was any indication. It would not be long before the handful of soldiers returned, if the mercenary could convince the Hebrews to enter the water.

If he learned anything from his days as Commander of Temple Guard, once a Philistine decided on a course, there was nothing to sway him. If Athaliah had hired the ruthless mercenaries to fight alongside her warriors she no doubt believed Joash lived.

A bowl clattered to the floor, startling him. He spun on his heel in time to see Joash pick it up.

He finished emptying the contents of the chest into one of the linen bags just as Joash disappeared into the hidden alcove. Mira's feet seemed rooted to the cave floor. He grasped her hand and tugged her behind him. It was not until they reached the secret tunnel pass that she found her feet. And then it was only to come to a swift halt.

"Mira," he whispered. "This is not the time for stubbornness."

"What of my parents?"

He furrowed his brow, trying to concentrate on the noises coming from outside the cavern as well as on her question. "They are well, but we must make haste." He tried once more to pull her toward the tunnel but her feet held firm. "I will tell you of their ordeals once we are safe, Mira."

"I cannot go in there." He felt her panic through the fingers clasped in his. Fingers rough and calloused from working alongside her mother and father.

"Why not?" This side of her puzzled him.

He had never seen her afraid. Not when she fought off a pack of wild dogs with a firebrand as he lay dying, and not when faced with menacing soldiers.

"I—I am scared." She ripped her hand from his and wrapped her arms around her stomach.

He laid his palm on her shoulder, the wet linen cold beneath his touch. She shivered. There was no time for her to sit by the fire and dry. "Mira, do you trust me?"

Her hesitation was like vinegar poured over tiny cuts. But it was the glittering tears in her eyes that tugged on his heart.

There would be much ground to gain if he were to ever have her faith again. "Mira, you must listen to me." He released her arm and adjusted the pack slung over his shoulder. "This," he said, waving his hand.

" Joash is much more than you and I could ever fathom. He is important to the good of Judah. Those men," he pointed in the direction of the waterfall. "They know this. If they do not return with the child as their queen demands, they will lose their lives. If they capture us, we will lose ours."

"It is dark," she countered as if she hadn't heard a word he'd said.

He sighed with a great deal of relief. Thankful that she fretted over the darkness, and not over her faith in his abilities to keep her safe. "Yes, I regret that I cannot light a torch. Not yet. I promise to keep you by my side, but you must listen to me." He grasped her hand, so small and cold. He gave her a reassuring squeeze. "All right?"

The sound of earthenware hitting the ground was like a sword thrust toward his chest. Without waiting for her to answer he jerked her forward. They raced through the hidden tunnels as fast as he dared to push them, all the while praying the Lord would keep them hidden within the bowels of the earth. Not that he thought Athaliah's guards would find them in the maze.

After traveling through the dark for an hour, Mira tripped and stumbled behind him. He halted, taking her baggage from her.

"Are you hurt?" he asked. Their breaths ragged in the still, dark air. Her only answer was to squeeze his hand. If the walkways had been wide enough he would have carried her. "There is a hollow not much farther. I am confident in the Lord that we can stop for a rest."

"How is it that you know this place so well, Ariel?"

He wanted to tell her the truth, the entire truth, especially when she reverted to his full name instead of the one she'd called him for the past several years. But he feared she would think he lied once again.

"A man does not survive without a way to escape his enemies," he answered as simply as he could. He knew once Mira felt more like herself, she would continue with her questions. However, he never expected the one echoing off the cave walls to his ears.

"How did you become guardian to Joash?"

"Now is not the time, Mira. Soon, I promise you will have answers to your questions."

After what seemed like another hour, an orange light began to filter through the walkway. Joash's shadowy figure moved toward it. Ari's faith wavered as he realized that the light could only be from a fire within. He tugged on Joash's tunic and pulled him backward. He let go of Mira's hand and knelt beside the child.

"If I do not return for you, you must go back twenty paces and turn north. And then forty paces to the east. There will be a blind man, his name is Seth. Tell him to take you high. He will know what to do. Do you understand, my young friend?" he whispered.

He hated causing the boy more stress, but no matter how much he willed it, if danger lurked in the cavern he wouldn't be the one to take Joash back to Jerusalem. That job would be left to the priests of Manna. He kissed the boy on either side of the cheek and bowed his head before he rose.

Reaching for Mira's hand, he leaned close. His heart thundered in his chest. Their breaths mingled between them. He should have accepted Caleb's offer and pledged his troth to her. "Mira, if aught should happen to me protect him with your life. He knows the way, but guard him well." He slipped his hand from hers and replaced it with the hilt of his dagger.

"Remember, twenty, then forty, and run if need be."

Joash's shadowy figure nodded. Ari straightened his tunic, pulled his sword from its sheath and crept forward.

He peered around the opening that led to the large cavern centered in the network of caves. A small fire flickered in the middle of the floor. A young girl knelt beside it stirring the contents of the kettle over the flames. A woman shuffled around carrying out various tasks as if she were expecting visitors. His gaze slid to one of the plaster benches that had been built into the walls hundreds of years before. Three men sat with their heads bowed and another woman sat at their feet. He drank them in having not seen them for near seven years. "Thank you, Lord," he prayed.

Without hesitation he returned for Joash and Mira. At the entrance he motioned for them to remove their sandals, as he had done. They placed them outside the entrance. Bowing his head he entered with Joash and Mira at his side.

"Shalom, my family" he offered.

*

The men lifted their heads at once. Mira regretted leaving her veil behind, even soiled as it was. Fearing her lack of proper manners would shame Ari, she sunk back into the darkness of the tunnel and tucked her hand into her tunic lest they see her imperfections. As if reading her thoughts, Ari wrapped his fingers around her upper arm. It wasn't a touch meant to reassure or comfort, but a silent command to heed his will.

She fought the urge to pull from his grasp. She started to dip her chin when the men closed their eyes and raised their hands heavenward. The women halted their movements and bowed. They didn't return to their tasks until Ari returned their greeting.

One woman, the older of the two, set a bowl of water at their feet. She dipped her cloth in the bowl and washed the dust from Joash's skin. She dried them before perfuming his feet with oil.

Mira had seen the honor of welcoming guests performed many times, but never had she been the receiver of such a welcoming. The woman knelt before Mira. Unaccustomed to the attention from a stranger, Mira shrank back against the wall and curled her toes.

The woman glanced at her before looking to Ari. At Ari's firm nod, the woman gently took Mira's foot in her hand and began performing the same ritual she had on Joash. With the same grace and care as she had the young king. After she perfumed Mira's feet she moved on to Ari.

Once their feet had been cleansed, the youngest of the three men rose and approached Ari. In light of Ari's recent command, wariness trickled over her and she wrapped her arm around Joash hugging him close. The man bussed each of Ari's cheeks. "Shalom, Ariel. I have missed you at the temple."

She choked. She was parched from their hasty journey. Her head spun. She pressed her fingers to her temples. What she'd just heard could not be true.

Ari, a priest.

"And I have missed you as well, Uncle." Ari hugged the man.

Heat flooded her cheeks at the realization of what the past years had held. Shame slammed into her belly. This man had served her father with the diligence of any son, and he was a priest? No wonder he taught the law with efficiency.

Her knees began to shake. She pressed her knuckles against the wall to hold her upright. She had known there was something different about him. Had known the Lord had set him apart for a divine purpose and not just to build her bridal home or help tend her chores.

In her naiveté she'd thought the Lord had meant him to torment her with his constant interference. Tears smarted the backs of her eyes. She blinked them back when the elder of the three men greeted Ari.

"Shalom, Ishiah," Ari grinned.

Her gaze traveled over the older man and then to the other two dressed much the same as this Ishiah. They each wore deep blue sashes around their waists. Were they all priests? They lacked the brightly adorned turbans her mother had told her about.

The older men were much shorter than Ari and their arms did not hold the same contours, they were not well muscled. And Ari's hair hung only to his shoulders, his face had been clean-shaven when he had arrived at her home all those years ago, and he had not once grown it back. Only now did his face contain a dark shadow from the lack of blade on his skin.

Ari explained the events of the last days to the people in the room. Leaving out portions about the child's ancestry. "Mira protected Joash where I failed."

Her cheeks warmed. It was on her tongue to deny her role but Ishiah grasped her hands with his papery ones. Heat seared her cheeks at the thought of this man of God, one who was holy and righteous touching her maimed hand.

"Shalom, Mira. It is a great fortune you were with the child when Ari was unable to be."

She blinked, and then looked at Ari. Returning her gaze to Ishiah, she responded, "It was I who was fortunate, for it was Joash who saved me from another attack."

Where had Joash gone? She found him on a bench with his legs crossed eating a cake of bread. It was nice to see him acting like a hungry child and not like a man beyond his time.

Assured of his well-being she returned her attention to the priests, feeling inadequate before them.

"I find the need to busy myself," she said, noticing how the women continued in their preparations.

Ari chuckled, his laugh rolled out of his chest and to her knees making them weak. "No one has ever accused Mira of having idle hands."

She answered with a glare. "What is it that I can help with?"

Ishiah laughed. "First, Mira, you must dress."

Her eyes widened in horror. She had forgotten about her disorderly and wet clothing during their frantic flight, but it was the way Ishiah stared at her hair that caused her the greater shame. "I beg forgiveness," she whispered with her head bowed.

"Nonsense, child," he replied. "After your ordeal, your state of disarray is to be expected." He motioned toward one of the women. "Anna, my wife, will see you properly clothed."

Anna approached them with a friendly smile and bowed her covered head in greeting. Her richly decorated veil shimmered in the firelight. The delicate woven blue sash around her waist looked as if it was made of the finest threads, and the trim on her tunic had beads tinier than grains of sand. Mira bowed in response.

"My thanks," Mira said to Ishiah and then followed Anna to one of the outer rooms off the cavern.

Several oil lamps lit their path illuminating drawings depicted in the limestone walls. She gasped at the ornate pictures. Some were simple with lines and circles, but many were...

"They are lovely, are they not?" Anna asked.

"Very much. This place is beyond any words known to my tongue. I've lived in this desert all my life and never knew..."

"There are not many who do know the depth of these crags. King David himself, with his soldiers, hid in these very caves when Saul sought to kill him."

Mira ran the tips of her fingers over the white lines. Had David drawn this very image? Had he written psalms upon these very walls?

"The priests have kept them to themselves. They have used these caves to hide from those who would destroy them. And to carry out God's will."

"Much like now?"

Anna lifted a fresh piece of linen from a box. "Here, let us unwrap you."

Mira shied away knowing her scars were not contained to her hand only, but twisted up her arm and over her shoulder. She did not wish to be rejected or worse pitied. However, Anna insisted and removed the damp tunic and the under binding from Mira's chest and replaced it with a dry, fresh, balsam scented cloth before handing her a new loincloth. Not once had the woman reacted or commented on the distasteful scars marring Mira's flesh.

"You do not fully understand what has occurred. Do not worry overly much. Ariel, he's never been one for words. It is why he was chosen. But he'll speak soon enough."

Anna draped a rich blue-colored tunic over Mira's head and then tied a gold sash around her waist. The soft linen whispered against her skin, but it was the woman's observations of Ari that left her shivering.

She had spent several years scorning the man, but that did not mean she didn't know his gait. The lyrical tone in his voice when he lifted up prayers to the Lord. The gentleness of his hand when he soothed a frightened sheep. The care he took with her father. How he ran a hand through his hair when he was perplexed. But this woman, this woman he had not seen once in the past six years seemed to know him better than she ever could.

"You know him well then?"

Anna stood in front of her, a delicate blue veil trimmed with gold beads in her hand. The cloth a perfect match to the tunic. She settled it on Mira's head, her fingers brushing through her hair.

"You are very lovely, child," Anna said, her eyes glittered with an emotion Mira had only seen in her mother's eyes. It was a deep love that only a mother could have. But why she looked at her thusly Mira could not fathom.

The moment drew long and Mira grew uncomfortable. She longed to return to Ari's side. To knead dough. Plough the mountainous terrain. Anything. "My thanks, Anna."

"No, Mira, thank you. You do my son proud."

Mira swallowed hard. "Your son?"

"Yes. Ari, he is my son."

Chapter Fourteen

Ari sipped the cool spring water from the cup offered him by his younger sister. "I am very grateful it is you who occupied this area and not one of Athaliah's guards."

"It is fortunate for you, my son," Ishiah, his father, responded. "Word spread quickly that they'd been terrorizing the area. I knew it would only be a matter of time and sought to offer our assistance."

"How did you know I would come this way and not make straight for Jerusalem?" Ari's curiosity had nipped at his tongue since he had spied his family, but he had let it lay dormant.

"Ah, my nephew," Daniel spoke. "We have our ways." He laughed as he lifted his own cup to his lips.

His Uncle Elam's eyes twinkled with mischief. "That we do."

Ari ignored his uncles and looked to his father and wondered if his father had broken his vow to keep silent about Joash. "Although I have no doubt in your abilities to know things that leave the best of spies baffled, even I did not plan our retreat thusly."

"This I know, my son. Your brothers and cousins are branched throughout the area." His father paused to take a sip from his cup. "If you'd not arrived when you had, we would have come after breaking bread."

"I near turned around and went to Seth's when I saw the firelight," Ari responded with a smugness that was overdone even for him. His father and uncles always knew things, even when he did not and it set him on edge. He lacked their ability to discern details. Details that often came in handy when one was on a mission.

"Is that so?" Elam asked.

Ari hid his smile behind his cup as he took a sip. He had not lied.

"You fool yourself, boy," Daniel added. "You have ever been curious. You would not have left without investigating further."

Ari conceded with a nod.

"Besides, your brothers Isa and Melchiah wait with Seth along with their wives. They will join us soon."

In the comfort of his family he had near forgotten that danger lurked. He rose from his seat, his eyes on Joash. His thoughts on Mira. "I must return. I must see to it they did not infiltrate and if they did…" He raked a hand through his hair as he turned from them and faced the opening in the cavern from whence they came.

A heavy hand gripped his shoulder. He did not need to look. It did not matter whose it was for it brought little comfort. "You have carried a heavy burden all these years, my boy," Daniel said.

Another hand, this one stronger, firmer, laid on his other shoulder. "Of course, I had not realized all you've sacrificed until recently. I did not even know you were alive until Jehoiada confided in me, something I should have learned from my own brother." Elam glared at Ari's father. The terseness in his voice set Ari on edge.

"Forgive me, Uncle. My father was sworn to secrecy as was I. If I hadn't been in need of his help he never would have known either."

"All that matters, now, is you are home, and fortunate, too as your burden has cost you much," Elam added.

What his uncle said held a great wealth of truth, but an image of Mira kneading dough, the comfort of her music offered during his sleeplessness contradicted the words, for he had gained a greater wealth than any man could have asked for, even if he might have to walk away from her in the end.

He heard his father rise from his seat. He shuffled to stand in front of Ari and looked him in the eyes. "Ari, it is time to share your burden. Besides, your brothers will see to it our hideaway is secure." He waved a hand toward the youngest of his children. "Lydia prepares a meal. You must rest and build your strength for the fight ahead of you."

"Your father is correct, Ari." Mira's soft-spoken words wrapped around every one of his muscles. His heart filled with a combination of overwhelming joy and tormenting pain. They seemed to fight for precedence. Fear of her rejection left him utterly helpless. Hope of her love had him spinning on his heels, dislodging the hands that sought to bring him comfort.

She was a vision to be treasured. The rich blue dyed linen set her eyes to flames, like a lamp lit with oil. Her cheeks glowed even in the dimness of the cavern, and her smile was the first genuine one he had seen from her since she had last spoken with her father. She left him breathless, and his heart pounded like a madman trying to escape the chains of death. He worked his lips to respond, but no sound came.

"You need your rest." Mira folded her hands before her. She seemed relaxed. Comfortable among his family, which was good. Her eyes sparked with mischief. "Even now circles grow beneath your eyes. You look as if you are about to faint from exhaustion. Tell me you did not carry my father around the fields."

For a moment, he thought she had been serious. He knew he must look like a wild animal, especially since he had pushed Caleb homeward and then raced to the spring. Not to mention their frantic escape through the tunnels.

"I see you have fared our travels well."

She bowed her head a little. "I have also rested." Mira raised her brow.

Ari rolled his shoulders before settling his fists on his hips. Restlessness consumed him. He feared it would continue to do so until all was well within Judah. "You," he said, glancing around the room encompassing his father, uncles, and Mira, "do not understand. It is obvious Athaliah knows of his existence or her guards would not now be searching the area as we speak. Until the child is in Jerusalem where he belongs, I cannot, and will not be at rest."

*

Delight curled her toes when Ari had looked at her with such great emotion, yet his scrutiny made her uncomfortable. Especially in full view of his family, which left her searching for a way to ease the tension building in the air. But when he turned serious, when he clung to his stubborn tendency and mentioned his duties it left her reeling.

It was as if he had tossed her words of affection to the ground and trampled them beneath his sandals. Of course, she had not uttered any such words for fear he would do just that.

He was not a man who would ever belong to her. There was no use in offering what would never be accepted or returned. She did not blame him. Nor did she blame the Lord for what seemed cruelty. Ari was a man loyal to his duties, not his heart. Instead, she would embrace the blessing of having known a man as great and honorable as Ari. And she would do all she could to help him in his quest.

"I overheard the guards. They talked of killing Joash."

Ari's gaze narrowed. "Why did you not tell me this before?"

She twisted her hands into the folds of her tunic.

"Mira, you have had a difficult day," Anna said, exiting the makeshift chamber behind her. "Why don't you sit and rest?"

Ari's mother wrapped her soft fingers around hers and squeezed. She offered her strength and courage in the face of adversity. Mira would take both. However, she would not sit by with idle hands.

"My thanks, Anna. I would prefer to help in any way I can. First, I must tell Ari what I know." Mira smiled at the kind woman and then glanced once again at the man who remained as still as a statue, the only evidence of life was the rise and fall of his chest and the slight ticking of his jaw. She'd angered him. Albeit unintentionally. It was just as well. The more distance between them, physically and emotionally, the better.

"Very well then, my daughter," Anna responded. "There are two tables by the earthen jars. If you would lay them out over there." She pointed to the east side of the fire.

"You'll find all you need once you are finished speaking with my son."

Anna turned her piercing gaze on her son before leaving them to tend to her chores.

"What is it you know, Mira?"

She felt the men's eyes on her and she swallowed. "On—only what I heard. The captain believed it to only be a rumor."

"But?" He clenched his jaw, his nostrils flared. If spears could shoot from his eyes—she fought back the tears threatening.

"One of my father's servants added suspicion by telling him of Tama's arrival with an infant. I know—" She lifted her chin and held her head high. "One of the soldiers saw us. I know he did. He was in the cave. He saw Joash."

Ari gripped the back of his neck and rolled his shoulders before reaching out with the pad of his thumb to wipe a tear from her cheek. "That is not your doing, Mira. You had no way of knowing they would follow you and Joash."

No, she did not. She hadn't even known where they were. But if it hadn't taken Joash so long to coax her into the water, would they have been followed?

She turned away, found the tables and carried them to where they would eat their meal. She untied the strap and pulled it through the loops that edged the round leather fabric. In the center were a stack of bowls and utensils. She set them out and then laid out the second leather table. Its center contained seasoned spices as well as several more bowls and cups. With the setting of the dishes done, she searched the earthen jars for one that held wine. When she found none she remembered whom she was dining with and grabbed the water jar.

She had just begun to pour water into the first cup when a booming voice sounded from one of the tunnels. Startled, she dropped the jar and rushed to Joash and enfolded him in her arms.

It was then that she glanced at Ari. His face radiated with fierce pride. And for a moment she thought it was directed at her, until a rather tall, muscular man ducked through one of the entrances.

"Jesse, my brother!" Ari beamed, clasping the man in a hug before kissing each cheek.

Ari was a tall man, but Jesse towered over him. His shoulders were much wider than Ari's, but his arms weren't as muscular. The color of their hair was the same silky straight strands, although Jesse's curled at his shoulders. Ari's barely brushed his. Where Ari's chin was clean-shaven, Jesse wore his beard in the same fashion as Ari's father and uncles. Their eyes were the same shade, their noses the same aquiline. And their smiles were identical, like Anna's. She looked to Jacob, and then to Anna and wondered how these two average people could produce giants.

"I see I have frightened our guest," Jesse said. "Look, I've brought another guest." He motioned his hand toward the opening. Her cousin stood in the entrance.

It was then Mira had noticed all eyes were on her and Joash, who squirmed within her arms.

She released him and he rushed forward giving Tama a quick hug before darting toward the men. Mira rose from where they had knelt. "Tama, you are well? What of my mother and father?" She pulled her cousin close.

"Ay, I am as are your parents. It is glad I am to see you two alive," Tama returned. Her gaze fell to Joash and she smiled. "And you, what a brave boy you are."

Joash tugged on her hand and pulled her to a bench where he proceeded to tell her of his adventures.

"Jesse," Ari said, sauntering to Mira's side and taking her hand. "This is Mira, the daughter of my master. Tama's cousin. Her protection of the child is fierce."

She took great comfort in Ari's presence. The warmth of his touch. The mint leaves that seemed to belong to him. She bit her tongue against any wayward speech that might threaten to spill from her mouth. The mention of her father, not knowing if he was alive, the idea of Ari, this priest, as a bond servant left vinegar churning in her stomach.

"A pleasure," Jesse bowed to her. She returned the gesture.

Out of the corner of her eye, she saw Lydia mop the spilt water. Mira made a sound of distress and pulled her hand from Ari's.

"My forgiveness." She knelt beside the girl and took the cloth from her. "Allow me."

"It is no matter," Lydia returned. "I have often spilt a jug."

"Or two," Jesse teased. The young girl's cheeks turned rosy.

"Jesse," Anna called. "Leave the child be. She is coming along nicely. She'll make some man a wonderful wife one day."

"Let us not be hasty, Anna," Ishiah spoke.

Mira rose with the dripping rag. She glanced around, unsure where to place it. Anna pointed her in the direction of an ornate blue hand-painted bowl, the same used to wash their feet when they had entered this cozy, dark cavern. From all that she had seen they were a very loving family. Not what she had expected from a long line of men dedicated to carry out God's edicts.

She had expected. . .what? Less love, more sternness? It was a pleasant surprise even if a double-edged sword, for it was something she would never be a part of. Not that her family wasn't loving. They were very much so, except for the occasional spat with Rubiel.

"Abba, you'll have to let her go sometime," Jesse answered.

"But only when she is ready, is that not right, Elam?" Ishiah turned the conversation to his brother. "You have been blessed with a quiver of daughters and not one remains."

"And you've been blessed with a quiver of sons and have gained only two daughters beside your own." Elam took a sip from his cup.

Mira found the talk of marriages disturbing. A son took a wife and brought her home to his parents. The reminder was like a seal upon an earthen jug. Ari would never be free to leave his family. Just as she would never be free to leave hers. And now that she fully understood that Ari's constant help with her chores didn't grow from pity but from a sincere kindness in his heart, now that she knew the sensation of his hand, she'd never be able to marry another. Not for love.

"Tell me, Brother, how was it serving your master?"

Guilt gnawed at her insides. Her father had never treated him badly. But she had, not as unkindly as Rubiel, but she'd been unkind nonetheless.

Ari laughed, sending a thrill of awareness to her toes. "It was more blessing than anything. The Lord's plans are much greater than anything I could have fathomed. As we will all see in due time."

His dark eyes forced their way into her soul. It was as if he were conveying a message to her. A message she wanted to reject wholeheartedly. Except for that one little piece that caused her heart to soar to the heavens. Surely, Ari knew the impossibility of their match. For he would never give up his ambitions. And she would never ask him to.

Chapter Fifteen

Two more of Ari's brothers and their wives, along with another uncle, a blind man by the name of Seth, joined them before the evening meal. Mira's stomach rumbled as she dished lentils onto the remaining plates.

The sound of Ari's deep chuckle startled her, but his tanned hands were there to take the pottery from her before she dropped it onto his lap. "How long since you have eaten, Mira?"

She swallowed past the invisible lump in her throat. "We are about to eat now."

Ari wrapped his fingers around her wrist. Heat flooded her cheeks as his family watched their interaction. "You did not answer my question," he said, his voice low and dangerous.

"We broke bread last eve, remember?" Joash spoke. "There's been no time today."

The glare she sent the child's way went unnoticed. How was it he, too, considered himself her keeper?

"Mira, come you must sit. Eat," Anna said.

She bowed to Ari's mother out of respect and tried to rise, but he did not remove his fingers from her wrist. Instead he scooted closer to his brother Jesse. "She will sit here with me, Mother," he said, his eyes never leaving hers. "I will feed her myself if need be."

"You wouldn't," she said, tugging on her arm.

"I would." He grinned, giving her unblemished arm a slight yank. She landed beside him. His shoulder brushed against hers. She sucked in a sharp breath and tried to scoot away.

How quickly his overbearing and unwanted kindness had turned to overbearing arrogance.

He released her and handed her his plate. The heat that had flooded her cheeks rose to the tips of her ears. She felt shamed, and in front of his family. Never had she seen him act this strong-handed and arrogant as if he were her...He had no rights to her. He was not her father. He was not her husband, nor would he ever be.

She spooned a bite of lentils into her mouth knowing he'd carry out his threat if she dared defy him. After her third bite he seemed appeased, and accepted another plate from his sister. The men around the table resumed their conversation. Not much of which she understood. Mainly questions about the activities in the surrounding cities and the well-being of relatives.

She continued to eat, red faced, in silence knowing she should not be sitting with the men. Then as if a shofar sounded, silence hung in the air. An icy chill infused her limbs, she froze.

Ari tilted his head. She heard an odd sound coming from the tunnel. The brothers and uncles dropped their dishes, rose from their seats and drew their swords from their belts. Without being ordered, she snagged Joash's hand and ran to the chamber where Ari's mother had taken her earlier. Anna, Tama and the rest of the women followed.

The hiss of swords as they sliced through the air echoed throughout the cave. A clang rang out and she drew Joash close. Her sanity threatened to lose its tether as grunts filled her ears. Somewhere a piece of pottery clattered, a man cried out in pain. Her heart dropped to her feet.

Had Ari been injured? An image of his old wounds pressed into her mind. The blood, the infection, the fever, the endless days of not knowing if he would live or die.

She squeezed her eyes closed. "Lord, cloak us in your wings. Protect us from our enemies."

Although a battle continued to rage in the outer cavern, peace settled in her heart. She opened her eyes. Tama and Ari's mother and sister encircled her and Joash. Each held a short sword in their hands. Even Lydia, the youngest amongst them.

Mira released a sigh. She was not alone in her desire to protect this young boy. This king child.

"Do not worry, my daughter," Anna soothed. "This place is well fortified, and we are well prepared for the danger."

She tried to hold on to the hope Ari's mother offered, but the truth rang in her ears. Clang after clang struck through the air, reverberating off the rock walls. In her mind's eye she envisioned Ari and his kin striking, defending their position. And then her mind saw Ari, injured, cut down. Fighting for his life. She'd watched him do so once before. Did she have the strength to do so this time? Now that he was more than a stranger? Now that she might be falling in love with him?

Fear sunk its sharp talons into her.

"Do not fret, Mira." Joash patted her hand clenching his shoulder. "Ari will not let anyone hurt you."

She offered him a tentative smile, wishing she had his faith. But in all her years, never had she encountered the likes of what had occurred in the past few days. Never had she seen the face of evil, not even during their trips to Hebron where all sorts of it paraded in the streets.

"Besides," Joash continued, "if you fear our enemies, you place more trust in their abilities than God."

The boy amazed her. In the midst of a battle he remained calm. And wise. A strength and integrity. A testament to the man who'd influenced him.

"How did you become so wise?" She mussed his hair.

His mouth curved upward showing a brilliant toothless smile. "I had an excellent teacher."

"You humble me, Joash." Ari's voice, although low, echoed off the cave wall and caused chills to race over her arms.

Her gaze flung to the entrance. She drank in the sight of him, damp with perspiration. His muscular chest expanded with each breath he took. He sheathed his sword and then dropped his arms to his sides. He looked exhausted, but well. No visible injury marred his skin, and no blood stained his tunic. She sighed in relief.

"Is it finished?" Joash asked.

Ari nodded. "For now, it is."

The boy pulled from her embrace and pushed past Ari. It was then she noticed that they were alone.

"Are you well?" she asked, her hands twisted in her tunic.

"I am."

His lack of words irritated.

She looked around the room, her gaze skimming the drawings left by men of old, anything to avoid looking at him.

"Mira," he whispered.

As if they had a will of their own, her eyes shifted to his. And before she could force them away she was caught by his gaze and the emotion pouring out of them. Her heart filled near to bursting, and then it deflated. *This will never do.*

"I should see to the wounded."

"No," he said, stepping closer. "The others will do what is necessary." He shoved his hand through his hair. "I never told you how your family fared, and you did not ask again"

"There was no time. Besides, I feared the answer." It was true. Even when Tama arrived and told her of her parents well-being she feared pressing further, afraid she'd discover that not all was, in truth, well .

He reached out and slid a hand down her arm until he twined his fingers with hers. "I should have been more considerate. I should have told you."

As much as she wanted to know they were all right, she did not want to know if they had been harmed. Not after what she'd just heard. Her family did not have the tools to defend themselves. They had no weapons among them. "How many soldiers were there?"

His brow furrowed in confusion. "Now?"

She blinked, fighting back the tears. "Yes."

"Four. Why?"

"Are they dead?" His hand fell from hers. The place where his fingers had been branded her in a way she could not explain.

He raked his palm over his face and hung his head. "They gave us no option, Mira."

"I see." But she didn't. These men, these priestly men, had fought like trained warriors, at least from what she had heard. And, they had prevailed over the enemy. Of course, she was not complaining, she knew ultimately the guards had sought Joash's death and anyone who stepped in the way, but she didn't understand. She didn't understand any of it. "Did they follow us? Were they the men from the pool?"

Ari furrowed his brow as if confused by her question. He shook his head and then lifted his hands to her shoulders. He stared into her eyes. "Mira, your family is well. Your mother was bruised a little when she sought to protect one of the slaves."

She nodded. A tear slid down her cheek. Her mother, so small, had always been as fierce as a lioness. "And the slave?"

"He died."

"Which one?" It didn't matter. What was done, was done, but she could lift a prayer of peace for those he was close to.

"Obed."

She closed her eyes against the sadness threatening to burst forth.

"Mira, you should know." He paused.

She opened her eyes, searching his. "What?"

"Athaliah's men," he said, motioning toward the cavern. "They've attacked other villages. Jesse said they did not leave one child alive in those camps. You must know, if you would have stayed," he gulped. "If you would have stayed with Joash, none of you would have survived. It is fortunate all the children from your village remain unharmed. Mayhap, because they were not of the same age as Joash. Mayhap because the soldiers chose to follow you instead. You did right by leaving. And as difficult as I know it was for you to stay hidden, you did right by that, too."

"Th-thank-you." Her resolve to remain strong began to crumble.

Ari wrapped his arms around and hugged her close, just like her father had done when she was a child, and sought to comfort her. "All will be well in the end. All will be well soon, I promise you."

She didn't know if it was his words, or if it was his embrace, but she wanted to believe him.

*

He would give all of his possessions to keep her near his heart. Her tiny frame fit snug to perfection against his. She was soft where he was solid. She smelled of henna blossoms and cinnamon, he smelled of several days' travel dust.

His mother had seen to Mira's comforts, for which he'd have to thank her. Now, however, he just wanted to hold Mira. He started to drop a kiss to the top of her head when he recalled he didn't have the right for such intimacies.

Not yet. Not until he signed the marriage contract. Not until she agreed to be his wife.

With great effort he pulled back from her.

"You must rest," he said.

She flinched and he immediately regretted his tone. It wasn't as if he meant to cause her distress. He only sought what was best for her, and she needed rest.

"I will rest when everyone else lays their head down."

"You are a stubborn one."

"There are things that need tending too. I will not sit by with idle hands. It is not in my nature."

He smiled. "I know, sweet. I know. We travel on the morrow to Manna. I do not want you dropping things in my brother's lap from weakness."

She snapped her head back as if he'd slapped her, but she wouldn't apologize. She was not invincible. Not that he thought her weak. She'd shown much courage and strength through the terrifying events that had occurred over the past several days. Her only failings were recognizing her need for sustenance whilst she cared for others.

"Will we be running for our lives as today?"

Ari held his gaze steady. The threat was even more viable than it had been before. "It is possible."

She moved around him, her arms crossed over her chest. He followed her with his eyes until she halted. She stood in front of the entrance as if to block his escape if he were so inclined. She looked the warrioress, armed with amber-colored eyes, full lips, and perfect curves. Although he could not imagine her brandishing a sword against the Philistine.

He stepped one foot forward and then chastised himself for such thoughts.

"I do not understand," she said, peering into the outer cavern. "If they are dead, how is it a threat still looms?"

A tick thumped in his jaw. He released a deep sigh. Danger was always possible but he was aware that more of Athaliah's soldiers were hunting them and had breached their sanctuary—a sanctuary no one knew of outside his kin. "Anything is possible, Mira. We should always be at the ready."

"Who knows of his existence?"

There was no use pretending that he did not know whom she spoke of. And by her stance, there was no use ignoring her question. Besides, he owed her a few answers. "Myself. Jehoiada—"

"Jehoiada, the High Priest?" A crinkle formed between her brows. "My uncle?"

"Your uncle?" This time he didn't stop himself from stepping forward. He grabbed her by the arm and dragged her back into the depths of the room. "What do you mean?" he whispered.

"Jehoiada is my mother's brother."

"Of course," he said, raking his hand through his hair. "And Tama?"

"Tama is my cousin on my father's side. We knew when she brought Joash to our village he did not belong to her. We just did not know who he belonged too, nor did we wish to question her. Only embrace her."

"What did your father think, her bringing a child not her own to his home?"

"I cannot say. Tama had lost her husband before she'd given birth and the babe shortly after its birth. She left for Jerusalem full of sorrow. Father thought it would be good for her. I knew Joash could not be hers. There'd been no time. . ."

High color rose in her cheeks at the turn of the topic. "The Lord allowed her to be where He needed her to save a child from the same fate Joash's cousins had met."

The images of the bloody massacre had left him with nightmares. The defamation of King David's house, and worse the defilement of the temple, which had been like tearing out his heart. It had only been by the grace of God that Joash survived.

"Ari?"

"Yes, Mira?"

"If Athaliah's guards are after Joash, then that means—"

"She knows of his existence."

"She hadn't come for him before which means she did not know of his existence, which means—"

"Somebody has informed her."

"But who? Who would do such a thing? And what do they have to gain by doing so?"

"The only people who'd been privy to his existence are my parents and Jesse, and recently my uncles and cousins." He pointed toward the cavern. It was not possible. Was it? His family would not betray the Lord. They would not betray him, would they? Anger burned hot. He moved forward, Mira caught his arm and stopped him in his tracks.

"No."

"I have to know. I have to know if one of my family has betrayed God."

"You know here," she said, placing her hand over his heart. "Jehoiada is my uncle. He could have told my father of Joash's existence."

Ari shook his head, because he didn't know. Not for certain. And if her father had known, he would not have told a soul, of that he was certain.

"Ari, somehow, someone discovered the truth." She chewed on her lip. Sadness entered her eyes, darkening them to the color of the sand just as the sun sinks beyond the horizon. "I cannot believe I am about to say this, but Rubiel, she is petty. Selfish. She hated that Tama was sent to Jerusalem and she was left behind to tend sheep and fields. Yet, why would my parents confide in her and not me? As much as they loved her, they knew her ambitions dictated her actions."

He drew her into his arms. "They didn't tell her because they did not know. Whoever has divulged information has given more than your sister or your parents ever could have known." He gave in to his desire and bent his head and kissed her brow. It seemed as natural as drinking water from a clear brook. "Ease your worries, Mira."

She pulled back, her gaze searched his. She looked puzzled, and she seemed not to have realized that he'd just kissed her brow.

"But who?"

Of course, her mind was on the dangers surrounding their young king. Just as his should be. He dropped his arms and immediately missed the warmth and comfort of her.

Mira crossed her arms over her chest as if she too missed the contact between them. "Our journey to Jerusalem will continue to be plagued with danger if we do not know who is betraying us."

She was right. He knew she was. How could one of his own family betray him? Betray the secrets handed down for ages? He had no doubt it was one of his kin, for the traitor knew the intricacies of the tunnels. Which meant it had to be someone in his family, but who?

He would think on it some more, but first…He lifted his hands and cupped her face, running the pads of his thumbs over her cheekbones. The oil lamps flickered and illuminated the gold flecks within her jasper-colored eyes. He wanted to lower his mouth to hers. To feel the softness and the warmth of her lips. To breathe in her life. To give her his.

Therefore shall a man leave his father and his mother, and shall cleave unto his wife: and they shall become one flesh.

The verse came unbidden, but there it was filling his heart. Whether she knew it or not, she was his. For eternity. And nothing, absolutely nothing would stop him from keeping his vow.

Not even her.

Chapter Sixteen

His lips were soft and gentle against hers. The air caught in her throat as a warm sensation coiled to her toes. She had wondered what it would be like to kiss a man, none of her imaginings had foreseen this light-as-air dizziness consuming her. Nor could she have imagined the way her chest welled with some unknown emotion. Is this what her mother spoke of when she spoke of true love, or was this something different altogether?

The comfort of his arms and the simple touch of his kiss made her believe she was worthy of marriage. Worthy of love. The emotions welling inside forced all the turmoil away. The soldiers, the queen's threats, Ari's lies.

Ari's lies. This kiss could not continue. He was a man with a calling on his life. A calling that left no room for a marred wife.

She slid her hands between them and shoved him away.

"You go too far, Ariel! This," she waved between them. "This cannot be. You, you are not my betrothed."

He blinked, his gaze focused. His furrowed brow smoothed. His eyes lightened, silver flecks she'd never before seen, vibrated and came to life. His chest rose and fell in rapid movements, his hands clenched at his sides.

He looked crazed, and she had the sudden urge to flee. She pressed her palm against her chest to halt the pounding. A pounding much stronger than when she feared the soldiers would find her and Joash.

What torment! To finally have found a man who liked her, not her father's land. A man she could respect and maybe even love. After all the years of her parents patiently waiting for her to choose, and he was unattainable. He belonged in Jerusalem, and she in her tiny village with her ailing father and a herd of sheep.

Their hearts could never mesh. Could never become one. He was a servant of the Lord and could never leave his duties. Even if Ari was inclined to take her as his wife, he'd be an outcast for her imperfections.

Her chest ached, no longer with the delight of Ari's attention, but with the crushing reality of a broken heart. She straightened her shoulders and lifted her chin.

"You should not have done that, Ari," she whispered.

"I know. You wanted to help with the preparations." He tugged his fingers through his hair. "I'll see what can be done." Ari slipped by her and into the outer room.

She sighed, crossing her arms over her chest like a breastplate to keep her heart from falling to the stone floor and shattering. If only she could go home. Return to her father. Ay, she had already tried and it had nearly cost them their lives.

She sat in the middle of the cold floor, pulled her knees to her chest and closed her eyes. Loneliness crept into her bones. She missed her family, even her sister.

"Sh'mira."

She opened her eyes at the sound of her name. Tama knelt in front of her, her head bowed. "Will you forgive me?"

Mira drew her cousin into her arms. "There is nothing to forgive, Tama. You were brave to carry the infant from Jerusalem and to our home. Even more brave to keep him hidden all this time." She squeezed her cousin's hand. "If not for you and Ari, Judah would have no hope of turning from her wicked ways and back to the one true God."

A tear slid down Tama's cheek. Mira wiped it away with her thumb. "You have been a faithful servant, Tama. Faithful to Judah, faithful to God."

"My thanks, Sh'mira." Tama kissed her cheek and rose. "I must prepare Joash for bed."

Mira smiled at her cousin as she left the alcove. What would it be like to sacrifice one's life for her people like Tama had done? All Mira had done was feed a few sheep and pick a few pieces of fruit. Tasks far from serving the good of Judah.

"Ari said you needed something to do." Anna swept into the room with calm assurance as if there hadn't just been a battle. This woman's entire family had sacrificed for Judah. How could she compare to such selflessness? Especially when she'd, only moments ago, been allowing thoughts of pity to enter her mind. A few days from her family was nothing compared to the years Anna had spent from her son.

"My thanks," Mira responded, resolving to embrace her circumstances with contentment. If only she could banish Ari's kiss from her mind.

"If you could lay out our bedding, I'll turn down the lamps. The girls will be in soon."

"Joash?"

Anna smiled. "You have a great fondness for the child?"

"He may have been Ari's constant shadow while at my father's, but we had our moments together as well." Mira realized that her words sounded too familiar. "My apologies, Anna. I do not wish to offend. Joash was raised as my brother."

"No, do not apologize. Your days have been wrought with worry, not to mention things that were yesterday are no longer today." Anna gazed past her shoulder as if she were thinking of another time. "The boy will sleep here with us and Tama if it will ease your mind."

"My thanks."

Anna left and came back moments later with Tama and a disgruntled Joash. Mira smiled at the scowling child. She took his hand and knelt beside him.

"Thank you for agreeing to protect me. After how well you've done, I did not think I could sleep without your presence."

Joash straightened his shoulders and held his head high.

"Come, we must rest. Tomorrow will have burdens of its own. The travel will be long," Anna said.

"How long before we reach Manna?" Mira asked, hoping that once they were there she could convince Ari to allow her return home.

"By day's end, however, much of it will be through the dark caves. The rest over the mountains."

Mira unrolled the beds as the women filed into the cove. Removing their tunics and veils, they laid them in a hole in the wall. They each carried their short knives to their beds. Mira couldn't help notice they had taken the beds closer to the exit, leaving her and Tama to sleep by Joash.

She lay down on her mat and closed her eyes, wishing she'd not given the dagger back to Ari.

"Rest, Sh'mira. My son lies outside the door. He'll protect us."

How could she tell Ari's mother that her lack of sleep would not come from fear, but from the memory of her son's kiss?

*

"Brother, drink?" Jesse offered him a cup of water as he sat cross-legged beside Ari. He didn't know whether to curse his brother or bless him for distracting him from thoughts of Mira. Thoughts that had no place entering his mind until she agreed to be his wife, which she wouldn't do until he asked, which he couldn't do until Joash was safely in Jehoiada's hands.

Ari took the cup. Pressing it to his lips, he sipped. "My thanks."

The low firelight flickered off the walls, illuminating history, while hiding bits and pieces in the shadows. It was much like the Lord's revelations, while certain things were clear, others were left unknown. Like when he had been sent from Jerusalem, he'd been upset at first, yet he had been humbled at being chosen. He never would have thought that the day he had left the gates of his beloved city that he'd never return permanently. And he never thought the reason would be his care for a woman.

"How long do you intend to stay at Manna?" Jesse asked.

He looked at his brother, his conversation with Mira fresh in his mind. The uncertainty that his family would betray God and Judah sparked anew with his brother's question. Even though he trusted his brothers completely, it wouldn't hurt to keep his plans as vague as possible. "That depends."

"On?"

Ari took another sip in an effort to stall. He really needed to confide in someone and he'd been closer to Jesse than any of his brothers. "I am not sure."

"What do you mean?"

Lowering his voice, Ari replied, "Those men, the ones we killed, how do you think they knew where to find us?"

Jesse took a few moments before he answered. "You think they had help?"

"I don't see how else they could have maneuvered the paths."

Jesse blew out a low whistle. "What you suggest, Ari. . . but who?"

"That is the question, is it not?"

Jesse tilted his chin and looked Ari in the eye. "Do you think it is one of us?"

Ari hesitated. He knew his scrutiny hadn't caused Jesse's air of discomfort. Jesse had always been diligent in his service to the Lord. "It is not one of our brothers. I do not like to think it is one of our cousins, yet, whoever it is has intricate knowledge of the passageways."

"You are correct." Jesse pursed his lips.

"There is something else that has been bothering me."

"What is that, Brother?" Jesse refilled his cup.

"There had been a Philistine warrior with those men near the pool."

"That is not unusual. Athaliah has kept many of the mercenaries."

"But that is not all, Brother. He was there. In the cave, he saw Joash and Mira and…" Ari rubbed his jaw. "Mira thought to go back home. I found her in the pool. The mercenary saw her. I have no doubt. Yet he did not alert his companions and he was not with the men we killed."

"Hmm, that is an odd occurrence." Jesse leaned his head against the wall. His elbows rested on his knees, fingers tented. "I did not wish to alarm you any further." He sighed and looked Ari in the eye. "After the attack, I scouted the tunnels. There were three more dead just beyond the bend toward Seth's."

Ari was not surprised. "Did you take care of them?"

"Someone had done it already. Their throats were slit. Not one of them looked like a Philistine."

"We'll have to keep vigilant and question this mercenary when we find him." Ari sat his cup near the fire.

"Would you like me to go to the spring?"

"No. I need you here. I need someone I can trust and see Joash to Jerusalem should anything happen to me."

"So be it, Brother." He patted Ari's shoulder. "I'll take the first watch. There could be more waiting in the wings."

"I do not think so, brother. You've checked, remember? Just the same, there will be no sleep for me tonight."

"Then there will be none for me either. I will make my bed near the western door."

Ari nodded his thanks and then leaned his head against the wall. It was a shame Mira could not play her lyre. Her music would help soothe his troubles. But then her fingers strumming over each string with such passion would set his heart to longing.

He stared up at the dome ceiling and traced each crevice with his gaze. Had King David lain in this exact spot? Had he looked at the cracks to keep his mind from wandering to temptation? But why was Mira a temptation? Because her father had offered her to him, and the more time he spent in her presence the more he realized how much he wanted to accept the troth. Of course, Ari would insist her feelings be taken into consideration before finalizing the contracts.

She had allowed him to kiss her, something she wouldn't do unless her heart was in the matter. She would agree to be his wife. So why could he not kiss her whenever he pleased?

Because she is not your wife, yet.

That could be easily rectified. He had the contract tucked in his bag. All he needed to do was add his signature next to Mira's father's.

You must focus on seeing Joash safely on the throne. And that was the core of the matter. If he married Mira, he'd be sneaking off to woo his wife with kisses, and wouldn't be able to keep an eye on Joash.

"What is wrong with you?" Jesse asked.

Ari blinked his eyes a few time and then looked at his brother. "What do you mean?"

"You look troubled." Jesse sat up, his gaze holding Ari's.

"It's Mira," he whispered as if he'd been given a great secret.

"Yes." Ari paused. "Not another word. Not until this is all done."

"On my honor."

Jesse's honor was the best he could hope for, but if any heard their conversation he'd receive endless taunts from the rest of his brothers.

If Mira had heard?

Then it would save him the effort of trying to find the words himself. Although the thought of never telling her the truth of his feelings left him reacting as if he'd taken a blow to the stomach.

Maybe they'd stay at Manna for only a day. Then four days to Jerusalem. They could be back to her father in a little over a week.

If only they could leave immediately. However, he'd seen the dark circles beneath Mira's eyes, and her terseness was a testament to how frayed her nerves were. If aught else, she needed her rest. And he needed her strength if they were going to make it through this ordeal.

Chapter Seventeen

The silent darkness plagued her with each step as tiny, furry creatures scurried across her toes. It took all her reserve not to scream in fright with each passing, their sharp claws the only sound echoing off the tunnel walls.

Before they had left the well-lit cavern, the men had agreed it best if they travel without a lamp to guide them. They had emphasized the necessity for quiet lest their enemies came upon them. Her only comforts were Ari trailing behind her and Joash's small hand wrapped in hers.

The child squeezed her hand, and for a moment some of her anxiousness disappeared. Not much in her life had caused her fear. Wild dogs were one. Tama losing her babe had been another. At least with the dogs she knew how to behave.

With Tama, there had been nothing she could do. She had felt so useless, so helpless. And even though oil lamps had flickered, it had been the darkest night of them all. It had seemed as if the stars would never yield to the light of the day. Much like now. It had seemed as if the darkness would continue for everlasting. It was enough to make her weep.

Another animal ran over her foot. She swallowed her scream and squeezed Joash's fingers. Once again, as he'd done several times since their departure, he patted her hand. She wished she could give him her thanks, but then if she could do such, she'd scream down the mountain they currently traversed.

Why, Lord? Why must I be forced to endure my fears?

Silence clung outside the thundering of her ears. She hadn't expected a response. One ray of light to rest her weary eyes from the darkness would have been welcomed even more than an answer. *Enough, Mira. You should be grateful in your circumstances,* she chastised herself as she closed her eyes. It was not as if she could see with them open. But then another critter scurried over her feet, and she flung her eyes open.

A sliver of light pierced the darkness. Her heart slammed into her chest. Were they about to be attacked again? Had her longing for light somehow cursed them to their deaths? Even though she couldn't detect tension from those around here, she removed her hand from Joash's and wrapped her arm around his shoulders.

The ray became wider with each step forward. The air changed from cool dankness to warmth and salt and…She bowed her head and gave thanks to the Lord, for He had heard her prayer. Perhaps, He had even answered her question as to why she must endure her fears. Where she sought comfort, God sought her trust.

She stepped into the opening of yet another cave, but this time natural light filled the entire area. Heat from the midday sun radiated through the opening. Ari's father, one of his uncles, his mother, sister-in-laws and one of his brothers were already there. The older men sat on the plaster benches deep in prayer. Ari's brother Melchiah carried an earthen jug, as the women readied the area for a meal.

She released Joash and watched him as he neared the elders. Sitting beside them, he too bowed his head. Assured that the boy was well, she began helping with the meal. As she had done the night before, she untied the strap around the leather tables and laid them out.

In under a day's time with Ari's family, she had come to understand a great deal about them. They loved each other deeply, and they were not above teasing one another—they actually took pleasure in it.

Ishiah poured grain onto what looked like an altar. Ari's family also took their vows seriously, which she could only reason that Ari would do so as well, even if he had kept his priestly identity a secret from her and her family for many years.

She understood the circumstances required secrecy. It was vital for the good of Judah. She only wished there was another way. Wished Ari had been what he had pretended to be. Wished she weren't deformed and below Ari's status. But as she listened to the prayers of this family she knew there could never be anything between her and Ari. Just as God required perfect livestock for sacrifice, so too, would Ari's family require him to marry a perfect, unblemished wife. It was decreed by the temple elders.

Ari entered the alcove. Her gaze met his as his sister Lydia offered him water. He drank deeply from the cup. And when he was finished he handed the cup back to his sister. His lips were shiny with moisture. She blinked as her toes curled at the remembrance of his lips touching hers. Did he recall with clarity the kiss they'd shared? Did the memory twist and turn his insides, too?

She tore her eyes from his and busied about with preparations. She would never last the trip to Jerusalem with him. She would constantly covet a life she could never have. Especially with his intense gaze following her.

One touch of his lips to hers, one small kiss, and she knew what it meant to desire something more than life itself. She had once thought she understood the looks passed between her parents when they thought no one could see. But after hours of traveling in the dark, with only the rustling of their clothes and the scurrying critters, with Ari's presence close behind her, she realized there was so much more to understand. A realization that dawned on her when the emotion swirling in his eyes tugged on her heart.

*

He wouldn't apologize for touching her with his gaze. He cared for her. And he would tell her once he'd made an offering to the Lord.

He moved toward his father and knelt beside him. He bowed his head and prayed silently. *Father God, thank you for our safe passage. I beseech you to grant us safety for the remainder of our journey. Bless thy servant with wisdom, anoint Joash as he learns to walk in your ways. May he help return Judah's heart back to You.*

The whisper of Mira's movements drew his attention. He opened his eyes just as she lifted her gaze to his. The bowl in her hand hovered above the leather table. Color rose in her cheeks. She quickly dropped her gaze and continued with her chore.

For some reason she had the look of shame. Why was that?

He rose from his knees and dusted his tunic. He untied the bag at his side and prepared his thank offering to the Lord. He added his grain to that of his father's and those of his brothers and uncles. If there had been too many more of them, they'd burn the mountain to ash.

All gathered around and watched as his father set flame to the grain. They muttered the blessing, and then they broke out in song. Even though the threat of their enemies continued to loom, and they shouldn't have, they did not quiet their voices as they lifted them in praise to the Lord, for He was their protector.

After a few minutes, their voices droned to a stop and then they discussed everything from the heat of the day to what they would do when this was all over. Lydia brought him another cup of water. Parched, he swallowed it in one gulp. "Do I look as thirsty as I feel?" he asked Lydia with a teasing tone.

She smiled, nodding. "Your lips are cracked, Ari. It looks uncomfortable." She took the cup from him and moved away.

He lifted his fingers to his mouth, running them over the sharp, jagged surface. His gaze sought Mira's. Had he upset her when he'd kissed her? Was that why she had erected a shield between them? Was that why, even now, she avoided looking to him?

His sister returned and pressed the cup into his palm once again. "Drink, it will be of aid. And, here," she said, removing the lid from a small pottery jar. "This will help. Your lips will soften in moments."

Ari glanced at the purple-colored balm. It looked to be one of her salves. He would not put that on, and he was about to tell his sister so, too, but then he licked his lips and felt the harshness of his skin. Once again he looked to

Mira. She bit down on her bottom lip, her hands at her sides where her fingers worried her tunic.

He shook his head, dipped his fingers into the thick salve and applied it to his chapped lips. He supposed he should be thankful that it tasted of pomegranates and not ashes.

"What is this?" Jesse asked. "Abba, your son is applying Lydia's lip balm."

"Do not be a jackal, Jesse." Lydia punched him in the shoulder. "His lips are dangerously cracked. He could sicken and die," she exaggerated.

"Then I would be your favorite brother," Jesse mocked.

"Lydia, child, you are one for dramatics, but you shouldn't call your brother names."

"Yes, Mama." Lydia tossed Jesse a sneer. "You could never be my favorite, Jesse. You think too highly of yourself."

Ari listened as they bantered back and forth. He had missed this. Had missed them.

"You think I'm vain?" Jesse dropped his arms to his sides. He looked sorely wounded.

Ari almost said something to ease his brother's sensitivities, but Joash, in his too-wise-for his age way said, "You do tense your arms and chest more than anyone I have seen."

"And have you seen many men such as I?" Jesse smiled, crossed his arms over his chest and inhaled causing his tunic to stretch tight over the steely strength."

"Ari's arms are much bigger than yours," Joash said with a twinkle in his eye leaving Ari speechless. He had rarely seen the boy tease. It was good to see him do so.

"I think not," Jesse argued lightheartedly.

"I do believe there is only one way to settle the matter," Ari's mother chimed in.

Ari rolled his eyes knowing exactly what would follow. "But, Mother, I did not argue the point," he added.

"No matter, my well-muscled sons. We need some entertainment." She laughed. "After we break bread you will wrestle. We need to show Sh'mira and Joash we do more than argue."

"But first, with your permission, Mother, I would show Mira the view." As much as he had missed his family and enjoyed them, he wanted to spend some time alone with her.

"Is it safe?" Ishiah asked from his corner of the cave.

"I do not know why it would not be," Elam answered.

"It should be safe enough, Abba," Ari added.

"Then you have my permission. She has done all I need her to."

He handed Lydia her jar and walked toward Mira. Her eyes widened like a cornered animal and he almost retreated. But he wasn't a warrior for nothing. He held his hand out to her. "Come, Sh'mira. I will protect you."

Mira released a deep sigh and placed her palm in his and rose to her feet.

Chapter Eighteen

Ari took her hand and led her out into the open. The view wasn't too unlike her home with the shadowy crags. But here, the great expanse of brine seemed to swallow them, leaving her breathless. The lapping of the waves as they crashed against the base of the mountain lulled her into a satiated peace much like when she played her music.

She closed her eyes and breathed deeply. Even though it had only been a day since their flight from the spring, it had felt like an eternity. The open air, even if it was thick with heat and salt, revived her from her time inside the dank and lifeless mountain.

She jumped when Ari pulled her against him, his arms about her waist like the girdle tied around her tunic. She tensed and prepared herself for the startling contact between them.

"Relax, Sh'mira. The ledge is narrow. I do not wish you to fall."

Glancing at her feet, she sucked in a sharp breath. The tips of her sandals were near the edge of the cliff. She scooted closer to Ari until her back met his battle-honed chest. "It is breathtaking."

"It is unblemished perfection. And very dangerous." He tugged her closer, encouraging her to lean against him. He buried his face into her hair and inhaled. "I wish I could stay like this for hours. I'd much prefer it over being chased by ruthless villains. I am weary of being ever watchful over my shoulder."

Mira didn't know what she'd expected him to say. Weary of his duty to God was not it? Perhaps, that he'd been weary of being subservient to a simple farmer. Even though she knew her father had been kind, the years as a bond servant could not have been easy, not when he loved his family as much as he did, especially since she'd been unkind to him.

If she could turn back the days…if she could stay within the strength of his arms, to feel his protective nature, to feel as if she belonged with him, but it was not meant to be. She had to consider her father and the people depending on her future husband. A man who could never be Ari, for Ari was destined to a higher calling, one that did not have room for a deformed wife.

She swiped a tear from her eye and then buried her hands into the folds of her tunic.

Ari pressed his lips to her temple. The firm pressure lingered, sending shivers over her arms. The lightheadedness consuming her proved his kiss was anything but fatherly.

"Mira," he whispered against her ear, eliciting another wave of chills. "I would like to kiss you."

"No." She shook her head against the longing building in her heart. "You should not." He was not her betrothed, could never be her betrothed. It was useless to encourage. Useless to hope when there was none.

Ari turned her in his arms and gazed into her eyes. The unspoken promises written clearly on his face. Promises he could never keep shone brightly. His request for a kiss sent a hundred little butterflies fluttering along her skin. From her nape to her knees and down to her toes.

Tension built within her, thundering in her chest like a thousand horses. But his request brought sorrow to her heart. She wanted him to break their eye contact, to relent in the unspoken promise, yet she wished to believe it was possible. Possible Ari could care for her and take her as his wife.

She bowed her head as a tear fell to the rocky ledge beneath her feet. A kiss should be an intimacy reserved only for her betrothed, her future husband. A husband Ari could never be.

The torment was too much. The wanting. The knowing they could never be. It tore her apart little by little, shattering her into fragments like the pottery she'd broken only days before.

She needed air. Space. Away from him. Unable to remain in his presence any longer, she tried to move from the circle of his arms, breaking their bond. She stumbled backward. Rocks tumbled over the ledge, crashing into the sea. He grabbed her arm just as her foot slid.

"Mira," he breathed her name. He yanked her against him, banding his arms around her waist. Their chests rose and fell. Hers was a little faster than his. He dropped his head to her shoulder. The weight heavy, firm, yet comforting. Ari sighed and spun her around. "You could have fallen."

She gazed out across the horizon, this time noticing the more intricate details. The highs and lows of the mountain peaks were unlike anything she had ever seen.

"It is breathtaking," she said once again.

The cavern of his chest expanded and released. "Yes. It is here, in this place that I first felt the calling God had for my life."

She bowed her head. This place was sacred to Ari. Shame crept into her toes, rose to her limbs and up to her cheeks. She had just defiled this beautiful, sacred place with her longing for a man she thought she might love but could never have.

"God is faithful, Mira. All you have to do is trust Him," he whispered near the cup of her ear. Severe pressure built within her chest, until it seemed as if it could expand no further, forcing tears to her eyes. It was as if her heart had been tied in knots like her mother's challah bread.

She looked up at him, words clung to her lips but she could not say them, for she didn't quite understand what Ari meant, although his caress and tone had been tender.

The Lord had been a part of her life for as long as she could remember, but she'd never had the same sort of intimacy with Him as Ari.

She turned in his arms and pressed the tips of her fingers to his mouth. The closest she dared to granting his request. "Lydia's balm worked. They are improved."

"Is that so?" He smiled and brushed the pad of his thumb across her brow. He showed her his digit, revealing a smudge of purple. She inhaled a sharp breath. "Do not worry yourself, Mira. There was only the one smudge."

The corner of his mouth curved upward, and something in her chest fought to break free and soar with the griffon. How was it that Ari's smile threatened to sever the bounds of her resolve to keep her distance? Every part of her being wanted him to kiss her once again, to feel as if she was cared for by someone other than her parents. To feel as if Ari cared for her, mayhap even loved her. But it was not to be, even if he did care for her--could love her--she could not allow it.

She relaxed against him and he leaned his head to hers, his lips hovering mere inches…

She twisted from his embrace and left him leaning against the rock fortress, along with her heart.

*

Ari clenched his fists. Were all women as hard to convince of affection as Mira was proving to be?

That was an answer he could not give since he'd never had a desire to woo a woman before. He'd never been free to do so. And now that he wanted to, she seemed to be running in the other direction, which left him confused. Their friendship and previous camaraderie should have made it easier. He raked a hand through his hair. She cared for him. He had no doubt in that matter. Perhaps even loved him. Why was she determined to ignore the affection growing between them? Mayhap because she didn't love him and he was only being fanciful that she might.

"All did not go well, then?" His father exited from the cave.

Ari did his best to school his emotions, but it was no use. His father had ever been perceptive. Besides he would never tell a lie beyond the life he had lived protecting Joash.

"I do not know where I have gone wrong, Abba." He pushed away from where he leaned and crossed his arms over his chest. He released a heavy sigh as he looked out across the sea. "I know she has great affection for me." He paused. "I can see it." He shrugged his shoulders.

"She has had a shock, my son."

"I know, and the blame can be laid at my feet, but..."

"You think she should accept the fact that you have hid from her who you are. She should accept the fact that you lied to her? That she's been dragged from her home, away from her family?"

Ari twisted his lips in thought. He had deceived her and her family, but she seemed to understand the reasoning. "I cannot help but feel there is more to her hesitation."

"Have you told her?"

Ari furrowed his brow in confusion, for he hadn't told Jesse of the contract. "You amaze me, Abba. How did you know about the marriage contract?"

His father smiled in approval. "I did not know, Ariel. But I am pleased. She will make you a wonderful wife. But I take it even she does not know of it."

"No. I will wait until my vow to Jehoiada is complete before I make another. If you did not mean the contracts, what did you mean, Abba? Have I told her what?"

"Have you told her you love her?"

The air rushed out of his lungs as if his father had swatted his staff across his midsection. His first thought had been to deny the very words his father spoke. Of course he cared for her, but love her? "I cannot tell her something I do not know myself and have her believe it the truth."

Ishiah laid his hand on Ari's shoulder. "My son, there is nothing wrong with loving your wife. Your mother is the very air I breathe. I would perish without her."

Ari placed his hand on top of his father's. "I know, Abba. I cannot deny that I feel something for Mira, and as strong as it is I'm still unsure of its origins." He thought back to Caleb and his excitement at offering his daughter to him. "Is it possible that I only feel this way because her father has offered her to me? Is it possible I only feel here," he said, thumping his chest with his fist. "Because I feel as if she is my responsibility? That is a truth I cannot live with. I want her by my side, Abba, but I want to be assured of love between us."

"I cannot give you the answers you seek, Ariel. Although, I believe you have just done so yourself."

Ari glanced at the vast landscape, so wild and so beautifully untamed, much like Mira. "Answers will do me no good if Mira does not feel the same."

"I would not be so sure, my son. You would stand in awe at what speaking your heart to a woman does to her knees," his father said with a knowing twinkle in his eye. He patted him on the shoulder. "We welcome her with open arms, my son, no matter what you decide."

"My thanks, Abba."

His father returned to the cave. Ari took a deep breath, confusion weighing heavy on his mind. He was pleased his family would accept Mira, but would they be as open when they discovered in order for Ari to marry her, he would have to reside with her father?

If he had been his father's only son, his considerations would have been different. But he had brothers, all of whom carried their father's legacy. Mira's father had no sons. Only Nathan, who had shown he would not care for Caleb's land. The thought of Mira at the mercy of him in the event of Caleb's death left a bitter taste on his tongue.

Chapter Nineteen

The batter sizzled as Mira poured it into a pan over the fire. Although it made her heart glad to have her hands busy, she would have much preferred something more taxing on her mental faculties. Her mind continued to wander to Ari.

She flipped the cake, taking note of the perfect golden hue, just like Ari preferred them. Ari, Ari, Ari. She thought of him much more than she should.

Mira shook her head. She had always thought of Ari, but where her thoughts once considered how to thwart his efforts when he helped her with her chores, they now moved to pleasing him with perfect cakes. Of course, those thoughts were interrupted by the renewed sensation of her hand wrapped in his. A simple, breathtaking, touch of the lips.

Heat flooded her cheeks. Incidents like that would not be repeated. She would ensure they never spent another moment alone. No more. Not even a peck on the cheek in greeting. Nothing.

"Is that cake mine?"

She squeaked. Her eyes widened in horror at the smell of charred cake. She hesitated to flip it over knowing it would not be the perfect golden brown, but as dark as the tunnels they had traveled through for the better part of the day.

Ari moved his plate toward her. She pursed her lips wondering if she should toss it away or place it on his plate. If she tossed it aside she would have to admit that she hadn't been paying attention to the task Ari's mother had given her. She smiled, scooped it up and plopped it onto his plate, golden brown side up.

She poured another helping of batter into the oil and watched as Ari sat his plate on the leather table beside the other men. Lydia set a bowl of figs and grapes in the center, along with a jug of water.

"We have only another two miles before we reach Manna." Elam's gravelly tone interrupted her thoughts.

"Yes, but it is over narrow mountain paths. And we would be walking in the heat of the day," Jesse added.

"I will rest much easier when we reach Manna." Ari broke off a piece of cake and popped it into his mouth. Mira winced. It had to taste awful. She watched in amazement as he chewed without spitting it out, or even making a face.

Lydia sat beside her and waited for the next few cakes to be finished. "I would prefer to stay here," she murmured.

"What is this Manna?" Mira asked, having never heard of it, which puzzled her since they couldn't be that far from her father's house.

"It is a secret fortress," Lydia answered.

"For the priests?" Mira asked, turning the cake.

"In a way, but not all know of its existence. Only a select few."

"Our position has already been infiltrated by the enemy. We take a risk staying here," one of Ari's brothers said.

"You are right, but I think the risk is equal," Seth, Ari's blind uncle, added.

"But no one knows of our destination," Jesse argued.

"And the obvious direction would be Jerusalem. It is why I chose to come this way first." Ari took another bite of his cake.

"Do you think he knows he is eating charred food?" Lydia giggled.

Mira blushed. Had everyone noticed the burnt cake? "I hope not." She lifted another cake off the fire and checked both sides to ensure it was perfect before placing it on Lydia's plate. "What is this Manna like? Is it another cave?" she asked wanting to change the subject.

Lydia giggled once again. "Oh, yes. But much grander. I suppose it can be overwhelming, but I've grown up there."

"It is your home, then? I assumed you lived in Jerusalem."

The girl shook her head. "We visit Jerusalem often, but Manna is home."

"Then why would you wish to stay here?"

"I do not wish to marry. And Abba says I must at least try to find a man I'm willing to live my life with."

"You do not wish to marry a priest?"

"Oh, that is not it at all," Lydia said a little too quickly. Her cheeks pinkened and Mira wondered if the girl already knew who she wanted to marry. "It is just. . ."

"You have found him elsewhere? Somewhere other than where your father has dictated?" It had been like that with her when she had come of age, her father had said much the same thing, but she knew her husband would never be found in the market place of Hebron, or anywhere else.

Lydia bowed her head. "Besides Jerusalem, we don't travel outside Manna for me to meet another. I have not found a man I could hold affection for, not like the kind of affection my parents hold for each other, or that you hold for Ari."

Mira sucked in a sharp breath. "You think I care for your brother?"

"It is obvious." She nodded. "I want to love my husband, and I want him to adore me."

She chose to ignore Lydia's observations. "From all that I've seen, your father is a kind and gentle man. Ari is much like him." She wrapped her arms around the girl's shoulders. "You should tell him how you feel."

Ari's sister looked her in the eyes. They were dark as night, much like Ari's. "Father would think me silly to expect a man to return feelings."

Mira's heart ached, both for her and for Lydia. It was their lot in life to marry and accept what affections their husbands chose to give. Most men believed marriage to begin with mutual respect, not love. Her father held a different opinion, and she believed Lydia's father did as well if the looks he tossed Ari's mother were any indication. "You must speak with your father."

Ari slapped his hands together, drawing her attention. "That was the most delicious meal I believe I have partaken of in a very long while," he said, wiping the crumbs from his face.

The cave filled with the song of laughter. Only Ari sat in silence, his brow furrowed in confusion.

*

Nobody had ever told him what they had found so funny, but from the redness of Mira's cheeks he had a feeling she had had something to do with it. At the first opportunity to get her alone he would ask her.

After much debate, they had decided to pack up camp and head to Manna. They sent Jesse and Isa ahead of them to scout the path, while Melchiah and Elam watched their backs. He wiped the sweat dripping from his brow, his clothes were near soaked, and his feet were caked with the dust of the road.

Only another mile to go, and he could order a bath. Of all the things he had missed over the years it had been his own cleansing tub. Not that he wasn't thankful for the spring the Lord had provided. It had its uses, but in his tub he could relax. And he was far from relaxed with the constant pricking at his nape, which had him continually looking over his shoulder.

He picked up pace, the faster they got to Manna the sooner they would be safe. The sooner Mira would be safe from his enemies and the temptations plaguing his mind. If he continued on with such thoughts, he'd never make it back to her father a sane man. And then he'd not only be denied the right to be called her husband, but he'd rot in a tomb with his ancestors for not keeping his focus on Joash and the mission given him.

"Look," Lydia called.

Ari snapped to attention, afraid danger loomed. But when he glanced at where she pointed he couldn't help but look upon Mira's face. The awe and complete rapture etched in the softness of her amber eyes took his breath away.

Manna had always been a source of pride, even more so than Jerusalem, but somehow he had forgotten just how unique Manna really was.

"It is more beautiful than where we left," she murmured. "I did not think it possible to find a lovelier place."

"God has blessed us tremendously," his mother responded.

Ari stepped closer to Mira and wove his fingers with hers. The sensation pulled on his heart like a bowstring pulled taut. She looked into his eyes, his lips parted. Like water beading to water, he felt drawn to her and bent toward her. Her eyes grew wide, she released his hand and raced to catch up to Lydia, looping her arm through his sister's. The bowstring snapped, leaving a distinct ache in the middle of his chest. And for the first time that he could recall, he felt the sharp pang of jealousy.

*

They were met with a procession of music, dance and food fit for a king. He turned to his father. "They know?"

His father drew his hand down his beard. "I fear your uncle interrupted a meeting with the elders. He accused me of lying in front of them and then proceeded to tell them of Joash."

No wonder the soldiers had increased patrols. With so many aware of the boy's existence it stood to reason Athaliah had found out through rumor. Had Elam inadvertently sent danger to their doorstep? It set Ari's mind at ease knowing there hadn't been intentional betrayal. Then how did the warriors know of the tunnels?

That was a question that would leave him alert.

"There shouldn't have been celebrations, Abba."

"It could not be helped, my son. The people of Manna cannot contain their excitement. Besides, Manna has always been full of joy."

"You are correct, Abba. However, the child does not even know who he is." Ari prayed it would remain that way until they met with Jehoiada.

"Do not worry, son. Only the elders know. The celebration is of our homecoming. They've had sentries on watch." His father pointed to the high places. "Waiting for our return."

A bevy of servants lined the entranceway, some kneeling beside bowls of cleansing water, others with cups of water to break their thirst. Their belongings were taken from them, as were their sandals. Their feet were cleansed, their stomachs fed and their minds nourished with song.

Used to the ways of Jerusalem, and then that of being a bond servant, Ari had forgotten what the welcomings were like here.

"No!" Mira shouted.

Ari looked through the crowd to see what had distressed her. He cut through the pressing bodies until he stood behind her. Her back stiff as a rock.

"Would you not have me cleanse the travel from the child's feet?" A young woman Ari did not recognize held onto Joash's hand as if she were about to lead him away.

"Not without his guardian's approval."

The young woman looked perplexed. "You are?"

The woman bowed her head. "Dinah, daughter of Omar."

Omar had been an elder in Manna for years. "Dinah, my thanks for your hospitality. I will see to the child myself." The woman glanced between them and shrugged her shoulders. Ari waited until the woman walked away before turning to Mira. "You do me proud. Mira.,"

Her shoulders relaxed a little. "I am sorry."

"Do not be." He laced a wayward strand of hair behind her ear. "You are right to be protective." He glanced around the people. Although it was not Jerusalem, it was still like a small city. And although each and every one of them should be worthy of trust, someone had betrayed them. "As it is I do not know who can be trusted." His gaze flitted to hers. "Except you, Tama, my father and Jesse. Come, I will take you to my father's house where you can bathe and rest."

She looked at Joash. "What about Joash?"

"I will see to him."

Joash crossed his arms over his chest. "I am not a child to be watched over, am I?"

Ari laughed. "Then it is I who must need watching."

"And who will watch over Mira?"

"That would be me," his mother said, entering their little group. "I near lost you, my daughter. I forget how busy it is here. Come," she said, ushering Mira away.

Lord, bring her comfort and safety.

For as much as being here should ease his mind, the pricking at his nape continued. He was certain someone watched him with malice. Or was it Mira who was watched with such murderous emotion? The idea set his nerves on edge. If any harm came to her...How was he supposed to be responsible for his actions? For he knew he'd have a difficult time keeping himself from murder if any harm came to her or Joash. He prayed the Lord was not tallying up his sins. He'd broken more commandments in the past few days than he had his entire life.

Lord, is this what it is to care deeply for someone? To remove aside all thought of yourself for someone else?

Chapter Twenty

With Joash no longer taking the focus of her attention, Mira took in Manna. When they had approached the city from the mountain pass, it had looked like any other ordinary mountain in Judea. Or at least any that she had seen. But then they had passed through what looked to be just another cave entrance, which left the bitter taste of bile rising. She had had enough of dark tunnels and scurrying critters.

Even the spectacle of celebratory dancers at their approach hadn't eased her fears. But she had gathered up every bit of courage she could garner. For she knew the sooner they reached Manna the sooner she could return home. The sooner she could put space between her and Ari. Then she could mend the pieces of her breaking heart.

But when they walked through the gates of Manna she'd forgotten about home. Manna was only a bit larger than her village, a village made up of her family. Her mother, father, Rubiel. Aunts, uncles and cousins. Were all these people kin to Ari?

People pressed and touched, kissed her cheeks and bowed. There was no room to move without bumping into another person. No room to breathe. She felt lost. Alone in a sea of ornately colored tunics. It was enough to make her head spin. She almost preferred the black, cold walls of the tunnels over the weight of friendliness.

Now she followed behind Anna's gracefulness. Marble columns were erected throughout the central area, reaching toward the ceiling. As if it reached into the heavens. Blue, purple, gold and red square designs decorated the floors surrounding the columns.

They passed rooms, upon rooms. Each seemed to be a home of some sort. Much grander than her father's house. A woman sat before a loom weaving fine linen cloth in front of a home. Another crushed grain. Her children ran circles playing a game of tag.

"Here we are," Anna said as they climbed a set of carved stairs.

Mira's eyes followed the line of stairs as she took each step. Something bubbled and swirled in her stomach. With no Joash to hide behind, she had to take each step on her own. Each step that would take her into the place Ari called home. A shiver ran down her nape and across her shoulders. It somehow seemed intimate. An intimacy reserved only for a wife.

"Since you have no belongings with you, I'll take you straightway to the bathing chamber. There you will find clean clothing."

"My thanks, Anna," Mira said.

"None is needed, my child. You have been through quite an ordeal. You'll rest easier once the dirt is washed from your limbs."

Mira smiled. As much as her body ached from the days of hard travel she felt as if she would never again rest easy. And with the possibility of crossing paths with Ari, she wouldn't find peace until she returned to her father's house.

"This is Sybil." Anna introduced an elderly lady with graying hair. Her smile was welcoming and her hands looked papery soft. "She'll assist you in whatever you need."

Mira bowed her head in greeting.

"You are with my Ari, yes?" Sybil asked.

Mira choked. "I am." Even if it wasn't by her choice.

"Lydia told me to expect you. He is a good boy." How long it had been since Sybil had seen Ari? There was nothing boyish about him.

Sybil led her through a narrow path lit by oil lamps and down a few steps. They entered a large chamber. Steam rose from the tub made of cut stone large enough to easily hold a man of Ari's size, although she knew this to be the women's cleansing room. Sybil removed Mira's veil and placed it with gentleness onto a stone bench.

"I recall the first time Anna wore this very veil. It was the day she left with Ishiah to meet his family."

"You have been with Anna for a long time, then?" Mira asked, as Sybil untied the sash at her waist.

Sybil laughed. "You could say that I have been with her since birth."

Mira glanced at the woman. Although sagged with age, her facial features were somewhat familiar, could she somehow be a relative of Anna's? "You must be like family."

"I am." Sybil lifted Mira's tunic over her head, leaving her standing in nothing but the loincloth and the strips of binding around her chest. This ritual was so reminiscent of what Anna had done when they had arrived at the cave.

"Sayta." Lydia entered bearing linens and several small jars. "I have brought all that you have requested."

Embarrassed, Mira wrapped her arms over her chest. This woman was Ari's grandmother?

"No need to be shy, my child," Sybil soothed.

This sort of hospitality was not unheard of. Mira knew it to be quite common, but she had never before—that was until only yesterday, twice in a short span —been treated with honor. What was more humbling was the fact that the actions of Ari's family were genuine, from the heart, not out of duty.

A knot formed in her stomach. Allowing Ari's grandmother to attend her seemed disrespectful. It was she who should be attending Sybil.

"You should not." Mira glanced at the slated floor.

"Why is it, my child? I wonder why you think I should not cleanse the day's travel from you?"

"You humble me. It is I who should honor you in such a way," Mira answered.

"Pash. It is an honor to meet your needs." Sybil returned.

Sybil gathered Mira's hand within hers and drew her to the pool of steaming water. The water percolated leaving bubbles on the surface. Did Ari's family think to cook her? "Will it burn?"

"No. See." Sybil sunk their combined hands beneath the surface.

Amazingly, although the water bubbled, it was only warm. Mira looked for the source, but found none.

"Here," Sybil said, untying the linen cloth around Mira's chest. "Once you are sitting in the tub, you will feel much better."

With Sybil's encouragement, she climbed up the few steps and then down into the pool of water. She sat rigid.

"Child, you'll grow wrinkles frowning as you are. Relax." Sybil nudged her shoulder to relax against the cushioned mat. Mira took several breaths of air. The water, warm and comforting, forced her limbs to droop. She gave in and closed her eyes.

"There now, is that not better?" Anna asked.

The feebleness of her limbs must have traveled to her mind for she could not form a coherent thought. At least no thoughts outside of Ari. His rugged handsomeness with his aquiline nose. The rich tan of his skin. The strength of his hands. . .

Mira rolled her neck as Sybil dumped water over her hair. The woman's fingertips massaged her scalp. Reminding her of Ari's earlier caress.

The rich scent of cinnamon teased her senses with each wave of the water. The cinnamon was followed by cloves. It was as if she were being prepped for sacrifice, but only unblemished offerings were given. And nobody could say she was without blemishes.

Why, her skin was too golden from days in the sun, not the porcelain complexion of his mother and sister. The palms of her hands were calloused. And if any cared to look, they would see the twist of her fingers on her right hand, the marred skin of her shoulder and down her arm, which none had spied outside of her mother and sister.

Mira's cheeks heated with shame. Would Ari's grandmother disapprove of her too? She closed her eyes and waited for the woman to say something, but Ari's grandmother cleansed Mira's skin without a word and when she reached the scars there was no sharp intake of breath or disgusted grunts, as was Rubiel's tendency when she saw the puckered skin. Ari's grandmother washed her with gentleness and not as one on a mission to scrub away her imperfections.

The kindness warmed her heart and forced tears to her eyes. For whenever her mother saw them she clucked in pity and her sister, well, she always had the look of disgust. As long as Mira kept them hidden they could pretend she was just like everyone else. Perfect.

And that was the water in the earthenware jar. When Ari was a bond servant he was like her, a human with imperfections. But now that she knew his secret, that he was a priest, a servant of the one true God, he deserved nothing but perfection.

She curled her fingers in the warmth of the water. The lone tear sliding down her cheek had nothing to do with the pain in her knotted knuckles as she clenched her fist.

Perfection was something she would never be.

Chapter Twenty-One

Mira stepped out onto the terrace and a peace settled over her. Flimsy cloth hung from the ceiling blowing in the breeze from the sea, tantalizing her eyes with glimpses of the scenery beyond. Curious, she moved closer to the edge. She slid her fingers down the gauzy fabric and tasted the salt from her lips a moment before she lost her breath.

White-capped waves of blue lay cradled within the wilderness. Mountain peaks rose on all sides as if to protect the secrets of the sea. Here, high above the landscape a sense of pride welled in her breast, a pride that rightfully did not belong to her, for it had not been her hand that had shaped the jagged lines and multifaceted hues.

An urge to fall to her knees shook her. *Father, God of all creation, I am not worthy of such a gift.*

The evening breeze danced across her cheeks and she drank in each detail, the sound of the waves crashing into the mountain fortress. The taste of salt. The puff of clouds cloaking the horizon.

How could anyone stand here and not see how gracious their Creator was? What beautiful blessings he offered to his people. And yet she'd seen too many people take for granted the offerings of the Lord. If anyone ever doubted God's love all they needed do was open their eyes.

The spicy scent of cloves danced along the breeze, teasing her. She wrapped her hands around the balustrade. Tilting her head back, she inhaled the salty air.

In this place, cleansed from the day's dirt, she could almost believe. She gripped the railing tighter, the sharp pain in her knuckles a swift reminder that she should not hope for Ari's presence. Although she knew he stood directly behind her.

Her heart pounded in anticipation. Would he lay his hand on her shoulder? Would he wrap his arms around her? Would he kiss her brow with tenderness?

What was she thinking?

The longing flooding her heart would only cause her more pain. She could not love Ari even from a distance. She would not encourage his attention, no matter how his kindness filled her heart. Since a man with any deformity could not serve in the temple as a high priest according to Levitical law, she could only reason that a priest's wife could hold no such deformity either, even if that priest served in a lesser fashion. She would not wish him cast from the temple because of her imperfections.

Nor would she have him ridiculed for taking pity on her and making her his wife. Where had that come from? It wasn't as if he had mentioned marriage. Just because he wanted to kiss her didn't mean he wanted her for a helpmate.

No, Ari was an honorable man. He would not kiss her if he did not wish to take her as his bride. Yet, he had a duty to the Lord, one he knew all too well, just as she knew hers to her father.

Straightening her shoulders, she turned and drank him in. His black hair hung around his shoulders. The waning sun graced each strand into a silvery sheen. Tiny creases crinkled at the corners of his eyes. The lines, depicting a hardworking man, enhanced the beauty of his being. His cheeks and chin were once again scraped smooth, which left her baffled since no Hebrew man cut the sides of his beard. Not that she complained. It was very pleasing to her eye.

"I have missed you, Sh'mira." The way her name rolled off his tongue like the melodic blow of the shofar sent shivers down her spine.

"You should not," she responded.

He took a step toward her. If her back had not been against the terrace wall, she would have retreated. As it was, she had no escape. She looked beyond his shoulder into his home for reinforcements, but none were to be seen.

"Whenever we are parted, I will always miss you." He closed the distance between them. He lifted his hand and cupped her jaw. The pad of his thumb slid along her cheekbone. She fought the urge to close her eyes. Instead, she sidestepped and faced the sea. If she could not see his eyes, if she could not read the emotion burning in them, she could deny him.

He leaned his arm against the rail in the exact spot she had just abandoned. She stared out across the white-tipped waves and tried to count their rise and fall. However, they seemed to move in time with her breathing, ragged and full of life. Her face heated as she felt his gaze focus on her. She swallowed.

Ari drew a finger along the curve of her ear and along her jaw. With the tip of his finger he guided her chin, until her eyes lifted to his. He bussed her cheek. "I like being in your presence."

"Do you not have duties to attend? What of Joash?"

Ari pulled away, and she sought his gaze. It had not been her intention to offend him, but she needed space.

"The boy is well." He flashed her a smile. "He is waiting for you so that he may break bread."

"Then I shall not keep him waiting." She turned and left him cloaked behind the flimsy cloth.

*

Her scent clung to him like honey. He should find his friends in the courtyard. It had been a few years since he'd seen them. But like a deer to water his eyes had to drink in her beauty. It was torment to see her and not touch her hand. And he was sentenced to an entire meal in her presence. Not that the thought was an onerous one, he didn't mind dining with her. He preferred, however, to do it alone and not with his family listening to their words, watching their actions.

Ever since his conversation with his father, he couldn't help but wonder if all his family thought the same thing. Did they all believe he loved Mira? Their interference would only make his wooing of Mira that much more difficult. He thought back over the past several days.

Something had changed. Why was Mira so determined to distance herself from him? He thought she might love him. But it was more than that. Deep inside, their souls recognized each other as the other's half. She was his helpmate. If he knew that, why didn't she? Weren't women supposed to know such things?

He smiled. Mira was special. She wasn't like most women, even if he had caught her many times during his bonding with that dreamy-eyed look. What had she dreamed of?

He would give all his gold coins to know if only to make them come true. And he'd give all his possessions to make things right with her.

For now, he would join his family in their homecoming feast and then he'd pray to God for guidance.

Ari entered the dining area. Although he enjoyed camping in the tunnels, the comforts of home had given him peace. Or they should have. This discord with Mira had left him feeling anything but peaceful.

Mira sat between Lydia and Melchiah's wife, Hannah. Jesse and Melchiah sat across from her. The only spot left to him was the farthest from her. A stab of jealousy pricked his conscience. He did not wish to share her attentions, but since she was doing her best to ignore him, what could he do? Sit, eat and watch her every move.

"Come, let us hold hands and thank the Lord for our safe return and ask Him to bless our food."

Ari listened to the words of blessings his father lifted to the Lord, but his mind wandered to Mira. Shame infused his blood. Had his time away from the temple demolished all his discipline? *Forgive me, Father God.*

Duty had always been most important to him, but now…his gaze shifted to Mira. Now she seemed to be taking precedence, at least in his thoughts.

"Let us eat," his father said.

"You have outdone yourself, Mama," Jesse said.

"Nonsense, my son."

Foods Ari hadn't seen in years graced the table. Almonds, apples, dates and figs. Olives and cheese. Roasted fish.

"Where did you get the fish, Anna?" Ishiah asked.

"One of the men at the market had them."

"It is delicious," Mira added.

Even more than having all his favorite foods, he enjoyed watching Mira poke and taste each item on her plate. He could tell by the way her eyes widened when she bit into an apple that it brought her sweet pleasure. Perhaps he'd talk her father into adding apple trees to their crops.

"How long will you stay?" his grandmother asked, reminding him of his vow.

His eyes settled on Joash who seemed to be enjoying himself. If only they could stay here until the boy became a man, but he would not risk the people of Manna as he had Mira's people. He *could* not risk the people of Manna, not even for the chance to convince Mira to be his wife. Instead, he would take her to Jerusalem. Since leaving her behind was not an option, especially if an enemy moved among them.

"I need to speak with the elders, Savta. Preferably tomorrow." He looked at Mira. Her eyes filled with an emotion he couldn't read. "The sooner I return to Jerusalem, the better."

For everyone involved.

Once Joash was back with Jehoiada, Queen Athaliah would no longer rule with terror. And then they could demolish her idols. The one true God would once again prevail over Judah. And Ari could begin wooing Mira.

"Will you hand me the olives, Melchiah?" Ari asked needing the bitter tang to remind him all his sacrifice was not in vain.

"You always did prefer olives" Melchiah passed the bowl.

"As I recall," his mother interjected. "Ari preferred to stick them in his ears."

Mira's face lit with a beautiful smile as his siblings laughed at his expense, but he wasn't going down alone.

"Mama! I believe it was you who showed me how," Ari teased.

Lydia giggled. "Mama taught me how to wake Jesse by tossing grapes at his head."

Jesse answered by tossing a grape at Lydia. They all broke out into laughter. He had missed this, and as hard as it would be to leave again, he knew he had to. At least when it was all done he'd be free to visit.

"Mira, Ari tells me you have a gift with the lyre. Would you mind playing for us?" his mother asked.

Mira's cheeks brightened much like they had when he'd asked to kiss her earlier in the day. She chewed on her lip and clenched her fists. Discomfort registered on her brow. Did her hand cause her pain?

A twinge of guilt nagged him. He'd told his mother out of a selfish desire to hear Mira play. To take delight in the gift of her fingers as they created comfort and peace. He had not intended on causing her distress.

"Mama, Mira needs her rest." He popped an olive in his mouth and chewed. "Our travels have not been easy, and we have a long road ahead of us on the morrow."

"Won't you stay a day or two?" his grandmother asked.

"We cannot."

"But, Ari—"

"Enough." Ari snapped. His voice hard, gruff to his own ears. His bevy of a family silenced as if he'd struck them down with a sword.

Did they not realize that he had given up his life? While they had each other, while they ate apples and olives, while they were able to keep the ceremonies, he had given up everything. His ambitions, his identity. Not that he regretted a moment of it because it had brought him to Mira, but Lord help him, he did not want to waste another moment of his life. He wanted to be done with his duty to Jehoiada, so that he could begin living the life he desired with Mira.

"My apologies for bringing an end to our camaraderie. I meant no disrespect." He rose from his seat and bowed to his parents, and then turned to his grandmother. "Savta."

Without a glance toward Mira he left.

Chapter Twenty-Two

She watched his retreating form. Head high, shoulders straight, his gait full of purpose. Someone should go after him. A glance around the table proved she wasn't the only one shocked over Ari's behavior.

"I have never before heard Ari raise his voice in anger, nor have I seen him show a hint of disrespect," she said, recalling all the times she'd lashed out at him and not once had he spoken in anger. "Even when it was well deserved." She looked at Anna wondering if she had spoken out of turn, and then to Jacob. "I fear the danger we've experienced the last few days has taken its toll," she defended.

Ishiah firmed his lips as if he was fighting back laughter but a twinkle of joy betrayed his intentions. "Danger has never before bothered Ari. Perhaps. . ." He trailed off, his gaze bored into hers. The occupants at the table remained silent waiting for his next words. "Mira, you would do me an honor if you spoke to my son. Perhaps, he'll speak to you about what bothers him."

Mira's eyes widened in horror. The thought of being alone with Ari scared the breath from her. Would he try to hold her hand? To kiss her?

It was something she could not allow. She chewed on her lower lip as she bowed her head to Ishiah. "Of course," she said.

She slid off the bench and walked from the room. A shiver of anticipation raced down her back.

Once out of sight of the others, she halted her steps upon the tiled foyer to gather her courage. She wiped her hands down the front of her tunic and wondered what it was she was supposed to say. Or why his family had chosen her when his brother Jesse seemed to be his closest friend.

"Sh'mira." She heard the soft grandmotherly voice behind her.

Mira faced Sybil and waited for the woman to speak.

"You are nervous, child."

Was that why the palms of her hands beaded with moisture? Was that why her stomach tumbled like a boulder slipping from a mountain?

"What I do not understand is why?" Sybil reached out and squeezed her hand. Mira halted the reaction to jerk her fingers back from the kindly woman's grasp. "It is obvious you hold deep affection for my grandson."

Mira swallowed past the lump in her throat, she cared more than she should. "It is not my rightful place."

"Then whose is it?"

She shook her head. "His mother's? His father's?" Mira shrugged her shoulders. "Yours or his brothers? I mean no disrespect, Sybil. I will do as asked. However, you must know I do not know what words to speak to Ari."

"Why, Sh'mira? If you love—"

Mira disengaged her fingers from the soft papery ones of Sybil. "This," she said, waving her hand, "has nothing to do with my feelings for Ari. I intend to ask to be returned to my father as soon as possible."

"You do not mean to travel to Jerusalem?" Sybil's eyes grew wide, her lips pursed.

"Sybil, I've not the Lord's wisdom. Whatever His purpose He brought Ari to my home along with Joash, but our lives. . .they can never be as…as one."

The elderly woman's gaze traveled over her. Mira tucked her fingers into the folds of her tunic.

"Sh'mira, my grandson is much like his father, ever a rock. His strength and fortitude know no boundaries." The woman paused, as if to relent in her argument. "I will not pry, Sh'mira, but my grandson draws his strength from you. It is evident in the way he looks at you. If ever he needed anyone, it is you. It is you, and it is now that he needs your support the most."

Sybil pressed a kiss to her cheek. When she pulled back, concern etched in the lines of her wrinkled brow. "Do not allow your pride to carve your future."

Before she could deny the sin of pride, Sybil shuffled away. Couldn't the woman see pride had nothing to do with her not wanting to be in Ari's presence?

She took a deep breath and fought for calm. She'd never been able to deny a person in need, not even if it meant much pain and inner turmoil. If Ari needed her to sustain his strength in order to see Joash to his rightful place then how could she walk away? Her heart was already broken, shattered. A few more missing pieces wouldn't matter. As it was, she'd never be whole again. Especially when the time came to part ways.

She strode through the entryway and leaned against the cut stones forming columns as she glanced around the terrace. She peered deeper into the shadows, and then stepped out onto the flagstones.

"Now is not the time, Sh'mira," he said. The hardness of his voice sliced through her.

She moved toward him, and squinted. He knelt beside the fountain. "Have I upset you?"

The rolling of the sea and the distant sounds of strings and flutes dancing in the air left a foreign intimacy skirting along her skin, but his silence left her hollow. Somehow she'd angered him.

Unwanted tears thrust to her lashes. She turned on her heel and swiped them away as she made to retreat to her room.

"Do not go." The harsh whisper pulled at something deep in the soles of her feet, halting her steps. She closed her eyes.

She waited for what seemed like an eternity for Ari to say something. Anything. When no words came she turned back and glanced at where he continued to kneel with his head bowed. An unknown force, a power greater than any she had known, drew her to him.

With tentative fingers she touched his shoulder. It was then she realized he wept. She slid her hand down his arm and to his hand as she knelt beside him. He cupped her hand in his and lifted it to his lips.

She had known this man of little words for many years. She'd felt many things toward him, perhaps even a young girl's love immersed in anger at his pity for her, but never until this very moment had she known just how deep her love was rooted.

They remained on their knees in silence, their fingers entwined. It was sweeter than any of his words. More intimate than his kiss.

"The priests here at Manna," he whispered. "Many of the priests have been trained in the art of war. Some are even spies."

As much as her curiosity begged to ask questions, she held her tongue.

"My Uncle Seth was attending duties at the temple when he was just becoming a man. There was a small rebellion when King Asa removed the detestable Asherah poles. Seth was speared in the eyes. My grandfather and his brothers moved their families here to save him from ridicule. Grandfather sought out the tribe of Benjamin and Philistine warriors to train our people in the art of war.

"Many agreed. Just because we were teachers of God's law did not mean we were to be defenseless. All first born sons were and still are sent to Jerusalem."

"But you are not your father's first born." She'd seen Melchiah and Isa. Melchiah's hair grayed at the temples. It was obvious he was older.

"This is true. Elam is the youngest of my uncles. My grandfather allowed him to return to the temple since he showed little ability in warfare. When his wife failed to bear him a male child…"

The oil lamps glimmered and flickered, lengthening the shadows. He lifted his face and turned his gaze on her. "I was supposed to serve in the temple under Elam's mentoring. It wasn't long before the elders realized my talent for combat. I became the youngest of the captains and soon commander of the entire temple guard."

It was no wonder Jehoiada had trusted Ari with Judah's future. For a man to achieve much at a young age, he had to be determined and loyal.

"Elam was not pleased. My training took time from him. To keep the peace, I trained hard under the warriors and studied diligently under Elam's watchful eye."

"Your uncle must have taught you well. You are a wonderful teacher, Ari." She caressed the back of his hand.

He shook his head. "The night—that night I was with Elam, if I'd been on duty maybe I could have stopped Athaliah's men."

"You cannot think to blame yourself, Ari. Her selfishness was not your doing." All the times he'd carried Mira's yoke for her, relieving the weight from her shoulders and he was carrying something much greater. She wished to lighten his burden if only this once.

"You do not understand, Mira, it was my duty, but when—when..." he stammered.

She'd heard some of the horrors that had occurred from Tama. Had Ari seen them with his own eyes? Shifting her position she knelt in front of him, her hands cupped his jaw. "It is all right," she said.

"No. I will not speak of such things. You must know Sh'mira I would protect Joash with my very life. Jehoiada sent us from Jerusalem. There was no time for instruction. We left in the dark of night beneath the city. We traveled here in hopes to hide the child. I left Tama and the babe in my father's care, while I went to seek the Lord's wisdom. My father knew they weren't safe at Manna, and now it seems he was right. When I returned, Tama and Joash were gone."

"My father had taken her to your father. I followed only days later."

"They did not arrive until later." She nodded, thinking back to that time and his struggle to remain alive. Tama had showed up with Joash right before Ari was able to have lucid conversations. Why?

"I did not travel along the mountain passes but instead went through the tunnels. Had I, I wouldn't have been set upon. I would have come across my father and Tama." He shifted and looked her in the eyes. "Sh'mira, I am a trained warrior, I was attacked and left for dead in your father's groves. I can tell you from experience the men who tried to kill me were not thieves. I do not remember much, and I first believed they were the queen's soldiers, but they knew our art of combat."

"And this is the urgency that fuels your desire to leave quickly?"

His lips pursed together as if he were about to deny her assumption.

"I am concerned for Joash's safety, and that of yours, here at Manna. I fear not everyone here is on the side of our God. However, my concern is not what feeds my desire to be done with my duty. The Lord is ever faithful. He will see Joash on the throne in Jerusalem with or without me."

"Then why? You have behaved in a way that I have never seen, and that has left your parents speechless. What is it that bothers you?"

He rose, and began to pace. She uncurled her legs and stood. "Ari, what is it?"

Ari halted and looked at her. Even through the darkness she felt his gaze bore through to her soul. "It is my selfish desire to finally begin living my life, Sh'mira."

As much as it hurt, she did not blame him. He had intended to serve at the temple, and ended up serving as a bond servant, no better than a slave. Commander of the temple guard was a high honor, one he greatly deserved for his service to the Lord and Judah. When all was done, and Joash was crowned, Ari would be free to return to his life as he intended. She would find joy in his happiness, even if it left her devastated.

*

He gave in to his longings and reached for her. Pulling her into his arms, he hugged her close. Her breath hitched in her throat at the contact, but no more so than his. Was this how it felt to love? A simple touch of hands, a touch of their lips. . . it was no longer enough.

"There are many miles between us and Jerusalem. I feel an urgency that I cannot explain." He took a deep breath. "I do not wish to hurt their feelings, but the time for celebration is not now. We must make haste, Mira."

She pulled back and searched his eyes. "Do you intend for us to go alone then?"

"No. Of course not."

Ideally he'd prefer to go with a contingent of armed men. "I must speak to the elders."

"Do they know, then?"

"The elders, yes. It seems Elam informed them only weeks ago."

"But someone must have discovered."

"There is that possibility. I had considered that it might be someone here at Manna. However, I am not sure how any would discover such information."

"If anyone in Jerusalem knew of Jehoiada's relation to my mother—"

"That would mean they've known about the child from the beginning." He shook his head. "No—I believe someone found themselves in trouble and the only way out was to offer information worth its weight in gold. One thing that troubles me is that Athaliah's guards knew the tunnels well enough to plan an attack, which means someone has shown them through, but they did not, or at least have yet to give up Manna's location."

"Who knows the intricacies of the mountains, Ari? Is it common knowledge among the occupants of Manna?"

Her question opened a door he did not wish to pass through. "No, it is not common knowledge."

"Then who?" she whispered.

Ari lifted his eyes to the heavens. The nagging thought that had plagued him ever since the attack pierced his chest. The answer to her question could only mean— "Lord, say it is not true." But he knew it was, knew as he knew he held great affection for the woman standing before him. He lowered his gaze to Mira. "My grandfather's sons, and their sons. Their daughters." He scrubbed a hand over his chin not wanting to believe that one of his kin had betrayed him. "We have been protectors of the mountain passes for ages."

"How is it the locals never knew of these passages?"

"Their secrets have been well hidden. My apologies, Mira. There are many things I, myself, do not understand. Many things I must ponder before I commit to action. I should speak with my father. I trust him above all others, only second to God."

He pressed his lips to her brow and released her. "Find your rest this night."

He turned from her and walked to the balustrade looking out to the sea.

"Ari," she said, laying her hand upon his shoulder. He felt her need to say something but she held her tongue.

"What is it, Mira?" he asked, staring at the reflection of the moon upon the choppy waters, the image, a mirror of his emotions.

If she were to invite him, he'd kiss her. Her hand slid off his shoulder. He turned and captured her in his arms before she could walk away.

He leaned his brow against hers. Their noses touched. "When this is over—"

She placed her fingertips against his lips. An unexpected pleasure at her simple gesture rocked him back on his heels, silencing the promise of love clinging to his tongue

Chapter Twenty-Three

It had taken two days for the elders to be gathered, which had given Mira time to explore more of the small city. The only place she hadn't seen was the inside of the temple. According to Ari it was much smaller and built of humbler means than the one in Jerusalem. The adoration in his eyes when he spoke of the temple affirmed her decision to keep her distance from him.

While Ari spent his time preparing for their journey, she visited the market with Anna and Ari's sister. It contained breads and fruits she had never before seen. Pottery with intricate artwork. Cloth fit for a queen, veils that would trail behind her in the dust made of the finest fabrics, with hand embroidered designs, such that a farmer's daughter like her would never have occasion to wear. The detailed craftsmanship of items amazed her. All made by the people of Manna.

Several rocks slid down the cliff. She gripped the donkey's mane and refocused her efforts on staying on the narrow path.

They had traveled over the mountains along the passes for the past three days instead of through the tunnels, the large sea their constant companion. With the steep, unstable terrain, she often longed to travel in the valley below. She understood traveling in the open plain would place their entourage in greater danger and so she pushed her fear aside.

The donkey in front of her struggled to climb a slight incline. The woman on its back swayed, and Mira held her breath until the beast found its footing and moved along. She would not like to see anyone perish. The only true comfort she had during their journey was that Ari's brothers, as well as over half of the occupants of Manna, men, women and children traveled with them. According to Anna, the elders thought it best to hide among travelers, and with the great Jubilee only days away what better excuse.

The woman in front of her disappeared as she descended. The path widened, opening into a valley. Mira glanced over her shoulder and took one last look at the rugged hills. If only she could see Manna one last time. To brand it in her memory. She would miss it.

Ari never asked her to keep its secret, but she knew she would take it to her death. Never would she be able to share the majestic fortress with her mother or her father. Instead, she would create a new song on the lyre.

"You look tired." Lydia maneuvered her donkey next to Mira's.

"Although I am grateful to not be walking, I am weary from holding so tightly," Mira responded.

Ari's sister laughed. "You are not used to riding?"

"The occasion rarely occurs. My father owns several donkeys, but whenever we ventured to Hebron, it was not far. There was no need to ride."

"I see. You should have told my brother."

He had enough on his mind. She did not wish to add to his worries. "What could he have done? I would only slow us down by walking."

"My brother, he loves you."

Mira grappled for her balance as she flung her gaze to Ari's young sister. "What makes you speak such nonsense, Lydia?"

"Anyone with eyes can see the way he looks at you." She smiled. "Besides, I heard him speaking with my father. Not about love. Men do not speak of such things."

"It does not matter." She sighed. Her fingers ached with the effort to hold her seat. "As much as I had hoped. . .there can never be a match between us."

"Why ever not?" Lydia asked.

Once, Mira thought things were as simple as just believing, but now she knew better. Ari's hopes and dreams of resuming his temple duties could never be realized if they were to become man and wife.

"It is not possible, Lydia." She firmed her lips and kept her eyes on the tunic directly in front of her. Thankfully, Lydia had taken the hint and had not said another word. Having his sister mention the possibility of Ari's love tore a chasm in her chest, especially knowing they could never be together.

She sought his position ahead of her. His body swayed back and forth with the motion of the donkey, Joash sat in front of him. Ari bent his head whenever the child spoke. At times he would point to an object in the distance. He was ever the teacher and would make a wonderful father someday. Just not the father of the children she had desired.

Ari touched his lips to the child's locks. Even if Ari did not wish to return to his temple duties, how could he walk away from Joash? He cared for him deeply. Surely he would want to stay near and keep watch over him.

Green spiked hedges appeared. An open clearing near a small spring rose before her eyes.

"This will be our last night of travel. Tomorrow we reach Jerusalem," Lydia told her as the riders ahead of them began to dismount.

"You have traveled this path many times?"

"Of course. We visited Ari quite often when he lived there."

"Come." Lydia slid from her donkey's back. "We must help ready the evening meal while the men set up camp."

Mira looked to the ground, and although the drop was not overly far, it was far enough. Before she could protest or garner up her courage, Ari was there lifting her down. Her breath caught, and her heart swelled. If she had been any other woman, other than her father's daughter, her father's disfigured daughter, she would take everything Ari's eyes promised. But she was not any other woman. She would be expected to marry a man who would take care of her father's land—as Ari had done for the last several years—and Ari did not belong in the wilderness tending sheep and pruning vines.

"You are well?" he asked, massaging her fingers.

"I am well," she responded. He should not pity her. Mira pulled her hand from his, and sidestepped. "I must tend my duties." She bowed her head and walked away

*

She scurried away like a frightened hare, although he did not know what he had done or said to scare her. He pulled on the donkey's lead and dragged him over to a corral built long ago by his grandfather. He removed the blankets and untied the rolled mats. Ari carried them to where they would make their camp.

If he had his way they would have pushed on to Jerusalem, especially since the city was only mere miles away. But he had to send word to Jehoiada, and he would attend Jehoiada himself, the only problem was that he would have to leave Mira and Joash in the care of his kin. The idea did not sit well with him, but he really did not have a choice. Jehoiada would not trust words from another's lips.

He searched for his father and Jesse but could not find them. Instead he found Elam, who was preparing an offering. "Uncle, I must enter Jerusalem."

"You worry for the girl?" Elam rose, his robes flowed around his ankles. His face was hard like stone, and his eyes betrayed no emotion.

Wariness rode across Ari's shoulders and he gripped the back of his neck. "My concern lies with Joash and Mira, yes?"

"They will be well cared for," Elam said.

"My thanks." Ari bowed. "If anything should happen to me. . .if I do not return…"

Elam laid a hand on his shoulder. "My brother's son, have faith. Contact Jehoiada. If you do not return to us, I will send us out in groups of seven. Your woman and the child will be amongst us. I will keep vigilance, and your brothers and cousins will guard them with their lives."

Ari kissed his uncle's cheeks. "My thanks."

"All will be well, Ariel. You will see."

God's plans were mightier than man's, even that of Queen Athaliah. If ever he needed to trust God, it was now. He shook off the uneasiness pricking his nape.

He found Mira near the fire once again cooking cakes. "I see my mother has entrusted you with our cakes."

She jerked her head toward him. "I did not think you had noticed the burnt cake."

"I had not. It was only later when Jesse had asked me how I could have stomached the taste." He smiled. "Imagine his surprise when I told him it had tasted of the sweetest of honey."

She giggled.

"I do not lie," he added.

He knelt beside her. He wanted to take her hand but feared she would once again shy from him. He did not wish to make the cakes if she were to run away. "Mira, I must enter Jerusalem this night."

"Oh," she said. "When will we leave?"

"It is only I that will go," he said.

Shadows flickered into her golden eyes. "Alone?"

"Yes."

"What if you are recognized?" She lifted her hand, placing it on his smooth cheek. The contact stopped the beat of his heart.

"It is a risk I must take," he said, laying his hand upon hers. He turned his face and pressed his lips to the palm of her hand. The bustle of activity disappeared over the pounding of his life's blood in his ears. If he could, he would take her to wife this very moment, but he would wait out of respect for her father. "My brothers will guard you. I need you to stay with Joash. Help Tama watch over him. Can you do that for me?"

Her eyes widened in fear, but she nodded.

"Call on the name your Lord God if you should need him," he breathed against her palm. "He is faithful. He will protect you. I know this here." He cupped her hand within his and placed it over his heart. Her tiny palm against his chest heated. It was as if she had branded him. "I," he stammered. Words clung to his lips. "I will leave as the sun begins to descend. And I will return in the morning."

The tips of her lashes brushed against the golden hue of her cheeks.

"If for some reason I do not return—" his words were interrupted as a small cry of distress passed her lips.

"You must not go alone," she pleaded.

"I have no choice, Sh'mira."

"Allow me to attend you."

"No, you must help protect Joash. It will be up to you and Tama to return him to Jehoiada if I do not return. Do you understand?" He caught sight of his sister hovering in the distance. He motioned for her to finish the task of cooking cakes, and then he rose with Mira's hand trapped in his. "Come, with me?"

She dug in her heels, and he believed she would refuse. He thanked the Lord when she moved her feet.

They walked a short distance, away from prying eyes and ears. Ari turned toward her. The curve of her lips drew his mouth to hers. He pressed his lips to the corner of her mouth before resting his brow against hers.

"Mira," he pulled back and gazed into her eyes. "If anything happens while I'm gone, any of my family, Jesse especially will take you to Jehoiada. He and Elam know how to enter the temple passages."

"There must be some other way, Ari. You should not go alone."

He pulled her back into his arms and hugged her. She trembled.

Her worry over his well-being set a smile on lips. It danced in his heart, leaving him filled with joy. He silently praised the Lord for bringing them together for he was beginning to think she was the perfect half to his whole. His intended helpmate.

If he ever doubted God's will, he would remember the touch of her lips, the thundering of her heart in tandem with his. If he ever doubted God's will, he would remember how much he wished to marry Sh'mira daughter of a farmer. If he ever doubted God's will, he would remember just how much she worried over his safety.

Even though she had never said the words.

Chapter Twenty-Four

"What is wrong with you?" Ari picked up a handful of desert and tossed it into the air. He sat on his rear looking up at the cantankerous donkey with his ears pinned back staring down at him.

"As if I did not have reservations of my own, you have to go and prove stubborn."

The donkey's nostrils flared. His sharp squeal rent the cooling air.

"Fine." Ari stood and pulled on the animal's reins. The beast brayed as he planted his backside into the ground. Ari rolled his eyes. "I should be halfway to Jerusalem. I'd much rather be sitting next to the fire watching Mira stew than fight with you, you stubborn donkey."

The donkey pulled back his lips, baring his teeth. Ari had never heard of a donkey hissing, but this one was doing just that. And he didn't think the donkey was offended as much as to say that Ari was the one being a stubborn fool.

"I should have stayed with Joash and Mira." It had taken every bit of faith to entrust them with his kin. Even after he had been firm in his decision, after all, he knew he was the only one for this particular mission. Jehoiada would believe no one else. Even then, Ari had still dragged his feet as he left the encampment.

Feeling Mira's eyes on his back had made it worse. He had known she stood at the edge of camp watching him go until she could see him no more. He had known because he kept glancing over his shoulder looking for any indication that he should stay.

And now he was here, fighting a losing battle with a beast that should be humble. Not full of pride.

He dropped the reins from his hand. "Well, if you will not move, I have no choice but to continue on without you." Ari scratched the spot between the donkey's ears hoping a little affection would be enough to entice the animal to move. All he received for his efforts was a baring of teeth and a flattening of the ears.

"So be it," Ari said as he headed in the direction of Jerusalem. "I hear the great spotted cat prowls the nights. You'll make a wonderful meal for her family."

He kept walking, his heart heavy at the thought of leaving this defenseless beast to his own devices. "If the cougar does not get you, the birds will be ready to devour you come morning."

Nothing.

"It would be in your best interest to at least follow along, you know. I will not make you carry me another step if that is what bothers you." He sighed and turned around to face the donkey sitting in the sand. The beast twitched his ears. Ari crossed his arms over his chest knowing full he would not be able to convince the donkey to move. He was as strong-minded as Mira. A vision of her behaving as the donkey lifted the corners of his mouth.

If she weren't as stubborn, would he care for her as much as he did? He would never know for she was as stubborn as they came, at least she had been until they had met up with his family. What had happened to his bold, courageous Mira? Had it something to do with his family? Or was it something he had done?

The donkey screeched, rising up on all fours he turned toward camp and pawed at the ground.

Ari lifted his eyes into the distance. The sight of his father and Jesse, along with another man, approaching on horses, left his chest thundering in fear.

Had something happened?

Dust and sand kicked up as they halted their horses. Ari eyed the Philistine he recognized from the spring. His hand slid to the hilt of his sword.

"Let not your heart be troubled, my son." His father slid from the horse. Jesse jumped to his feet, while the Philistine remained seated, staring down at Ari.

"You ride as if a great wind is nipping your heels, with a Philistine no less, and you tell me to not be troubled?"

"I am surprised you had not made if further, brother," Jesse teased.

Ari glared at his brother. "The beast would not cooperate."

A look passed between his father and brother. "What? What is it that brings you here?"

"Your brother and I surveyed the area surrounding the camp. No," his father held up his hand, "we did not find anything. When we returned to the camp your brother paced." He paused. "He tends to do that whenever he is troubled."

"I was not troubled, I am never troubled," Jesse argued.

"You were." Ishiah turned his eyes back to Ari. "I myself had a stirring deep within my gut. An uneasiness."

Ari's eyes flicked to the warrior who had yet to speak. His discomfort grew under the man's watchful gaze.

"I decided to check the area once again." Jesse crossed his arms over his chest. "Not because I was troubled.

"And you found him?"

"No," Jesse answered.

What did he mean by no? "Then why is he with you?" He wished his father would say what was to be said and halt the churning in his stomach.

"He came upon us when we decided to seek you." Jesse said.

Ari shoved his fingers through his hair. "You mean to tell me you thought to travel to Jerusalem with me when you came upon a Philistine and decided to bring him along?"

"No." His father and Jess answered together.

He scrubbed his hand over his face. His level of frustration rose, his virtue of patience sunk to the ground.

"You must return to your camp." This came from the Philistine.

Ari glared up at the man. A sharp warning stabbed him in his chest. His gaze bounced between his father and Jesse. "Has something happened to Mira? To Joash?"

"No, not as of yet, but we," his father said, motioning between himself and Jesse. "And," he waved toward the warrior, "he feels the danger is imminent."

"Since when do you listen to a Philistine, Father?" Their people may have helped train the men of Manna, but that didn't mean they trusted them. And Ari would not trust this one, especially since he'd seen him with the queen's soldiers.

"After I listened to what he had to say, Ariel."

The donkey brayed as if to laugh. Ari's cheeks flamed with embarrassment. He knew better than to judge a man, even a Philistine, without cause. He nodded toward the man. "What is it you had to say, Philistine?"

The warrior dismounted his horse and removed his helmet. He stood a head taller than Ari. He tucked his helmet beneath his arm, his bald head glistening in the setting of the sun. "My name is Ianatos. I was with the queen's guard when the child and your woman slipped into the waterfalls." His hard eyes settled on Ari. "I killed several when they followed in the tunnels."

Air whooshed from Ari's lungs, relieved at having an ally in the enemy's camp. "My thanks, Ianatos."

"None needed if we do not return to camp and save your Hebrew king. Suph, the captain of the queen's men is determined to kill the child. A man came into our camp shortly before I found your brother and told Suph of the child's whereabouts."

Ari's jaw slid open. He wanted to ask about the man who dared betray the rightful king of Judah, who betrayed Ari's trust, but there was no time. "Then we should not waste a moment. Let us return with haste."

"First, we must build an altar and make sacrifices," his father said.

Jesse, Ari and even the Philistine gathered up a pile of dry brush and some wood. Ianatos retreated to his horse as they gathered up three stones, one for each of them. They laid them together and waited for their father to prepare the grain offering.

His father laid a small dish upon the stones and then they each added a portion of grain. They knelt around the altar with their heads bowed. "Father God, maker of the Earth.

You alone are God. Grant thy servants protection and wisdom. Divert our enemies. Amen," his father prayed.

"Amen," he and Jesse repeated.

No second thought entered Ari's mind about whether or not the cantankerous donkey would move with haste. He doubted the beast would so he rode with Jesse. The closer they drew, the more anxious he became. "Father God, forgive thy servant for my obstinacy. I pray it has not caused harm to my king and my love," he muttered beneath his breath.

Soon the camp's firelight rose in the distance, yet he hesitated to breathe a sigh of relief. They drew ever closer, and Ari could hear the song lifted up to God in praise. He closed his eyes and thanked God. If his family and friends were in such joyous celebration, then naught could be wrong, could it?

Ianatos pulled on his reins, bringing his horse to a halt. His father's and brother's beasts did the same.

"Wait here." Ianatos disappeared into the darkness, leaving Ari to wonder if they'd misplaced their trust in the Philistine.

An uneasy feeling turned in his stomach as they waited in the shadows of camp. He was about to demand Jess ride on when the clop of horses' hooves pressed into the desert. He peered into the darkness as one shadow after another appeared, all with Philistine helmets on their heads.

*

"What is it I can do for you, Sh'mira?" Elam asked. The tone of his voice and the way he watched her sent chills chasing down her spine. It was no more than she expected being that she was imperfect in many ways.

She bowed her head to the elder, keeping her eyes firm on her toes and her hands folded in her tunic. "Tama is busy. I would take Joash to the spring for his evening cleanse, if you approve."

From the corner of her eye she watched him run his fingers over his beard. "I will take the boy," he responded.

"Forgive me, as Ari has asked me to meet the child's needs and to not leave his side. For anything," she added. She would not shirk her duty to Ari, not even for his uncle who scared her, even if Ari did hold him in high regard.

"I see." Elam rose from his seat and said something to his companion, a man she hadn't seen before but assumed him to be from Manna. "After we've broken our fast, we will go."

Sometime later, Mira took Joash by the hand and followed Elam. Twilight beckoned in its pale darkening beauty as the sun dipped beyond the western sky leaving it cloaked in pinks, yellows and blues. Thousands of white lights twinkled in the east, along with that of the moon. It was as if she stood in a canyon, dividing day and night. And although they remained within hearing distance of camp, a sense of unease warned her to beware. She tossed a glance over her shoulder where the evening campfire glowed less and less with each step away. She could make out Lydia and Anna as they cleared away the dishes and folded the tables.

"Sh'mira," Joash whispered as he tugged on her hand. She leaned her ear low. "I am frightened. Shall we return to camp and cleanse on the morrow?"

Normally she would have thought the boy was seeking a way out of his bath, but she too would have liked to return. Yet, she allowed her feet to continue on their path behind Elam, taking a reluctant child king with her. "Have faith, all will be well," she soothed. "Besides, we leave for Jerusalem even as the sun will rise."

"If you say, Sh'mira," he responded.

The trickling sound of the spring brought a semblance of relief. It was as if their destination brought peace, although she knew it best to keep a watchful eye.

"Joash, you may remove your tunic and lay it on the ground beside the stream." Elam watched the boy move away, then he turned his eyes fully on her. "You should not coddle him. It will only make for a weak king."

"Yes, of course," Mira responded.

"You may sit at the edge. I will be over by yon rock if you need something."

He walked away and then knelt beside the indicated rock, his example of diligent prayer did not pass her. Guilt gnawed at her stomach. His love for the Lord was evident in the time he spent in prayer. Much more than the others, proving she had no reason to fear him.

She ensured herself of Joash's safety as he entered the brook. Seeing that the water did not pass his knees she began to relax and focused her energies on praying for Ari's protection.

"Lord, if you will, I ask thee to grant Ari wisdom with each step he travels. Hide him from his enemies that he may carry out Your will." A sense of overwhelming fear gripped her body. Perspiration beaded on her brow, her stomach churned. She shook off the feeling. "Forgive thy servant for my lack of faith, my Lord God."

Elam's words bounced around in her head. Had she coddled Joash too much? Had she done so because she felt a kindred with him? He was alone in this world with no parents and no one to love him but her, Tama and Ari.

She blew out a breath of air.

Were they the only ones who truly loved this child beyond what he offered Judah? The thought left her saddened for the child. How could she leave him in Jerusalem, returning to her loving family, when he had no one to truly care for him? Of course, Ari and Tama would remain close by, of this she had no doubt, but would it be enough? Could she stay with Ari if he asked her to and care for the child, too? Her father would forgive her, give his blessing, even if she were to follow Ari to Jerusalem as his wife.

Could she leave her father with no sons to care for his land? Pain gripped her fingers, reminding her of all the reasons she could never spend the rest of her life with the man she loved. There would be many more men, such as Elam,, who would not hide their scorn of her and her disfigurement Although he had not spoken them aloud, she knew he did not approve of her. It was always there in his eyes.

The ground began to shake beneath her feet. She laid the palms of her hands on either side of her, thinking that the earth was about to split in two.

"Mira!" Joash cried.

She rushed to him and gathered him in her arms. She twisted around hoping to catch sight of Elam but he was nowhere to be seen. She turned back. A score of horses with menacing riders bore down on them. Curved swords rose. Her scream caught in her throat, refusing to break loose.

She should have listened to Joash and returned to camp. She should have heeded her own instincts. But she had not trusted them.

They stood in the middle of the stream when she first saw them kicking up the desert sand. Frantically she glanced around for a hiding place. Brush, reeds, anything. Not even a blade of grass poked from the riverbanks.

She twisted and turned, holding on to Joash. Where had Elam gone? Instinct roared at her to shout for Ari, but she couldn't utter a word. Not with the sight of twenty of the queen's guard barreling down on her with their swords raised.

How was she to deny fear when terror dogged her footsteps? She dropped to her knees beside Joash, circling him with in the folds of her tunic, her face buried in the crook of his neck. *Father God, please protect us from our enemies.*

The thumping of horses hooves pounded in her ears. Tears slid down her cheeks.

She was going to die a coward, and she hadn't once told Ari what was in her heart. He would never know that she loved him.

The smell of horse and man reached her and she tightened her grip on Joash. If she could not tell Ari of her love. "Joash, my brother," she whispered against his ear. "I love you, brother."

"And I you, Sh'mira." His small childlike voice held a slight quiver and she couldn't help but think what a wonderful king he would have made.

Chapter Twenty-Five

Ari watched as the last firebrand arched across the sky, propelling downward until it crashed near the bank where it exploded and roared to life. Ianatos dismounted. "At my command." He held up his hand and then sliced it down.

Ari crossed his arms over his chest and listened with satisfaction as the multitude of sinews thwaped against the air, releasing their deadly weapons. The queen's guard had not a chance against the Philistine mercenaries' superior warfare, especially given the guard's swords glinted off the firelight, revealing their positions.

Pops, as the arrows pierced the leather armor followed by their grunts, sliced through the crackling of the fire. The queen's men were dead before they'd even laid eyes on the future king of Judah.

Ianatos tucked his helmet beneath his arm and issued a command to his fellow warriors. The mercenaries swung their bows upon their backs and headed toward Jerusalem where Ari knew they'd spread out along the walls and keep a watchful eye for any who'd wish the boy harm.

Ari approached Ianantos and held out his hand. "My thanks, friend."

"It had been fortunate I'd been at the Hebrew camp when the messenger arrived with news of the child. Fortunate I was able to leave unnoticed and contact my companions."

"No matter, I owe you a great debt." Ari shook his hand.

"My vow is to my ancestors and their vow to protect the line of King David. Nothing more." Ianatos sat his helmet on his head and laced the strap beneath his chin. He mounted his horse. "I'll wait for word in Jerusalem."

Ari mounted a horse given to him by the Philistine. Jesse, he and his father rode toward the stream where Mira hunched in the middle of the spring, fire lined either side of the banks, encompassing her and the child wrapped in her arms.

A soldier and his horse flew across the spring, his face pale with fear. The guard fell from his mount and lay on his back at Ari's feet, and arrow embedded in the leather armor. The guard's eyes stared unseeing, his chest unmoving. With his hand on the hilt of his sword, Ari glanced to see if any other survivors roamed.

"Elam!" Mira hollered. "Elam? Where are you?"

Ari dismounted and splashed into the water. He grabbed Mira's arms. She shoved him away. She took a step toward the shore and stumbled to her knees. "Elam! Joash, where are you?"

"Here, Mira." The child touched her shoulder.

"Thank God," she whispered, dropping her head.

"Mira?" Ari moved toward her again.

She blinked her eyes as if trying to focus. "Ari? Is that you?" She held her free hand out in front of her as if to feel her way.

Ari reached her and pulled her and Joash from the water. "It is I." He pressed a kiss to her lips. "Are you well?"

Her hesitation alerted him. He squeezed her tight against him taking joy in the fact that her heart continued to beat.

"What has happened?" Joash asked.

"The queen's men attacked, but some Philistine warriors helped us thwart them," Ishiah said as he came upon them.

Mira gasped and pulled from Ari's arms. "Elam? He was here with us. What has happened to him?"

"Do not fret, Sh'mira." His father patted her shoulder as if to soothe her.

"If anything has happened to him. . ." she continued.

"Jesse is checking the area."

Mira moved completely from his embrace drawing Joash along with her. She fell once again. "Are you well?" Ari asked her once again.

"I do not know, Ari. I cannot see."

"What is it you mean that you cannot see?" Ari asked with concern.

"I do not know," she responded. "It's as if I stared at the sun too long."

He glanced at Joash. "Can you see?"

The child nodded his head. "When I first saw the fire descending I buried my face against Sh'mira."

"Fire?" she asked.

"It is quite simple, my child," his father offered. "The Philistines lit firebrands and shot them with their arrows. You must have stared at the fire."

"Come, we have no time if you are to make it to Jerusalem before the next wave." Jesse walked toward them.

"What do you mean?" Ari asked.

"One of the men was alive. He spoke of a traitor among us. Not that you are surprised, brother," Jesse answered.

No he was not surprised.

"Who?" his father asked, shocked.

"Did you find Elam?" Mira trembled against him.

"No, I did not find him. Perhaps he ran back to camp to gather forces."

Perhaps, but why would Elam leave their king to the mercies of armed soldiers?

Jesse scratched his bearded chin. "Since I was not able to obtain the name of our traitor, we must make all haste to Jerusalem at once. Before anyone discovers the boy is still alive." Jesse crossed his arms over his chest in a commanding manner. Ari for once was glad to let someone else shoulder the burdens and take control. He just wanted to hold Mira.

"I will not leave them again," Ari argued. "And I doubt Jehoiada will listen to anyone but me."

"That, my dear brother, is why we will all go." He smiled. "We have horses." His smile broadened. "Father can ride one. Joash can ride with you, and Sh'mira may ride with me," he said with an obnoxious grin.

"I think not," Ari returned.

"Jealous, brother," Jesse teased.

Ari eyed his sibling. "Never. However, I trust you to keep the child well." The knowledge that his mission would be complete, sooner than he could have hoped, brought him relief. He guided Mira to one of the horses. He helped her mount and then pressed his lips to her knuckles before climbing behind her.

Chapter Twenty-Six

As if not being able to see clearly had not been bad enough, she found herself tossed onto a beast much larger than the donkey she had ridden from Manna.

Even the presence of Ari could not soothe the nausea building wave upon wave with each jolt of the horse's hooves. She would have preferred to keep the giant to a simple walk for her first time on its back, although she understood Ari's urgency.

After the attack she was quite anxious to be done and return home, back to the safety in her father's house where the most adventurous thing that had ever occurred was a wild dog stealing sheep. However, the sooner she returned there the sooner Ari would be gone from her life. And even though she knew that they could never be together, she was not looking forward to saying their goodbyes either.

Ari's arm tightened around her waist like a steel band as if he could read her thoughts. The horse tossed his head. She dug her fingers into Ari's arm. They smarted with the movement. She grasped her disfigured hand with her other and ran her fingers over her knuckles, the heat from the firebrands had aggravated her scars.

She sighed.

"Are you well?"

She nodded. Other than feeling sick to her stomach, a renewed ache in her hand and darkened vision, and the fact that she'd soon be parted from his strength, she felt wonderful. "I am fine, Ari."

"How much longer before we reach the temple?" she asked seeking anything to keep her mind from dwelling on what could never be.

"I must take Joash to the temple alone."

She gripped his forearm.

"Do not let your heart be troubled, you will stay with my father. I will send Jesse back to alert the camp. They will be with you before the sun rises."

Had he forgotten about the traitor?

"And if God wills it our traitor will be ousted before they do."

"And if he is not discovered, what then?" she asked, her nerves, added to the rocking motion of the large horse, were getting the best of her. She didn't know how much longer she could keep from obeying the commands of her stomach and discarding her evening meal.

"Have you no faith, Mira?" he whispered.

Ari's words were a reminder that the Lord had answered her prayers in more ways than one, for the Lord had protected her and Joash from their enemies. Although she had feared to see death coming in the image of horse, rider and curved sword, she had peeked through her lids. There'd been nothing but an inferno, and she could not tear her eyes from the flames, not even when she felt the heat on her flesh, nor when she smelled burning of her tunic. She had feared an enemy would swoop down upon them and she didn't want to be caught unaware.

If God had answered her prayers in a great time of need would He answer her other prayers too? Would He find a way for her to stay with Ari?

Ari pulled up on the reins. The beast danced around, quivered and snorted. Mira tightened her hold once again on Ari's arm.

"What is it?"

She shifted, her ears attuned to his breaths. His chest rose and fell in short, shallow rhythms.

"Jerusalem." The word was no more than a whisper. A whisper of adoration. Devotion.

Jerusalem.

Ari's home. His destiny.

That one word for God's holy city squeezed her insides with the efficiency of a wine press, leaving nothing but empty skin. All her hopes for a future with Ari crushed.

"If only you could see…" The air in his lungs hitched, expanding his chest.

She stared in front of her and willed the bright spots dancing in her vision to lessen, willed the dimness in the corners of her eyes to lighten. It was like she'd stared at the sun too long.

"Tell me," she urged.

"Torches line the gates. The stones look as if they're made of gold."

"Are the gates as big as Hebron's?" Hebron had once been a holy city and still maintained much of its fortifications.

"No, they are much grander. Larger and wider. Wider than the breadth of your village, Mira. The towers seem to stretch to the heavens."

She'd heard the stories from her parents and had longed to see the city. She sighed. Perhaps God protected her from herself. If she could not see the city she couldn't fall in love with it. Couldn't be tempted to leave her father's house and stay with Ari if he asked.

"We are approaching the eastern wall. It is nothing like you've ever seen." He flicked the reigns. The horse jerked its head and snorted as it moved forward.

They rode for many long minutes before they halted once again. The saddle dipped and creaked as Ari slid to the ground. He placed his hands around her waist and brought her down alongside him. Although they had not been riding overly long her knees wobbled, threatening to tip her over. Ari held on to her.

"My thanks, my brother. I will forever be in your debt." Ari leaned forward as he held on to her arm. She heard the smack of Ari's lips as he kissed his brother's cheeks.

"I will remember you said that, Ari." Jesse chuckled and then grabbed her hand. He gave her a gentle squeeze. "If you need anything at all, Mira, you know how to find me."

"You are leaving then?" she tilted her head.

"I am heading to camp, but I will return if God wills it." He kissed her brow, she felt, more than heard the growl rumbling through Ari's chest. His hand banded around her waist. "I will miss you, sister."

"And I you, Jesse."

"Abba," Jesse acknowledged.

"My son, may God go with you," Ishiah said.

"And with you too, Abba." Leather creaked as Jesse mounted his horse. They stood there until she could no longer hear the clopping of hooves.

Ari twisted her in his arms. Sensing his gaze, her face warmed. "You must go with my father and enter the city through the gates. I will come to you as soon as I can."

"Ari," she whispered, placing her hand on his chest. All the words she wanted to stay clung to her tongue like honey. There they would have to stay, left unsaid. "Be careful."

He swept in, his lips firm against hers. Before it began it was over and he was gone.

Two things bombarded her thoughts, she hadn't hugged Joash, and Ari had not said his goodbyes.

*

He hated leaving her, but the choice had not belonged to him.

"Joash," he said, tearing off a piece of his tunic. "I must bind your eyes before we go any farther."

"I understand. There are some secrets that must be kept," the child responded.

Ari smiled as he knelt by the boy. "How did you gain much wisdom?" He wrapped the cloth around the boy's head and tied it in a knot.

"I have had an excellent teacher, Ariel. Even if you, too, are stubborn as a mule."

Ari straightened, his eyes narrowed, he glared at the boy even if the child could not see it. "What makes you say such things?"

"You should have told Sh'mira of your love."

"I will in due time, Joash." He ruffled the boy's locks. "The way of love is not always an easy road to travel. You will see. Come, let us go and find Jehoiada."

They skirted along the outer walls of the city until he was a hundred paces from the main gate, and then they walked out into the wilderness for another two hundred paces where a large fig tree stood. There they traveled east until he found a bit of bramble.

"Beware. You'll receive a few scratches," Ari told him as he moved apart the thorn bushes and ducked between them into a tunnel. They entered the hollowed-out tunnel and followed it back to the city walls. Beneath the rocky desert the air was moist and thick, but the tunnels had been kept well, which set his mind at ease.

After many minutes, Ari came to a locked gate. He reached beneath his tunic and pulled out a leather strap with a key. He unlocked it. The hinges made not a sound, although he did not fool himself that Jehoiada was not aware of his presence. The man seemed to know all sorts of things.

They slipped through the gate. Their footsteps and the occasional dripping of water were the only sounds as they moved through the tunnels until they came to a lit corridor. The once decorated room with mosaic floor tiles, now lay in a deserted shambles. The tiles shattered, left where they crumbled. He'd known the temple had been damaged by Athaliah's cruelty, he hadn't realized how much.

"Come." He guided Joash to another room much the same condition as the previous. The scent of myrrh teased his senses reminding him of a time long ago passed. He breathed deeply seeking to brand it firm into his memory lest he never experience it again.

A torch beckoned him from a small alcove. He peered inside. This small area seemed untouched by the cruelty. Ari stood outside and untied his sandals. He then knelt beside Joash and removed his sandals. Ari dipped a cloth into a basin of water and cleansed the boy's feet. Then he anointed them with fragrant oil. "I am honored to call you friend, Joash."

The child held out his hand, Ari furrowed his brow. "What is it you wish?"

"I will wash your feet, Ariel," Joash said with compassionate authority.

Ari closed his eyes against the kindness in this child. "You humble me, but it is not necessary," Ari argued.

"Am I your friend?"

"Of course." Ari bowed his head even though the child could not see him. If the child knew who he was would he still seek to wash Ari's feet? Of course he would, it was a part of who he was.

Ari placed a dry cloth in the boy's hand. Joash dropped to his knees and felt around for the basin of water. He took care with each swipe of the cloth.

"The oil?" Joash asked.

Ari complied, knowing any argument would be for naught.

"It is I who am humbled." Joash poured oil into the palm of his hand. He rubbed his hands together and smoothed the oil over Ari's feet. "Ari, I will never forget the service you have offered our great God and Judah. I, my friend, will ever be in your debt for you have loved deeply enough to give your life for God, your country and your future king."

Ari sucked in a sharp breath and glanced at the child. "You know?"

"Of course, Ariel. I've known for a while that I was set apart for a purpose. When Sh'mira fell to my feet, I wondered why. It did not take long to discover why your people treated me with such reverence." The corners of his mouth slid upward in a mischievous grin. "Besides, there is nothing wrong with my hearing."

Ari laughed. A tear slid down Ari's cheek. "I am going to miss you."

He rose from his knees and hugged Joash to him before leading the boy into the alcove.

"It is time to kneel and give thanks to the Lord."

They bowed their heads in silence. The last he had been here and had given thanks, the words had been meaningless. Words repeated from memory.

Now he spoke from his heart with sincere gratitude for all God had blessed him with over the past seven years. Broken was not a word he would use for what he felt, but aware. Aware that God had cared enough to show him His ways even through difficult times. Loved him enough to prove Himself to a mere man who had been lost in the dictates of the law. The difference was not just in his clean-shaven face instead of the levitical beard, but his heart had changed too.

"Lord, my God, creator of all the Earth. I stand before You in awe of Your Almighty greatness. May Thy hand continue to touch Thy servant, that I may walk in all Thy ways. Abba God," he cried wrapping his arm around Joash. "anoint this child with your wisdom. May he rule in obedience to You. May he rule with Your grace and authority. Amen."

"Amen," Joash repeated. "May I remove the cloth, Ariel?"

"Soon, Joash. Soon." He rose, drawing Joash along beside him. "Let us greet Jehoiada."

Chapter Twenty-Seven

Mira walked beside Ishiah with her arm wrapped around his. "How much farther?" she asked, the bright spots in her vision had lessened. And although she could now see the shadowy figure of Ishiah beside her, it remained difficult to see.

"Not far. I see the sentry at the gates. Here," he said, handing her his cane. "Use this. Pull your tunic over your head, and above all take courage."

She thought to ask why she needed to cover her eyes, but his last words gripped her. She had not felt courage since she'd left home.

"Hail! What is your business?"

Ishiah drew her close wrapping his arm around her shoulders. "My daughter, she is ill. We seek a physician and to bring sacrifice."

"Your name?"

"Ishiah of Ziph." Ishiah grumbled the words.

Mira was not surprised he did not speak the truth. The truth would bring danger to them.

"Ishiahand daughter," the sentry said. "Move along."

A loud snap, as if a branch had broken from its mooring, caused her to jump.

"It is only the latch releasing from the gates," Ishiah whispered.

The groan of heavy wood skittered along her nerves. Ishiah drew her forward, the tension in his arm relaxed beneath her fingers. His calm pats did not give her assurance all was well.

Once they were through the gate, the atmosphere changed. Her spirit shirked within her, cringing from the discordant noises. Cymbals and horns, boisterous revelry. With her eyes veiled, and only her heart to guide her, she could see no reason why Ari wished to call this offensive place home.

The stench of unwashed people left her nauseated as their bodies pressed against her. Afraid to be lost among the crowd of revelers she gripped tighter to Ishiah. Lewd comments were tossed in the air. Her arms were pinched. She cried out as her tunic was pulled back and her veil ripped from her head. One man even stopped them, offering to purchase her from Ishiah for a piece of silver. She wanted to weep, for this was could not be the Jerusalem she'd heard of. It could not be God's holy city.

Ishiah patted her arm, offering her encouragement. "We are almost home," he whispered. "But I do not think it best to enter through the front."

It did not matter which direction they entered as long as she was free from the eyes she sensed leering at her back.

She cried out as another person yanked on her hair, causing her to trip on the cobblestones beneath her feet. She released Ishiah's arm and fell to her hands and knees. "Ishiah!" She froze, unable to move due to the pressing bodies closing in on her.

Her fingers were smashed beneath someone's foot, and then she felt an arm around her waist lifting her to her feet. The man squeezed the air from her as she tried to break free. "You've caused my master a bit of trouble, Sh'mira, daughter of Caleb."

Mira stilled at the low voice rumbling near her ear. What master did he speak of, and who besides Ishiah knew her? She tried to look at her captor and catch a glimpse of his features through her dimmed eyesight but he jerked her close against his chest. Fear gripped her, and without thinking of what she would do once she was free, she jammed her elbow into the man's mid-section. He dropped her to her feet, and another hand, this time a familiar one grasped her and ran with sure footedness.

Ishiah turned a sharp corner and pressed her against a plastered building. He heaved deep breaths, hers matched his.

"I think we lost him," he huffed. He tugged on her hand and pulled her farther away from the street they had been on. The ground beneath her feet was no longer cobbled but smooth and soft.

After a few twists and turns he placed his hand on her head. "Duck, Sh'mira."

She did so, and the smell of baking bread made her mouth water making her forget she had been near abducted.

"Where are we?" she asked.

"Do not worry yourself, child," Ishiah said. "You are safe here."

"My son," a woman's voice called. "I did not think to be blessed with your presence so soon." Mira blinked as the firebrands lighting the room tried to break through the dark spots dancing in her vision. She heard the smack of a kiss and couldn't help but smile at the greeting between Ishiah and his mother.

"Hello, Mother." He pulled Mira close. "May I introduce Sh'mira to you. She is the daughter of Ariel's master."

Mira flinched at the reminder of how hard Ari had worked for her father. All the while he should have been taken care of by her father and his family.

"I see," the woman clucked. "What a beautiful girl she is."

Heat rose in her cheeks.

"And very courageous," Ishiah added.

Mira opened her mouth to argue but he squeezed her hand. "Mira, this is my mother Sara, Ari's grandmother."

"My pleasure," she bowed her head.

Papery fingers held her chin as the woman placed a kiss on her brow. "Come, come sit by the fire while I mix up a salve."

"A salve?" Mira asked.

"Yes, my child, you've burns on your face," Sara replied as she moved away, and Ishiah led her to a stool. He helped her sit. Mira brought her fingers to her cheeks.

"All will be well, you will see," Ishiah offered comfort. Fool her, she believed him even as she felt the tender flesh around her eyes. Had she been so focused on protecting Joash that she hadn't realized how close the flames had been? At least her skin was only tender to the touch and did not blister, which would have surely left scars, ones that would not have been as easy to hide.

*

Ari had searched the temple for the high priest, but was met with more destruction. Some of the smaller pillars had been demolished, pottery broken. All of the lampstands had been removed. The ten bronze basins and the laver were gone from the outer court. Even the bronze pillars at the entrance of the temple had been stripped.

The desolation filled Ari's heart with sorrow, yet the hand held in his was a reminder there was hope for Judah once Joash was crowned king.

He led Joash out of the temple courtyard and into the streets. Ari gasped at the revelry taking place. He knew his beloved city had been turned into a den of wickedness but he never quite imagined anything this terrible. He knelt beside Joash. "Keep your eyes to the ground as we make our way, and do not let go of my hand."

Ari rose to his full height at the child's agreement. He tried keeping to the shadows and away from large groups of people lest they get caught up in a mob.

After several long minutes, Ari and Joash stood in the center of the priest's courtyard surrounding his home. They were greeted by several men Ari recognized from his days of service as temple guard. Without a word, a servant stepped forward and then led them into Jehoiada's private chamber. He released a sigh of relief at the sight of the high priest leaning on a staff in the center of his room as if he were expecting them. Jehoiada's aging eyes fell to Joash. "This is he?" His eyes glittered with joy.

Ari nodded, and Jehoiada lifted his hand waving to someone hidden behind a curtain. It took all of Ari's strength of will not to push the child behind him, but when Jehoiada's wife stepped within sight, Ari relaxed.

He squeezed Joash's hand. "This is Jehoiada, your high priest, and his wife Jehosheba, your aunt. She rescued you along with Tama." He hadn't told the child of his kingship as he grew up, but he and Tama had told him about his survival. The boy needed to know who his greatest enemies were.

Jehosheba fell to her knees with her arms stretched out. Joash looked to Ari for reassurance. Ari nodded. She hugged the child to her and kissed his cheeks as she cried.

"You may take him," Jehoiada told her.

Ari watched with a mixture of sadness and relief as the boy was no longer under his protection. Joash turned back and bowed his head to Ari, and Ari did like in return. The boy and his aunt disappeared.

His look must have held some concern, for Jehoiada addressed the issue of Joash's safety. "He is well guarded."

Ari nodded.

"You have done well, Ariel. I do not know how I will repay your service."

"None is necessary," he replied.

"I can place you in charge of training our warriors. Of course," he said, waving his hand, "you must first grow your beard."

"We both know the law prohibits me from returning to do my duties. I am defiled. I have shaved my beard, which is the least of my impurities."

"Ari, your service—"

"It does not matter. God has been faithful and just. He has shown me another path that I must take."

"I see." He scratched his beard. "What is her name?"

Ari was taken back. Was his love so plain for all to see?

"Do not worry. I know there is only one thing that would keep you from what I offer. Your heart belongs to a woman."

"Her name is Sh'mira."

"Ahh." Jehoiada smiled. "Her name means protector."

Ari smiled, knowing that she had been suitably named. "And rightly so," he added.

"My niece will make you a wonderful wife," Jehoiada said.

"I am anxious to see to her well-being. She was attacked protecting our king not far from the city gates. Although she will not speak a word of it, I am sure she is frightened. And I am not sure she came away unscathed."

"Your vow is complete. However, before you leave Jerusalem, I would ask that you help in removing Athaliah."

"Of course, I would like nothing better than to offer my assistance, especially after what she's done to the temple."

"It is a shame, but with Joash as king we will restore the temple to Solomon's glory. We must act quickly, before Athaliah realizes Joash is alive and in Jerusalem."

"I fear she knows." Ari told the priest of the events leading up to their arrival in Jerusalem, even of the Philistines who helped them fight the queen's men. "I would give all my possessions to know who betrayed us," Ari said.

"As would I. No matter, the Lord will reveal all to us in due time, of that I have no doubt." Jehoiada paced before him. "The last word I received, Athaliah had near one hundred faithful in her ranks."

"After the fight outside the city you should be able to reduce that by about twenty or thirty."

"That gives us the advantage."

"God is on our side. That alone gives us the advantage. My family will enter the gates on the morrow and will be whatever assistance you need. They've come to celebrate Jubilee." Ari smiled.

Jehoiada chuckled. "And what a grand Jubilee it will be, too. We'll begin the next fifty years with a new king and the promise of restoration." The staff Jehoiada leaned against began to tremble. Ari rushed to his side and aided him to his bed. The high priest patted him on the arm and smiled up at Ari. "You've done well, my boy. You've done well. On the morrow at the setting of the sun, when she is offering worship to her god, we will act. I will call upon those who have not turned from God. How many have come from Manna?"

"Fifty men and their wives and children," he said with thought. "I dislike putting them in harm's way, especially knowing there is a traitor in the midst, but I understand the necessity."

"So you believe the traitor has come from Manna?"

Ari closed his eyes, and then opened them. "Not only am I certain the enemy has come from Manna, but I'm certain it is one of my own closest kin."

Jehoiada raised his brow. "You say this with reason?"

"Whoever betrayed us knew the intricacies of the tunnels near En Gedi."

Jehoiada emitted a low wheeze. "Even I do not know the passages."

"None do, but my grandfather's sons, and their sons."

"That makes things difficult, does it not?"

Jehoiada did not say anything Ari had not already felt, but how was he to explain all to his father when the traitor was ousted? Especially if it was the man he suspected.

Chapter Twenty-Eight

Mira sat in silence as Sara packed a thick salve over her eyes. Tears stung the backs of her lids but she refused to allow them to fall. She would not cry over the discomfort caused by the salve on her burns, not when she worried over whether Ari had delivered Joash safely to Jehoiada.

If only she could have gone with them, but if their entrance into the city had been anything like hers then she understood. Ari could not have divided his protection. His focus needed to remain on Joash.

She exhaled, feeling deflated, weary from the events of the past week. Had it been only a few days ago that she had dropped an oil jar on her feet? Had it only been a few days ago that she had discovered Ari's secret? Had it only been a few days ago that she'd become aware of Ari as a man and not just as an annoying servant?

"There," Sara said with one last swipe across her eyes. "The pain should be alleviated. I will cut some linen strips for bandages."

"My thanks." The sound of Sara's feet shuffled away, and then something in the air shifted. She lifted her chin, wishing the salve did not keep her eyes shut. She longed to see him standing there.

"Ari?"

A scented oil clung to his person as he entered his house, and she knew he must have had his feet anointed.

"It is I, Mira." His voice. His feet shuffled across the floor. He took her hands and raised her to her feet. He pressed his lips to the backs of her knuckles and then to her brow. His fingers caressed over the contours of her cheeks edging along the thick salve covering her eyes and upper cheeks. "I must ask your forgiveness. I should have been there."

"Shhh," she whispered. "I am not sorry. Neither should you. And you were there when I needed you for I do not know that I would have been able to contain my fear without your strength."

He brushed his lips against her brow once again, and she sighed. He pulled away. She felt the discord within him. "Is all well?" she asked.

"Joash is safe. My duty to Judah and Jehoiada is finished." Hesitation choked his voice.

"Something bothers you, Ari. And I do not believe it has anything to do with saying goodbye to the child."

"I'll miss him greatly, have no doubt, Mira." He pulled his hand from one of hers and she knew he raked his fingers through his hair. It was something he did often when concerned. "I cannot speak of things. Not here. You must know it is not because of my lack of faith in you, but that in others."

"I understand, Ari."

"I would take you from this place. It is not the same as it had been when I left. As much as the desolation bothers me, I know a change is to come and Jerusalem will be restored. But the danger has not passed. I expect uprisings to follow. Many will not be happy when the queen is ousted."

She would not tell him of her near abduction or he might abandon all reason and leave Jerusalem before he should. And if she listened to the voice in her head, Ari needed to be here. The high priest may have released Ari from duty but she knew God had not released him, yet. Once he was released, then he would hold his vow to her and take her home. Then he could return to his destiny and serve in the temple.

"Ariel, my grandson, you have come," Sara said from behind her.

"Of course, Savta. It is my home." Ari helped Mira to sit and then he moved away.

"You have a lovely girl, here," Sara said as she wrapped linen over Mira's eyes.

"That I do."

Heat filled her cheeks and flowed into her limbs, flickering a glimmer of hope within her heart. She quickly tamped it out.

"Your father asked to speak with you when you arrived. He is on the roof."

"My thanks, Savta," Ari responded. He bent and kissed Mira on her head. "Where is your veil?"

If she could have blinked she would have. Her mouth moved trying to form words but none came out.

"The streets were crowded when they entered, someone pulled her hair, another stole her veil," Sara spoke for her.

Ari's fingers ran over her locks. "Are you harmed?" His voice gentle, filled with concern.

"No, Ari. I am well."

"You are sure?" he asked as he handed her something soft and silky. "It is the one my mother gave you. I'd have you wear it, Mira, since you've lost another."

"How did you—"

"It does not matter, Mira." He smoothed a strand of hair behind her ear. "Are you sure you are well?"

"Ariel, go see your father." She stiffened her back, thankful she had once again found her obstinacy.

He touched his lips to her head, and in her mind's eye she saw the love he had yet to speak of shining there. If only she could accept it.

She listened to his movement as he climbed the ladder leading to the roof. A hand dropped onto her shoulder, startling her. She had forgotten she had not been left alone.

"You do him good, Sh'mira," Sara soothed.

Mira sighed, her heart shattering like an earthenware jar. "It can never be, Sara. It can never be."

"Hello, Mother."

Mira snapped her head up in surprise.

"Elam!" Sara squealed. "What a pleasant surprise it is to see my youngest son."

"I worried over your well-being, Elam," Mira said. "I am glad you to find you alive."

"My thanks for your concern, Mira." His voice was ragged as if he'd been running through the crowded streets like she and Ishiah had. She heard the brush of fabric as he moved around the room. It sounded as if he paced in front of her.

"You are well, yes?" she asked.

"Other than a bump to the head," he said. "I am fine."

"Oh, Elam, let me see. Come sit and I'll tend your wound," Sara crooned.

"I am fine, Mother."

"At least sit and drink."

Mira heard Sara dip the ladle into a jar and then pour water into a cup. "Would you care for bread? Curds?" Sara asked.

"That would be nice, Mother," Elam replied.

"Sh'mira?" Sara asked.

"No thank-you." Mira heard Sara shuffle away, the scent of cloves and cinnamon followed her as she left the room. A fire crackled in the pit. Much as the warmth filled the room, so did Elam's leer. What was it that caused this man to dislike her?

At first she thought it her disfigurement, and perhaps it was, but… Her conscience prodded her to speak. "I know you care deeply for your nephews." She twisted her fingers within the folds of her tunic. "Do not trouble your heart, *ladonee*," she said, using the endearment for master out of respect. "I will not discourage Ari from his destined duties at the temple."

"You concern yourself over the wrong thing, child." His voice sharp, deadly. The rustling of his tunic drew closer to her. He lowered his voice. "I have come out of fear for Joash."

She tilted her chin. "Why is that? Ari returned him to Jehoiada only this evening."

"And Jehoiada handed the child to his wife. A follower of the queen's gods."

"No," Mira cried. "It cannot be." She began to rise from her seat. "We must inform Ari at once."

"I am afraid, it will do no good. Jehosheba has seen Ari and would not allow him entrance." Elam paused.

Silence hung in the air pulling her already taut nerves to their limits. Is this what caused Ari to worry?

"However, you might be able…No, Ari would never allow it."

She stood. "Ari is not my lord. He does not make my choices. If there is anything I can do to save Joash, then so be it."

"I am not certain it is wise, Sh'mira. Ari would never allow you to leave."

"Then we'll go before he discovers our plan." She tucked the veil inside her tunic and held out her arm for him to guide her. "You'll have to help me find my way."

"Are you certain?" he asked tucking her hand over his arm.

No she was not certain. Her stomach quivered in fear, but whether from fear for herself or for Joash she did not know. She had vowed to protect Joash with her life. If there was a chance he was in danger, then she would do all in her power, with the help of Almighty God, to protect him. "I have never been more certain."

"Then let us go," Elam responded.

*

The reeds covering the roof ground into the flesh of his knees, but he continued to pray. The Lord's faithfulness filled him with an abundance of joy, so much so it burst forth from his lips, and leaked from the corners of his eyes. Even though she had suffered minor burns, the sight of Mira had set him at peace. He no longer harbored doubt within his mind.

All was well. Tomorrow, Athaliah would be removed and Ari could take Mira home and make her his wife.

The creaking of the ladder broke his concentration and he turned to find his grandmother's head peeking through the hole in the roof. His father turned also.

"Savta, you should not be risking your limbs. What is it?"

The soft wrinkles paled under the light of the moon. She gripped the top wrung and closed her eyes before looking to him. A lump formed in his throat blocking the air.

"I had hoped Sh'mira had come here, but I can see she has not," his grandmother spoke with solemnity.

"What do you mean?" Ari asked. The fierce pounding in his chest did not bode well. He clenched his fists at his sides. The look of concern in his grandmother's eyes kindled a furnace. There was no one to blame but himself. Only a handful of men could have entered his home without sounding the alarm. He had no doubts about who had her. None at all. He scrubbed his hand over his eyes.

"When I returned to the courtyard with bread and curds for Elam, they were gone?"

"Elam was here?" Ishiah asked.

"Yes, he came in a short while ago."

Ari glanced at his father and saw the speculation in his eye.

"He had been hit upon the head, although he refused to allow me to attend to it."

"That is because, Mother," his father said, scratching his chin, "Elam has not been attacked."

"What are you saying, Jacob?"

"He is saying that Elam has, for some reason, chosen to betray us."

And now he had Sh'mira within his clutches, which could only mean he meant to exchange her for Joash. Ari's chest expanded with the pain of loss. "God, help us," he whispered. How could he choose between the good of Judah and the woman he loved?

Chapter Twenty-Nine

"This girl, this child, is the one who has thwarted my attempts at killing my grandson?"

"She is."

"I would be careful not to be so smug, Elam," Athaliah crooned. "She not only thwarted my soldiers but you as well."

The fullness of the woman's hatred penetrated Mira's thoughts. "What have you to say for yourself?" A rustling of silks, and the clicking, of what seemed to be a staff on the flagstones alerted Mira of the queen's movements. The heavy scent of fermented wine invaded her senses. Athaliah stood directly in front of her. "Be careful with your answer lest you commit even more treason than you already have."

"Punishment for treason is death by sword, your majesty," Mira bowed, giving her the respect due her position even if it was not deserved, but she would not keep her tongue silent. She would even play on the queen's superstitions and strike fear into her heart. "You already believe me guilty, so therefore I will speak the truth. It is not I who has thwarted your efforts, but the Almighty Jehovah, the God of Israel. For it is He who allowed the jar of oil to break, spilling over my feet. It is He who led me to the well to cleanse, and it is He who carried Joash to safety when you would have had him killed. It is the God of Abraham that warned of an ambush, leaving your men to perish. It is the God of Isaac Himself who came down and cloaked the rightful King of Judah and me in His glory, shielding us from your armed soldiers. It was the Lord God Almighty who sent men to fight your warriors, leaving them to their deaths outside Jerusalem's gates."

"The girl is mad, your majesty. All those events were by chance, not her God."

"No matter your disbelief, Elam, it is Jehovah God who will crush your bronze and wooden idols beneath His fist. It is Jehovah who will hand all who've hardened their hearts to Him to your enemies. Even you, Queen Athaliah, demolisher of Judah."

The heavily scented perfumes cloaking the queen shifted as she slapped Mira across the face. "You speak boldly for a blind sheep herder."

"Prepare her," Queen Athaliah commanded.

"What is it you would prepare for her?" For once Elam sounded wary, but Mira hadn't a thought of pity for him given all the hurt he caused Ari.

"My bronze god will find her pleasing, do you not think, Elam?"

"You promised no harm would come to her."

"Do not worry yourself, Elam." Athaliah circled Mira. "You have done your job. Once I have the boy in my clutches, you will get your reward. Although, I'm sure Jehoiada will not be too happy." She caressed her fingertips along the side of Mira's stinging cheek.

Mira jerked.

"A feisty one. Too bad she'll be consumed when we sacrifice her." Athaliah pulled on Mira's hair, wrapping it around her fist until her nose buried against Mira's head. She sniffed. "My *god* will find her pleasing, indeed."

A bubble of laughter rumbled within Mira's chest. The hand gripping her hair trembled. The laughter spilled from Mira's throat. Her stomached fluttered in joy, not fear of this pitiful queen.

Athaliah shook her hand from Mira's hair as if she'd been burnt. "She's mad. Take her away!"

Elam tugged on her arm to take her from the queen's court. Boldness filled her, strengthening her courage. Her tongue became thick, heavy. "Your greed has twisted your thoughts. It is not too late to seek forgiveness, for it will always be yours if you only call on the name of your Lord God."

"You speak of what you do not know, Sh'mira." He jerked her arm, causing her to stumble over her feet.

"You know God has no mercy for the faithless. Not even one who calls himself a priest."

"Enough," Elam spat.

"Remember this, Elam, you have denied God, He will deny you."

She heard the opening of an iron gate and she was shoved forward. She fell to her hands and knees.

"You are naught but a crippled beggar. Who are you to tell me what God will do?"

She stood to her feet, and shoved her hair from her face, the strips of linen kept her from seeing his scorn. "God does not discriminate against afflictions such as mine, only against decaying hearts."

The gate slammed shut, echoing against the inside of her cell. The key turned in the lock. "Where is God now, Sh'mira? Will he deliver you from the queen?" His voice quivered as a man facing a lion. "No. I think not. Soon my queen's attendants will retrieve you. They'll shave the shame from your head and paint your eyes with kohl right before they tie you to the altar and set it on fire," he hissed. "Will God grant you mercy then?"

*

Sh'mira lifted her head from the rolled tunic and blinked. She pressed her fingers against the cloth covering her eyes. She pulled the bandages away and blinked again. Thankfully, the flesh on her cheeks no longer smarted with discomfort, but she was even more thankful that her vision had returned.

Several times through the night she'd paced the humble cell and waited to be retrieved. Yet nobody had come. Not even to bring her a meal. Her body had grown weary and exhausted and she gave in to sleep. Now, with only torches for light she had no idea the hour for she had no idea how long she'd slept. Nor, how long she had before Athaliah carried out her punishment.

Her hair fell over her shoulders as she curled her legs beneath her. She ran her fingers through the strands.

"It is her," a feminine voice called out from beyond her cell. "Come, woman. It is time," she said over the sound of the keys grating in the lock. Thick black kohl traced the woman's eyes. Tint the color of blood shaded her lips. Gold rings looped through her ears and nose. Her white, loosely draped gown left little to the imagination, but it was the shiny smoothness of her head which concerned Mira the most.

She would not harbor fear in her heart.

She would not doubt.

She would trust God.

Rising to her feet, Mira draped her tunic over her clothes, tucked the veil Ari had given her near her heart and waited for the gate to swing open.

"First we must bathe you," the woman said, wrinkling her nose. "Then we shall shave your head." The smile curving her lips made Mira think of a leopard ravenous for a sheep.

She led her down a corridor. Palace guards flanked either side of her.

"It is a shame your Ari chose to deny her majesty's request for an exchange."

"Ari?" Mira choked.

"The temple commander, Ari."

"Your queen expected that he would?" Mira held her head high, refusing to allow doubt to enter her thoughts. If there had been a way, Ari would have come for her. She knew he could not endanger Joash, no matter the cause. Yet, knowing the truth did not ease the sharp pain deep within her chest.

"Elam assured her that Ari would do all in his power to keep harm from your head."

"No," she whispered, not realizing she had said the word aloud until the woman stopped and turned on her.

"Did you not please him?" The woman reached for Mira's hand. "We were told you were disfigured." She lifted it to her inspection. "Perhaps your Ari decided against a marred woman."

Mira lowered her eyes at the weeping of her heart. She knew he'd rescue her if it was possible, but she could not stop the pain the woman's words caused. It was difficult enough knowing their hearts could never bind. She did not need this woman giving her reasons for Ari's abandonment when she knew full well why they must part ways when this was all over. For she had no doubt she'd return home to her father's house.

"It is a shame your God has abandoned you." The woman turned a corner and continued down the corridor.

"My God has not abandoned me."

She knew God would never leave her nor fail her. A renewed peace settled around her shoulders like a cloak to ward of the rain during the latter season.

Chapter Thirty

"It is near Shabbat," Jesse pointed out as if no one had realized the fact. They walked up the hill toward the temple where they were to prepare for battle.

"Yes, and Jehoiada believes we'll catch the queen off guard," Ari explained.

"There is no complaint from me, brother. I am surprised, Jehoiada and the others would break tradition."

"All is possible when God dictates a man's actions," their father said, looking Jesse in the eye. Although Ari's thoughts remained firm on Mira, he sought comfort in his father's teasing chastisement. "Whether he be priest or no."

"Here we are," Ari interrupted whatever Jesse thought to speak. His brother had yet to gain wisdom in how to choose his words with care lest he sound disrespectful.

"It is I, Ishiah and my sons Ariel and Jesse."

The sentry nodded his head to the pair of soldiers standing between the pillars. They moved apart. Just as Ari was about to ascend the stairs, the sentry blocked their way. "Welcome, my friends," he said, kissing either side of Ishiah's cheek. He repeated his actions with Jesse and Ari. "We are all joyous for God's return to our city." His eyes twinkled.

"As are we." Ari tapped the man on his shoulder and walked between the gates as he had done hundreds of times before. Masses of men stood in three groups, each with some sort of weapon. Jehoiada stood before them, directing their steps. "Ah, Ariel. It is glad I am to see you." The high priest greeted him. "Here is your weapon." Jehoiada handed him a spear. "You will go with those to the palace.

Rescue my niece. It is the least I owe you for your service to God and to Judah."

Ari bowed over the priest's frail hand. "My thanks, Jehoiada."

"Ishiah, if you will bless us by guarding Joash until all is settled?"

"I consider it an honor," his father replied.

"Jesse, I send you with your brother." Jehoiada handed his father and Jesse each a weapon, and they separated. "See to it that Althaliah does not leave Jerusalem alive. It would not do for her to regain forces and return."

Congregated together, they stood in their ranks and waited for orders. Jehoiada stood before them, between what should have been bronze pillars. He lifted a prayer of blessing over them. Collectively they banged the butts of their spears upon the ground and shouted, "Praise God!"

Jehoiada raised his hand for silence. "I have assembled you here for a greater purpose than any could ever imagine. On my command you are to kill all who would protect Athaliah. Kill her guards, and any who would follow her. The terror of Judah and her servants must perish. Demolish the Asherah poles she has erected in your city. Cleanse Jerusalem of her defilement. Do not allow anyone within the temple walls that is not one of us. Blood must not spill within the temple."

Jehoiada waived his hand, a hundred Philistine mercenaries streamed into the courtyard, each carrying a giant spear. Ianatos stood at their head.

Between them, Joash strode, attired no longer as a shepherd boy, but as a king draped in purple and gold.

Jehoiada, motioned Joash forward. An attendant handed Jehoiada a gold crown and a vile of oil. "The Lord your God has preserved the line of David as He promised. He has set before us a child." Jehoiada poured oil onto his fingertips and drew his fingers across Joash's brow. "I present to you Joash son of Ahaziah" The high priest sat the gold crown upon the boy's head. "King of Judah."

The curling sound of the shofar wound into the air, followed by one and then another, until every trumpeter blew his praise to the Lord God, creator of the heavens and earth.

After a few moments of the shofars resonating into Jerusalem, Jehoiada raised his hand for silence.

"What is this!"

Ari turned toward the palace, as did everyone else. Athaliah stood on the steps of the palace, her face red with rage.

"Treason! Treason!" She rent the neckline of her garment. "Kill them," she ordered the guards standing beside her.

Ari and the group of warriors he was with turned upon her and her guard. Her men fled back into the palace. Ari raced after them, cutting with his sword and jabbing with his spear those who fought for their queen. He pushed his way through the palace gate. His movements, that of a battle-honed warrior, were sure-footed, yet his mind focused on finding Mira. Desperation gnawed at him with each guard he dispatched, warring with the faith and trust he placed in the Lord.

It was like a double-edged sword twisting in his gut. The doubt that had crept in, sliced deep, leaving a gaping wound in his heart. "Sh'mira!" He sidestepped a sword as it threatened to crash against his head. Ari swung the flat of his own blade against the knee of his opponent, sending him to the ground. "Sh'mira!"

Lord, guide my feet to her.

He turned a corner, his instincts prodding him to run. His feet flew over the flagstones. His gaze fell to a pair of women. One lay on the stones, another crouched over her. The muscles in his legs froze, refusing to move another step. Was he too late? If only he had not taken too much time in fighting his opponents. If only he had been quicker.

"My Lord," he whispered, pleading with God. Sweat poured over his brow and into his eyes, causing them to sting, yet he could not take his eyes off the women out of fear they'd disappear.

If I have lost her. A knot curled in his belly at the anguish of losing her, leaving the taste of vinegar clinging to his lips. Ari sheathed his sword as his knees wavered in their strength. He shoved the flat end of the spear against the ground and leaned against it for support.

*

Just as they had entered the large bathing chamber, a shofar sounded. And then another sounded, and another until the palace walls vibrated with the intensity of the horns. Mira had feared the walls would tumble around them. The guards flanking her had tensed, their hands gripping their short swords. A thunderous shout arose from outside. "Praise God!"

Athaliah's shrill screams echoed through the palace, and the warriors raced away, leaving her alone with the arrogant woman.

"Praise God!" Mira looked heavenward and placed her hand over the beating of her heart.

The woman who only moments before had ridiculed God, trembled in fear.

"Did I not tell you my God has not abandoned me. Nor has he abandoned Judah."

The woman fell at Mira's feet. "Forgive me," she cried.

Mira knelt beside her, cupping her hand beneath her chin, she lifted the distraught woman's face to meet her eyes. "It is not I from whom you should seek forgiveness, but the Almighty God of Israel."

"Sh'mira," his voice, a mere whisper, echoed over her flesh. She swiveled and rose. Her heart swelled like a bladder of water near to bursting.

"Ari, you have come."

Afraid her eyes played tricks, her feet refused to move. And then he smiled. She ran across the distance, flung herself into his arms and pressed her lips to his.

Settling her on his left side, he buried his nose into her hair. "I have missed you, Sh'mira." He dropped a kiss to her brow, and then grabbed a hold of her hand. "Come, we must go."

"What of Athaliah?" Mira asked.

"She will not escape."

"It is over, then?"

"Yes. We may now go home." He dropped another kiss to her brow.

Home. Back to her father's. A blessing and a curse.

Ari drew her out into the palace courtyard. Slain men clothed in palace attire lay in various places. They exited through the gate facing the temple of God. Tears pricked her eyes as her gaze fell upon a crowned Joash in the center of the temple court. She leaned her head against Ari's shoulder. *God, anoint Joash the King of Judah with Your wisdom. And Your mercy.*

As if he heard her prayer, Joash turned his eyes upon her and Ari, giving them a slight bow. "My soul is filled with joy that all is as it should be. Yet, it is filled with sadness for I will never see the child again."

Ari looked down upon her, his eyes soft, filled with emotion mirroring her own heart. "If God wills it, you will see him again."

"Not as the child who lived among us," she said with solemnity.

"No, not as that child." He tugged her down the steps and into the streets. "Perhaps, the Lord will bless you with a bevy of sons. If you are truly blessed, perhaps He will grant you daughters as well, Sh'mira daughter of Caleb."

Even though his words tore at her heart, she smiled. If she were truly blessed, God would grant her an eternity with Ari. Children created of their union would be a double portion, whether they be sons or daughters for she would have none without Ari.

Chapter Thirty-One

Ari handed his spear to the first temple guard he came across and wished him well. His cheeks hurt from the permanent smile on his face.

The people of Jerusalem crowded the streets, destroying the queen's manmade gods They were more than ready for Joash to lead them with Jehoiada at his side and God at the command.

Seeing with his own eyes that his prayers had come to fruition was a soothing balm to his soul. A shadow moved across the sky and Ari looked up to find white puffy clouds moving over the city of Jerusalem. A drop of rain landed on his lips. He licked the salty sweetness.

Mira's fingers clenched into his hand and he glanced at her. She too looked up, her face glowed. She wiped a drop from her cheek, and then another. Then the clouds opened upon them. The people of Jerusalem danced in circles singing praises to God, their arms raised in worship.

"Ari, God is pleased."

He pulled her into his arms and danced her around in circles, just as those around them were doing. She laughed, her pleasure contagious. "I believe you are correct, Mira," he said, spinning her around. Their feet splashed in the puddles soaking their sandals.

"Come, let us go home and wait out the rest of Shabbat with my family. Then we will leave for your father's house."

The smile fell from her face, and she pulled from him. He reached for her, but she slipped from his touch. Ari watched helplessly as she pushed through the throng. Away from his home.

He gave chase, shoving the revelers out of his path. What had he said? His thoughts tumbled over in his head searching for any insensitivities, but he could not imagine...he thought she'd be happy to return home. Did she wish to stay in Jerusalem?

"Sh'mira!"

The woman did not know the curved and twisted streets. This was not her village where she could roam at will. Dangers lurked in the shadows, especially for an innocent such as her. He searched the streets, the shadowed alcoves, and the market place but to no avail. He was about to turn home when Ianatos blocked his path. Ari glared at the giant.

"I have word," he said.

Stretching to his full height, Ari peered around the man's shoulder and over the heads of those crowded around him. "I do not have the time. I need to find Sh'mira."

"Your uncle has taken her."

Ari grabbed the man's tunic at his neck and pressed his face close to his and then released him. He had no reason to distrust this Philistine. "How do you know this?"

"I saw him drag her through the Eastern gate. I could not go after them." He crossed his arms, his face solemn. "We were fighting those who surrounded Athaliah."

A heavy hand dropped to his shoulder. Ari turned, prepared to fight. "Brother, it is I, Jesse."

"I see it is you," Ari growled.

"Whatever is the matter?"

"Elam has taken his woman from the city." Ianatos rolled his shoulders.

Jesse scrutinized the man. "Then we shall go get her."

Ari began walking toward his home. "You should stay until after Jubilee. It is enough that I ignore tradition."

"I do not celebrate your Hebrew ways," Ianatos grumbled.

"Bah! Tradition will always be here. I will go." Jesse blocked Ari's path, halting his steps.

He assessed Ianatos. "You should stay. Guard our king. We would be remiss in thinking my uncle is the only one who wishes the boy dead. There may be uprisings among Athaliah's faithful."

"Of course." Ianatos nodded and then walked past them.

"Ianatos," Ari waited for him to turn around. "Thank-you, may God bless you greatly."

"My thanks." He pushed through the crowded streets toward the temple.

Jesse clapped his arm around Ari's shoulder as they neared their home, both were soaked from the rain, their feet caked with mud. "With the queen dead, there should be no problems."

Ari glanced at his brother. "She's dead?"

Jesse smiled. "Saw to it myself, just as Jehoiada asked. When do we leave?"

"As soon as I gather supplies, and dry clothing for Mira."

"I have horses. It shouldn't' take us long to find her."

Perhaps his brother did not notice the rain. "Any tracks would have been washed away. Besides, do those horses not belong to the temple?"

Jesse chuckled as they entered into their home. Ari began gathering weapons. He had not meant to joke, he meant all seriousness. The horses did not belong to them and should not take them from the city.

"You think little of me."

Ari stopped shoving necessities into the leather bags. "I did not mean offense, Jesse—"

"Of course not," Jesse said. The hurt in his tone wounded Ari. "They were given to the priests of Manna."

"I seek forgiveness."

"It is given." His brother smiled, but Ari knew he had hurt his brother deeper than he showed. "Come, we must make haste if we are to rescue your bride."

"What have you done to the floors?" Their grandmother asked.

Ari and Jesse looked to their feet even as their faces turned red with their grandmother's chastisement. "We are sorry, Savta," Jesse offered.

"P'sh," she breathed waving them off.

"Grandmother, Elam has taken Mira from the city," Jesse sought to explain.

Her dark compassionate eyes lifted to Ari's. "What are you doing here, boy? Make haste, find your bride!"

*

She fell into another puddle of water. Wet strands of her hair clung to her face making it impossible for her to watch her footing. It was the third time she'd fallen since they'd left the city. Her tunic began to shred from the abuse. Her knees and the palms of her hands bled from their scrapes, tiny pebbles of sand bored into her wounds.

Fear should have consumed her. However, anger took precedence. If Elam had not bound her hands with twine and jerked on the lead as if she were a willful donkey, she would have been able to maintain her footing without issue.

"What a crippled beggar you are," Elam said, looking down upon her.

With all her strength she jerked her wrists, pulling the twine from Elam's hands. She rose to her feet, bare and bloodied, Elam had disposed of her sandals shortly after they departed Jerusalem. She cursed herself a fool for leaving Ari's side, for what reason she could not even remember. If she had stayed. . . "I have never been a beggar, Elam."

He sneered and reached for the rope, but she pulled away. "Do you think to run from me? In your condition? I think not, scourge of Ari."

She spat.

He slapped her. "You heathen."

Raw emotion bubbled in her throat. "You should look at your reflection in the spring, Elam."

"You speak of what you do not know." He snarled, his eyes bulging.

"I know I have not betrayed my family, my people and my God."

"Be quiet!" He grabbed the braided rope dangling from her wrists and tied it to his waist.

"What are your intentions, Elam? Your queen is dead. Her gods destroyed. You have no one to sacrifice me to."

The rope jerked between them as he climbed onto another rocky path. "Come, the eve grows dark. I care naught for your comforts, I however do not wish to remain in the open lest my nephew comes after you."

Mira did not say another word as he forced her along a slippery path with jagged rocks that cut into her feet. She bit her lip with each stab of pain. She lifted up her eyes to the heavens, even as they continued to rain. *Thanks be to you, Lord of Creation, for the blessed rain.*

She stumbled over a rock, landing on her hip. Elam did not wait for her to gain her footing before he tugged on the rope. They climbed farther up the jagged mountain. The last place she desired to be was within the dark confines of yet another cave, and something told her Elam would not risk lighting a fire to dry their clothing, if he even knew how to do so.

If only Ari were with them.... If Ari were here, Elam would not be, or at least she would not be the one bound. Elam shoved her into the mouth of a cave. "Are there any creatures in there?"

She tightened her hands into fists. "If there be, it has not eaten me alive yet," she returned.

"You show disrespect to your elders, girl. Ariel should thank me for doing away with his intended bride," he said, entering the cave behind her. He yanked a small lamp and oil from a bag tied at his waist. He poured the oil and lit it. The soft glow danced upon the walls.

"Sit, there." He pointed to a small space away from the entrance. She obeyed and fought against the fears creeping along her limbs. Fought against the tears threatening to spill from her eyes. She focused on what Elam had said. "Your nephew never intended to take me to wife."

"Foolish, girl," he said. "He brought you to his home in Manna. And he brought you to his home in Jerusalem."

"Only to protect me from those who would seek to harm me and his king." She refrained from using Elam's name or the fact that it was his betrayal that had led to the danger.

"Why would he care for a cripple such as you? You are dispensable for the greater good of God's kingdom." Elam sat and rummaged through his pack. He pulled out a chunk of bread and began to eat.

"You do not know your nephew well," Mira argued.

"I know him. I know him well."

"You love him?"

Elam looked at her with a startled expression. "Of course, I love Ariel. I love him as my own son."

Mira pinched the bridge of her nose, confused at the man's confession. "Then why did you betray him?"

"I. Did. Not. Betray. Him," he emphasized. "It was Jehoiada. You and that, that child were nothing but pawns. Everything I did I had done for Ariel." He broke off another chunk of bread and stuffed it into his mouth. Mira's stomach growled as he chewed.

He uncorked the stopper of a bladder skin and drank. It was obvious he did not intend to share with her so she waited patiently for him to speak again. "I have no sons of my own. Daughters, a quiver full of daughters, none of whom married well. Ariel was like a son. My only son. The day after the massacres I went to the temple to speak with him. He was gone.

"Ariel had worked hard for his position. He would not disappear without speaking to me. He held much promise.

"I had my suspicions. There had been rumors, and I had many of the villages searched." He glared at her. "Even yours. No, do not look surprised. If Jehoiada was to hide the boy, he'd send him to your mother. The child was not there, but my nephew was. The men I hired tormented him, seeking information. My stupid nephew said nothing. We left him for dead. I figured the child was nothing but a rumor since Ari hadn't given him up."

Mira remembered well the broken and beaten body. If she'd not found him, he would have died.

"A few moons ago I overheard Jehoiada speaking with his wife about the child. It was a ruse. It had to be. None of the heirs survived. None. Jehoiada had taken the high priesthood from me. He took my Jehosheba, too." His eyes glazed over as if he were remembering, and Mira wondered how that was possible. "It was then I discovered Ari had survived. Jehoiada had intended on making a fool of me by using Ari."

Elam turned his gaze full on her, his hatred evident in the blackness of his eyes even with only the small glow of his lamp. "Then he brought you to Manna. No priest brings a stranger into our midst without making his intentions clear."

Elam was wrong. Ari had no choice but to bring her. "But you betrayed him before he brought us to Manna."

"Yes. I had not seen my nephew in many years. My brother refused to share with me. Their lack of trust wounded me. I was the one who taught Ari the law while Ishiah taught him the sword. When I discovered Joash's existence, and that Ari survived, it did not take me long to reconsider the connection between Jehoiada and Joash's nurse. That would make you her cousin, yes?"

Mira nodded even though Elam had not expected an answer.

"I knew then without a doubt Jehoiada had hidden them away in your village or nearby. I went to the queen. She promised if I delivered the child into her hands, she would see to it Jehoiada was killed for his treason and I would become the high priest. I would take from the man all he'd stolen from me and my Ariel."

Lord God, how can a man be so blind?

Had Ari ever wanted to remain in Jerusalem, or had he only wanted to please his uncle? Would Ari have been satisfied serving God no matter where?

Resting her head against the rock wall, she closed her eyes. One man's jealousy and ambitions had marred so many lives. Children had been killed for what he called the greater good. How could he be so deceived? Even her own mother had suffered abuse at the hands of this man.

She blew out a gentle sigh. What was done was done. Praise God that His will superseded Elam's twisted mind. Just as God's will would be victorious when Ari came for her.

Chapter Thirty-Two

"It should not take us long to catch up with them," Jesse said from beside him. The good humor in his voice grated on Ari's nerves.

"If you had not noticed, brother, it is raining."

"A blessed thing it is, too," Jesse replied.

Rain poured and his beloved wandered the desert with a mad man. No doubt she was soaked, if his own clothing was any indication. And his brother thought the rain a blessing? Every drop erased any trace of where they might have gone.

"Look, what is that?" Jesse pointed, catching Ari's immediate attention.

He turned his glare from the horse's ears to a piece of fabric pooled in the mud. Ari jumped to the ground. He crouched beside the blue cloth and lifted it. It was heavy with rain, matching the heaviness in his heart. He buried his face in the sodden, soiled cloth and breathed in her scent.

"I wish I could kill him." Even to his own ears his voice sounded not as his own, but the anger throbbing through his blood was very real.

"Do not say such things, Ariel. You have never been one to act brashly. That is I, if you remember."

Ari rose, turning on his heels he stared at his brother. "What did you say?"

"I said you have never behaved as such, why begin now? It is not in your character."

He scrubbed his hand over his face as the fullness of the revelation smacked him in the chest. "Oh, God," he cried, lifting his eyes heavenward. Raindrops splattered on his cheeks mixing with the salt of his tears. "What have I done? How will you ever forgive thy servant for his sins?"

The skies closed, leaving not another drop to fall. Before he knew it, Jesse's hand was on his shoulder. "Of what do you speak, Ari? What have you done?"

He squeezed the veil in his fist. "All of this," he said, holding the fabric for his brother to see. "All of it is because I have acted rashly."

Jesse's brow furrowed. "I do not understand. You have always been an example of how your brothers should live."

Ari laughed. "It is all an illusion, I tell you. For if it had not been for my rashness we would not now be standing in the muddied desert looking for a woman whose heart is purer than any I have ever known."

"Enough with the riddles. Tell me if you will, but do not waste our time. Mira's life remains in danger."

He shook the self-pity from his head. "You are correct. There is naught I can do about my past sins other than offer up sacrifice to the Lord."

"What will we do?"

"We will rescue Mira, and then I'll take her to her father." Ari said with a heavy heart.

"You intend to leave her there? I do not understand. If you love her—"

"The sins of a foolish man have brought this upon her and her family. Her neighbors' sons were killed. I should have taken Joash from the village when I realized the danger." He shook his head. "How could she ever forgive that of me? I should have listened to my instincts and not remained planted by fear."

"Ari, if she is as pure as you say, as pure as I have witnessed with my own eyes, she'll forgive you. How could she not?"

He pondered his brother's words of wisdom, knowing he was correct but unable to accept the truth of it in his heart. She would forgive him, there was no doubt in his mind, yet could he forgive himself for the pain he had caused her? Could he move beyond his sins without letting his guilt interfere with their future?

Obviously sensing his indecision, Jesse said, "Besides, the queen's men did not need an excuse for their terror.

They thrived on causing fear. The only sin is believing you are guilty and in control of such matters."

"You are correct, my brother." Ari clasped him in a hug. "I will nonetheless rectify my conscience with a guilt offering." He wrung out the veil and draped it around his neck, tucking it beneath his tunic. With all settled in his thoughts, he mounted his horse.

"You know, Brother, perhaps God allowed all this to happen to purge the evil from Judah. You were one of many vessels to carry out His will, as was your Mira."

"Perhaps you are right." He flicked the reigns. "Nonetheless I will go back to Jerusalem and make my guilt offerings after I see Mira home."

Jesse mounted his horse. "Offerings?"

"I'll beg forgiveness of Caleb for deceiving him all these years."

"Shall we find your bride?"

Ari smiled. He liked the sound of Mira being his bride. He prayed they found her before Elam harmed her.

They rode in silence for a few minutes. Only the click of their horses' hooves and the light patter of rain sounded on the rocky desert.

"Did you see that, brother?"

Ari shook his head. "I see naught but the darkness of shadows."

"Look to the cast near the top of the hills. Do you see the flickering of a light?"

Ari peered toward the direction his brother indicated. A faint glow brightened, and then disappeared before brightening once again. "Mira," he whispered.

Ari did not say another word not even when they dismounted and began the climb up the hill. Only then did he lift up a prayer that their feet would be silent, and most of all that they would find Mira and not a shepherd seeking refuge from the rain.

*

Elam's loud snores shattered the silence, leaving her to consider her options. She could stay and see what he had planned for her, or she could take the opportunity and flee into the night. At least she knew the threat before her inside this cave, where as she hadn't a clue what might lie in wait for her out there in the dark.

Could she remain with Elam when the opportunity to escape had so easily presented itself? Mira scooted away from the wall and watched for any hint of movement from Elam. Certain he continued to sleep, she lifted her wrists and bit at the twine binding them together.

It was of no use.

She glanced around for something that might cut her binding. If she held her wrists above the flames she risked more than a simple loosening of the twine. She didn't relish the thought of having them burnt. She pressed her face into the palms of her hands. With her hands bound she could not easily climb down the rocky outcrop. Even now, her hands were raw from the cuts and scrapes she had received when Elam had forced her up the rocky hill. If she could not brace herself when she fell, she'd more than likely tumble to her death.

At least she'd no longer be in Elam's grasp. *God, what will you have me do?*

She heard a slight inhale of breath, which could not be one of Elam's snores. She lifted her face from her hands. Silhouetted in the mouth of the cave stood her answer. Even in the glow of the firelight, she could see the ticking of Ari's jaw as he ground his teeth. His gaze flicked to her eyes and his lips parted, relaxing, until his eyes roamed over the rest of her.

He glared and in one fluid motion, he bent at the waist, grasped Elam's tunic and lifted him from his feet.

"What—what," Elam sputtered, and then his eyes focused on his attacker. "Ariel, my nephew."

"It is I, Uncle," Ari growled, his anger evident in the way he shook.

"You would not hurt me. The Law demands you honor your elders."

"Honor is not for cowards," Jesse said, pushing his way past Ari. "Hello, Sh'mira, I trust all is well with you."

"All is well," she responded, her eyes pleading with Ari not to do something he would later regret.

"Here, brother, allow me." Jesse peeled Ari's fingers from their uncle's garment. "Unbind Mira."

Ari rolled his shoulders as if to release the tension, and then stepped deeper into the cave. She curled her feet beneath her tunic lest he see their condition. He knelt beside her, and she prayed he would not see her wounds, for she feared Ari's rage would ignite to an inferno.

"Never. Leave. My. Side. Again," he spoke, his voice hard and raw with emotion.

Since she did not know what the future between them held, she refused to acknowledge his command. Instead, once he loosened the twine from her wrists, she wrapped her arms around his nape and hugged him close.

"What now?" Jesse asked.

Mira released Ari as he turned on his heel. She peered around his shoulder and saw that Elam was bound hand and foot and tied to Jesse's belt.

"We wait until the sun rises. We'll go south. You'll take him," Ari said with disgust, and then added, "to Jerusalem to the tribal elders for his judgment."

"Have you no mercy?" Elam squealed.

He ignored his uncle and turned back to her. "Are you sure all is well?"

She curled her fingers into fists, biting back the cry of pain the cuts caused. "I am fine, Ari."

He released a breath of air and then removed his cloak. He laid it out next to the fire. Grasping her hand he helped her to her feet and drew her into his arms, tucking her head beneath his chin. His breath warmed as he spoke. "I have brought you dry clothing. Tomorrow, I will take you to your father's house."

She wanted to ask how they would achieve such a feat since it was several days walk, and with her lack of footing, she'd make their travels even slower, but the steady pounding of his heart, along with the rise and fall of each of his breaths, lulled her into a peaceful security. He pressed his lips to her brow, released her and moved toward the entrance of the cave, taking with him the warmth and comfort she'd felt in his arms. He returned with a bundle and handed it to her. Without another word, he and Jesse, along with a bound Elam, left her alone.

Soon she was dry and laying on a cloak that smelled like Ari. And tomorrow, if what Ari said was true, she'd be back within her father's house. Alone, much as she was now. How would she ever let him go? *Why, God, why would you even ask this of me?* A tear slid down her cheek. How was she going to survive the heartache of letting him go?

Chapter Thirty-Three

He could have offered her his mat, but he was reluctant to allow any space between them, even for a moment. It had not taken her long to relax against him and fall into a deep rest. Anger renewed within his breast at the scrapes and bruises marring her skin.

Her hands curled beneath her chin, and he longed to twine his fingers within hers. The warmth of her smile as she lay sleeping spread to the beating of his pulse, causing it to hitch momentarily. His fingers hovered over the length of her arm, wishing he could touch her just as he had done several times since he had done when he'd found her unharmed outside the scraped and bruises marring her skin.. Her fleshly imperfections had never mattered to him. They'd only made her more beautiful, especially when she carried her weight with her chores, never once complaining.

The corners of his mouth lifted. Her only complaints came when he insisted on helping her.

"You realize if you insist on a guilt offering before you marry her, you'll be parted." Jesse's low whisper stormed into his thoughts.

"Yes. I know. I do not wish to leave her even for a moment." He ran his fingers through her tresses. "However, I vowed to return her to her father's house. And I will do so."

"Then return her. With the rising of the sun we will part. When I take Elam to Jerusalem, I will send word to have your possessions prepared for departure."

"My thanks, brother."

"What of your house, Ari?"

He twisted his lips in thought. "It is our grandmother's home. I cannot very well move her. Besides, if she did not leave when Abba moved to Manna, she will not move now." He looked at his brother. "I give it to you."

Jesse laughed. "Is this your way of relinquishing Savta to me as well? You bestow a great honor upon me, and a great responsibility."

"It is not as if I have taken care of her these last years, brother. From what I have been told you have done well keeping our grandmother. It will be no different except you have the privilege of a home to call your own. A place where your kin may visit when they enter Jerusalem."

"You are certain?" Jesse asked.

Ari looked down upon the woman who firmly held his heart and smiled. "More than certain, Jesse. My life would be nothing without her by my side. I cannot ask her to leave her father when he has no sons."

"Caleb will be proud to call you son, Ariel."

"As I will be proud to call him Abba." He'd miss his own father, but there was always room for another man after God's own heart within his own.

"Manna will not be the same without you."

Ari looked at his brother with confusion and moved away from Mira lest he wake her from her peaceful slumber. He sat beside his brother and reclined against the cave wall. "Jesse, I will now have the freedom to travel to and from Manna at will. Of course, there will be seasons when I must stay at Caleb's, but my visits will be more frequent than when I resided in Jerusalem."

Jesse twisted his lips. "I'm not sure that is a good thing for me. Our grandmothers and mother will fuss over you when you come, ignoring my needs," he said with a smile. "And they will do even more so once you have a wife at your side."

He glanced at his beloved's face so soft and serene in sleep. "Soon, you will have a wife of your own."

b"It is not likely I'll find a wife in the near future. I have had the choicest of the lot from Manna and yet none have caught my eye. I have had the same result with my ventures into Hebron and Jerusalem."

"Certainly someone has caught your eye," Ari reassured.

"Many have caught my eye, but none have caught the attentions of my heart."

Ari thought of the woman who slept nearby. Had he known from the beginning that he loved her? "It may take more than a moment's notice."

"This, my brother, I know." Jesse looked at Mira, his eyes held an emotion Ari knew all too well. "There is beauty, and there is beauty, I want the kind of beauty that is rooted deeper than the flesh. Deeper than the calculating eye. Deeper than what they think I may offer. I do not want a woman who wishes to increase her position by marriage, Ari. I want one who loves me, as Sh'mira loves you."

Ari blinked in surprise. "You think she loves me?"

"Is it not obvious to you?"

"Most assuredly, yet a part of me believes it is nothing more than a young girl's foolish desire to have a handsome face to husband," Ari teased his brother. He would never assume Mira to be as shallow.

"If that were the case, she would have fallen out of her foolish desire for you once she laid eyes on me."

Ari bit back the rumble of laughter and smiled. "The sky is beginning to lighten," Jesse said.

Ari lifted his eyes and looked beyond the mouth of the cave. Although the midnight sky spread across the horizon, grays and pale blues began to illuminate the Earth. "Then it is time for us to part, my brother."

He woke Mira as Jesse nudged their uncle. He unbound his feet and pulled him to stand. "May God go with you, Ariel."

"My thanks, Jesse. May God guide your steps as well. If the Lord wills it I will see you in a day or so."

After hours on horseback, they rode into her father's village and his heart filled with gladness for Mira as they were met with cries of jubilation. He halted the horse outside of the stone walls. One of her cousins ran up and held his hand out, his silent offering asked to take the horse's lead.

"You will take good care of him for me," he said with a smile as he handed the lead to the eagerly awaiting child. Dismounting, he lifted Mira from the back of the horse. She braced her palms against his chest as if he was going to set her down, but he'd seen the condition of her feet. Even now his muscles tensed with anger at the abuse his uncle had inflicted. An urge to race back to Jerusalem fired his blood. He needed to know his uncle met justice.

"Shh," he murmured when she pushed against him. He readjusted his hold and cradled her in his arms as he carried her beneath the arch of her home.

"Sh'mira, my daughter," her mother squealed. "What has happened to you, child?"

"Nothing, Ima."

"Then why does Ari carry you so?" Her mother eyed him, deep concern and disapproval etched in the lines of her brow.

"Allow me to sit Mira down. I will explain all soon enough."

Ari followed her mother into the inner courtyard and waited for her to roll out a mat. He bent his knees, and her arms flew around his neck. The softness of her fingers against his nape sent an awareness of her through his soul. He fought the desire to pull her closer, to meld her into him. Instead, he sat the other half of his whole upon the woven wool mat and slid his arms from beneath her knees.

His gaze bored into hers. The words he had yet to say stuck like honey to his tongue. Words bursting from his heart. Words he could not yet speak.

He regretted leaving her for any length of time. If it weren't for his conscience, he'd stay. However, he could not ask for her father's blessing without seeking first his forgiveness, and then providing the highest of guilt offerings on the altar at the temple.

He brushed the tips of his fingers through her tresses. The veil around his neck burned through his tunic. Any promises he thought to convey by draping her with the silk left him when he recalled its soiled condition. He knew she'd understand the gesture, as would her parents, yet he could not bring himself to pull the draped veil from around his neck and cover her hair.

Hope welled in his breast as she touched the blue cloth, humbling him, filling his heart with joy. It was as if she understood the vibration deep inside him. And although his mother had placed the same veil upon her head, giving her blessing to their union, his act would mean more. The covering would depict a promise to her. A promise to her father.

He wrapped his fingers around hers, giving them a gentle squeeze. Ari hoped his touch would reassure her, that it would dispel any doubts she might have. That she would feel the intensity of his love for her, even if he had not spoken the words.

Ari released her hand and rose. A shadow flickered in her eyes. Her disappointment hit him in the gut. *Lord, help her understand.* Her eyes pooled with tears and he near lost his resolve.

"Sh'mira, my child, it is glad I am to see you with my own eyes, daughter." Ari turned as Caleb wobbled from his chamber, leaning heavily on his staff. Ari had never seen him so weak. Was this his doing? The sight before him cemented his resolve to return to Jerusalem.

"And I you, Abba," she said with a quiver in her voice.

"Caleb, I have returned your daughter as promised."

"My thanks, Ariel." Caleb's all-knowing gaze squinted beneath the afternoon sun. "Is all well?"

How should he answer? How could he answer? When Caleb's daughter sat on a rug with battered feet and tears in her eyes. "May I have a word with you, *ladonee?*"

"Yes, of course. But there is no need to call me master. Come, my son." Caleb pulled back the curtain and motioned with his arm that they should enter his chamber for privacy. With a heavy heart, and the knowledge that Mira watched his back, Ari followed her father.

He waited until Caleb settled himself on the edge of his bed before he knelt beside him. "Caleb," he began. "I seek your forgiveness for the wrongs I have committed against you and yours."

"What nonsense is this Ariel? You have been nothing but the humblest of servants."

"No, *ladonee.* It was a deception."

Caleb laid the palm of his hand on Ari's shoulder. "My son, Tama told me all I needed to know. Your guise may have been deceiving, but trust an old man when he says, character such as yours, character that I've watched carefully, as a shepherd his sheep, over the years can be nothing but genuine."

"My thanks, Caleb. My sins have brought harm to your family."

"I do not know what sins you speak of. It is naught to me, but between you and our Creator."

"Just the same, I would return to Jerusalem and lift up my guilt offering."

"If that is what you must do, then you must."

Ari kissed Caleb's knuckles. "My thanks, *ladonee*." He stood to his feet and prayed Caleb would not broach the subject of the contracts.

"Ariel," Caleb called just as he was about to leave. "You are a free man. Remember you have no master but God."

He dropped his gaze to his feet and nodded. "Yes, of course."

He slipped through the curtain, his gaze immediately going to where he had left Mira. The woven mat was bare. He looked around the courtyard, and for the first time in his memory, it was devoid of people. Pinching the bridge of his nose, he walked to where the young boy had tied his horse.

As much as he wished to say his goodbyes and blessings, if all went well, he'd return before the setting of the sun.

*

Rubiel yanked on her ankle. "You are such a child, Mira," she chastised.

"Forgive me. It is not a pleasant sensation having my open wounds scrubbed clean."

"It is necessary, lest you wish to gain an infection," her mother chided.

"I know, Ima." She turned her gaze to the blue sky, hating each moment she had been confined to her room. Even the simple chores requiring only the use of her hands had been banned from her. Since her mother and sister had duties to attend they often left Mira to her thoughts, which often drifted to Ari and his absence.

"Daughter, you must not draw into yourself."

She shook off the haze of loneliness creeping into her soul and looked at her mother as she passed between the fabric covering the entryway.

"You think of Ariel," Rubiel said. "Sh'mira, you should not hold out hope of his return." Her sister's eyes flitted to Mira's lap where her fingers were folded. "You are nothing but a farmer's daughter."

The words Rubiel left unsaid cut deep. Her sister believed Ariel was too good for her. "Ari does not consider such things, Ruby."

"Can you be certain?"

"As certain as I am that you sit washing my feet," Mira bit. But her confidence wavered like the shifting of sand. And although Ari had made no vows, there had been hope in his eyes when he departed. A hope branded upon her heart. However, he had left without a promised return. His lack of shalom shoved aside her hopes, cementing doubt.

"My apologies. It is not in your character to behave solemnly."

Mira crossed her arms over her chest, hoping to keep her heart from being ripped to shreds. If she accepted Ruby's words as truth, she would have to accept the increasing pain within her heart. She would have to accept that Ari's hopes had been dispelled by the reality of who he was.

"If he were coming back, he would have accepted Abba's offer."

Mira snapped her gaze to her sister. "Offer? What offer?"

"I do not wish to distress you further, Sh'mira, yet I can see it does you no good to remain idle. Perhaps if you understood the fullness—"

"The fullness of what?" Ari had entered their family under the guise of a bond servant. Had there been more to his deception?

"Abba gave Ariel all that was promised under the law when he freed him."

"This is not unusual."

"No, it is not, Sh'mira," Ruby agreed as she wrapped her foot in a clean cloth. "Yet, Ari did not take one kernel. He did not take one grape, nor a seed. He took nothing."

Mira smiled, even as she felt tears prick the corner of her eyes. "Ari is an honorable man. He would not take what he felt did not belong to him."

"It was his right by the law." Ruby tied the length of linen in a knot and sat back on her heels. She pressed her palms against her thighs and looked directly at Mira. "That is not all. I heard Abba say he offered you as Ari's bride."

Mira's breath caught in her throat as the *fullness* of Ruby's words slapped her in the face. Her gaze fell to the brightly woven mat surrounding her, reminding her of the veil Ari's mother had draped over her head, the very veil Ari had worn around his neck when he had returned her to her father's house. She bit down on her lip to keep it from quivering.

"Abba had contracts drawn the day before the attack upon our people, yet your Ari did not accept them. He did not even mention them before he left for Jerusalem."

Silent tears slid from the corners of her eyes.

"I will leave you to your grief, Sh'mira." Ruby rose to her feet. "On the morrow you will shore up your courage, and you will begin to pull your weight again. It is not fair to Ima."

Guilt at her selfishness piled on her like stones. If Ari had not accepted her father's offer it was akin to rejection. He did not want her for a wife, more pointedly he did not love her as she had loved him. Perhaps, Ruby had been right. Perhaps, Ari did look at her as nothing more than a farmer's daughter.

Chapter Thirty-Four

The yoke dug into her nape as she carried the empty water jars to the well. The slowness in her gait had nothing to do with the bandages wrapped around her healing feet. She had hoped the pain in her soul would ease with each passing day. But not even the antics of her young cousins brought her happiness.

Kneading dough in preparation for challah, a task, which had always brought her joy, left her with a hollowness that threatened to bury her in the depths of despair. It had been a simple household pleasure she'd hoped to perform for Ari. And now that too was gone.

The worst of it had been her lack of desire to play the lyre. Although it soothed her father, helping him find his rest at night, she couldn't do it. Not when she'd miss Ari's rich baritone singing along.

The pale stones of the well came into sight, and a small tear slipped from her eye. The last time she'd been here, it had been over spilled oil. It had been the beginning of her realization of who the real Ari was. The beginning of the end of their contact, even if it had meant nothing to him.

She lifted the yoke from her neck and laid it within the branches. The dark earthenware jars swung back and forth like pendulums, reminding her of the color of Ari's eyes. She slumped onto the stone bench. *Shore up your courage.* Ruby's words pounded in her thoughts, just as flashes of Ari bombarded her. Even now, her soul ached from the loss of the tender promises in his eyes.

Why had he lied? Yet, she knew he would never lie. He had not spoken vows. Had not signed the contracts. Had never said that he loved her. And she had never said she loved him either. Her stubborn pride had kept her from saying what was in her heart, and now she would never see him again.

The pounding of feet upon the pathway broke through her pity. She swiped the back of her hand across her eyes. Rising, she turned the wheel to draw up water.

"Mira, Mira, your father begs you to come quickly," one of her young cousins called, the urgency in his voice set her heart with fear. She turned, releasing the wheel. The bucket dropped into the darkened sheath.

"What is it, Yousef? Has something happened?"

The boy bent at the waist heaving for air. Mira approached him and knelt beside him. She placed her hand on his shoulder. "You must tell me, is all well?"

"Oh, all is well. It is wondrously so." He straightened, and took a few slow deep breaths. "We have visitors."

"Visitors?" she asked, peering into the boy's brown eyes. Surely, he had been mistaken. Other than their closest neighbors, which her cousin would have announced, visitors did not come to her father's house. The terrain, as magnificent as any, was too harsh.

"Oh, yes, Sh'mira. Goats. Lots of goats. And sheep. And even cattle."

"Animals? Our visitors are animals?" Mira teased. She rose to her full height and allowed him to take her hand. She had nearly forgotten about the earthenware jars until the warm desert air blew across them causing them to clank against their perch. She turned back to the well drawing Yousef along with her.

"Of course not. There are men, and women." He tilted his head and looked at her. "There are even girls," he said in a hushed voice.

"It that so?" She removed her fingers from his and brushed her hand over his mop of curls. "Come. Help me fill the jars with water, so that our guests may find sustenance from their journey."

Mira watched in amusement as he tried his hardest to pull up the bucket of water. "Here, allow me to help you."

She wrapped her fingers around the handle right beside his. Together they turned it. Yousef stood on his toes and peered over the edge of the well. "Careful. You do not want to be lost down there do you?"

He cocked his head and looked at her with curiosity. "Is it far?"

She laughed, even as it caused her pain, for it was a question Joash had once asked. "I do not know, for I have never fallen in," Mira said, giving the boy a wink.

They filled the jars and then Mira settled the yoke onto her shoulders. They began down the path to her father's house, her young companion rushed ahead in excitement.

If she were to believe Yousef an entire village descended upon them. Mira locked her knees, her feet refusing to move. Nervousness grasped ahold of her that several long releases of breath eased.

Dare she hope Ari had returned? Had not Yousef said goats, sheep, and cattle were among the visitors? She swallowed against the tears threatening to spill. Whoever their rare visitors were, Ari would not be found amongst them, of that she was sure.

With another deep breath and a swipe at her tears, she steadied herself. It mattered naught who they were, they deserved hospitality, and she had tarried long enough.

The farther she moved along the worn path the louder the baaing cries became. Intermixed among it all were voices calling out to the herd. She turned her ear for a familiar voice even as she knew it would not be there. In light of the recent attack on her family she hoped the visitors were not bent on mischief.

She strode up the hill and rounded the curve. Here she halted at the sight before her. The vineyard south of her home burst in bright greens, flourishing from the recent rains. But it was the vision surrounding the courtyard that left her in wonderment. There were not just a few sheep, there were many. Near a hundred, maybe more.

Her gaze trailed to the pen where their lone lambs had been housed and found it occupied by goats. Several oxen were tied outside the pen, to the posting fences. Men, twenty or so, milled about erecting a larger fence while others corralled the sheep with their staffs to keep them from wandering into the wilderness.

Something caught her attention as she glanced across the sea of activity. She shielded her eyes with her free hand and peered deeper into the group of women. Was Lydia among them?

Before she could ascertain the truth the woman turned away from her. Perhaps it was only her foolish heart longing for something that could never be. Why would Ari's family travel among livestock?

She dropped her hand, and straightening her shoulders walked home, her sore feet crunching pebbles as she went. Each rounded and jagged object pressed through the sole of her sandals. The cuts and scrapes on her feet rebelled with every step, especially now with her extra burden, yet it was no more painful than the chasm ripping her heart into two.

Everywhere she walked Ari had been at one time or another. Even here, he had oft taken the earthenware from her, carrying it for her. And as she gazed upon the men digging holes for the posts, she could not help but feel bereft, for that had been one of the many chores Ari had tended to when he lived among them.

Her memories prodded her to run from this place, to close her eyes and her heart to her father's house, for it was filled with dreams of Ari. However, she could not abandon her family with so many guests to tend.

Lord, grant me courage.

She neared the stone structure she called home. A man she did not know in blue and purple robes and a turban knelt before her. She looked upon him with curiosity. Then another man, as finely adorned, did the same. Even though she could not see his face, he, somehow, seemed familiar. As did the next and the next. She narrowed her eyes.

Who are these people? God, why do they honor me so?

And then the last knelt, his graying beard tucked against his chest. He tilted his chin and looked her full in the eye. His own were filled with merriment. The other men glanced at her as well and recognition dawned. The earthenware jars swayed as she stumbled.

"Hello, Sh'mira daughter of Caleb."

Warm desert air caught in her chest, expanding to uncomfortable proportions as she stared into Ishiah's eyes. What was Ari's father doing here? Her body trembled such as a fig leaf in a windstorm. Her heart thundered like that of a drum. Believing her senses played tricks upon her person she squeezed her eyes closed.

Someone relieved her of her burden, leaving her to drop her hand to her side only to find it grasped with the warmth of another.

She lifted her eyes.

*

Caleb had sent for her when they first arrived. Her slow pace had given Ari time to negotiate a bride price. His anxiousness had led to impatience, his impatience had led to worry when she had yet to show.

Of course he had not been pleased to discover Mira had been up moving about on her feet such as they were, for he had no doubt they remained raw. He had been ready to seek her when young Yousef ran down the hill.

He waited for her to appear. What seemed like long moments had passed. He held his breath. Waiting.

Now he looked deep into her amber eyes. Her tearstained cheeks told him that her days had passed much like his; in pure agony. He had wanted to curse his delay, yet there was a need to finalize the details of his former life.

When Jesse had failed to return to Jerusalem with their uncle, Ari had to know why. Feeling responsibility weigh heavy upon his shoulders, he left Mira to God and went in search of his brother whom he never found.

"Sh'mira," he whispered. Finally she moved, taking a deep breath of air.

"Is it really you?"

Halting the movement of his thumb over the back of her knuckles, he gave her a slight squeeze. Over the course of the past few days he had dreamed of this moment. He had memorized each of the words he would say. Now, however, all thought beyond pure joy failed him. Any words that may have been meant to pass his lips remained locked inside him.

She lifted her free hand and swiped away the tears. "I did not think you would return."

With a will of their own his eyes closed. He had feared insecurities would grip her. "You knew it here," he said, tapping his chest.

"Yes. I did, but then—then. . .my sister told me of the contract, and how. . ."

Aware of the pairs of eyes watching him, he pulled her into his arms and buried his face into her hair. He inhaled her cinnamon and honey scent. "There were things that I had to take care of."

She leaned back, peering into his soul. "This?" she asked, waving her hand indicating the livestock.

"And more." He stepped away from her, yet his eyes did not break contact. "I sinned against your father with my deception. It was necessary that I seek his forgiveness and then make my sacrifice."

Mira tilted her head, her brow furrowing. "Sheep are your way of restitution?"

"No."

"The goats?"

"No."

"The oxen?"

"No."

"Do you intend to take them to Manna?"

"No, Sh'mira."

She fisted her hands onto her hips and glared. "Then what, Ariel? Why have you brought them here?"

"It is my bride price."

Her brows lifted and then she shook her head. "Certainly, one sheep would have sufficed."

Reaching out, he drew his finger behind the cup of her ear, tucking a stray strand. "You, *ahavah*, my beloved, are worth all of my possessions."

"You gave all you had?"

Ari would have laughed if she had not looked truly appalled. The truth of it was he would have given all. However, wise words had kept him from doing so. As his father had advised, he would need some of his wealth to provide properly for his future family.

"No. Although, I would have if your father would have been reluctant to relinquish you."

He witnessed the hesitation in her eyes. He watched as her eyes pooled with tears. She closed them and bowed her head. His heart beat erratically within his chest, even as she took slow, deliberate breaths. Would she reject his intentions? He had been so very confident in her answer that he had brought his family and the documents.

Ari pulled the laundered veil from his neck and held it within his hands as if it were precious pottery. The delicate blue cloth shimmered in the breeze. "Sh'mira, if you will allow me to adorn you with this veil, it would be a sign of the covering of my love for you the rest of our days." He stepped forward and lifted it above her bowed head. Just as he was about to drape it over her, Mira held up her hand. She lifted her eyes and shook her head.

His heart stopped beating.

"Ari, you honor me." She closed her eyes momentarily. "We," she said, looking at someone beyond his shoulder, "cannot accept the bride price you offer, for I can never leave my family."

"I—"

"No! I have always known my duty is here. I have no brothers. My father has no sons to carry on our way of life. It is my duty to marry a man. . ."

"Daughter," Caleb said even as he stepped forward. "Your willingness to sacrifice yourself is admirable and I love you for it. However, I will not allow it. If your heart belongs to Ariel, then so be it."

"I will not abandon you, Abba. Nor will I abandon all of your hopes and dreams to live mine." Her eyes shifted to Ari's. "No matter how big they are."

Ari motioned to one of his kin. He waited until his cousin brought forth a small wooden table, and then he knelt before her. He reached into his girdle and pulled out a leather strap and an awl. With the objects, he raised his hand to her. "Then I will remain forever your bond servant, Sh'mira daughter of Caleb."

For a moment she only stared at him, and then she fell to her knees. "You would be willing to give up everything for me?"

"Yes. Mira, I love you with all of my soul. All of my being, if only you will take me as your husband."

"What of your family?"

"I have many brothers. My father has many sons." He smiled. "Certainly we can visit often."

"You are certain?"

"I have never been more certain of anything, ahavah." He pressed his lips to her brow. "Will you take me as your husband for eternity?"

"For eternity." She wrapped her arms around his neck.

"For eternity."

Don't miss A Warrior's Heart. Read the first chapter below.

Chapter One

Judah
Circa 835 BC

The sound of horses' hooves thundered into camp. Abigail's pulse hammered in her chest at the commotion outside her tent. She tucked her hands into her sleeves and paced. Had the warrior priests who had attacked the palace and killed her mother found them?

"What is happening, Bilhah?"

Her cousin sat on a pile of furs, her knees drawn to her chest. Black kohl trailed down her cheeks. Abigail knelt in front of her and tried to imitate the strength she had seen her mother exude. "Bilhah, now is not the time for weakness. What if we must make haste?"

Soulless amber eyes stared at her. "There will be no mercy."

A chorused bellow startled Abigail, sending a tremor racing through her blood, until she realized what she'd heard had been a cheer of victory among her men. Uncertain of her new role as future queen, she forced a smile and rose. "Of course, there will be none. Jehoiada and the usurpers will pay for killing my mother." She inhaled a shaky breath. "And my brothers all those years ago."

Bilhah's brow furrowed as if she was confused. Many such looks had tainted her cousin's beautiful face since their flight from the palace and Jerusalem. She tilted her head and scanned Abigail from head to toe. "You misunderstand me, Abigail. The God of the priests, the God of our forefathers Abraham, Isaac and Jacob, will not grant us mercy, not if we continue in our rebellion."

The hot desert wind rippled the canvas around them. Gooseflesh rose on Abigail's arms and she hugged herself to ward off the omen. She'd heard the servants speak of a god greater than the ones her mother had worshipped, but she'd yet to see him with her own eyes, as she'd seen the wooden and bronze statues in the courtyard outside the palace. "You've had a great shock, Bilhah. You do not know what you speak."

"If they did not spare your mother, the Queen of Judah, they will not spare us, Abigail." Bilhah's shoulders sagged as she pressed her face into her hands. Abigail swallowed her fear as the memory of the frantic cries of the servants assaulted her. It was the one time she had willingly crawled into the wooden chest in order to hide from the warrior priests.

It was no wonder the confident, alluring woman who prowled the palace at will crumpled into another round of sobs. The change in her cousin's behavior since the priests and temple guards had stormed the palace was disconcerting. Abigail was having a difficult time being cast from her home, too. However, if she hadn't been forced to abide by Captain Suph's demands, Abigail thought she might actually enjoy her freedom from the palace.

A dark shadow passed outside their tent and then pressed against the fabric. "Princess," Micah called from outside. "The captain requests your presence."

As if her nerves weren't already taut, now the captain requested her presence. He'd not been kind since their flight from Jerusalem and he'd always made her feel less than human, as if she were a stray dog begging for scraps. How could she make him understand she was his rightful queen, would be his queen once her throne was restored in Jerusalem, and as such deserved his respect?

Abigail dried her palms and pulled back the flap. "In a moment, Micah."

The young servant nodded and crossed his arms over his linen tunic; although no more than a child, he'd been one of her only constant companions for the past few years. One of the only people her mother had allowed to attend her. Abigail faced her cousin. "Once you've rested and I've taken my position as Queen of Judah, all will be well. You'll see." She took two steps, bent at the waist and started to press her lips against Bilhah's smooth head before halting. If she was to go on as her mother had, if she was to succeed as Queen of Judah, such comforting gestures would no longer be allowed. "Rest, while I see what Suph requires of me. And dry your eyes, Bilhah. Our people need you. You cannot perform in your current state."

She shook out her tunic and brushed a hand over the dust-infested tunic. With a trembling hand, she patted down her hair before slipping between the folds of her tent. She scanned the desert encampment, pleased that many of her mother's subjects had followed their exodus during the priests' attempt to take over Jerusalem. Soon, with Suph's help, she'd see them returned to their beloved city, where she would reward their faithfulness with a banquet to rival her great ancestor King Solomon. Of course, she'd have to gain Bilhah's help since she'd no idea how kings and queens dined.

"Come, Micah, let us see what Suph wants, shall we?" She smiled at the boy. His black orbs sparkled before his lashes dipped against his tanned cheekbones. She followed behind him, twisting and turning through the maze of tents that had been hastily erected after their flight from Jerusalem. The people lowered their heads as she passed as if she were already queen. Their actions humbled her. And disheartened her. Until a few days ago many knew not of her existence. Those who did had slighted her, not even treating her with the acknowledgment a servant receives.

Now they looked to her to lead them, to give them back Jerusalem, a task that seemed near impossible given she'd rarely been allowed outside her chambers.

Micah halted and Abigail stumbled into his back because she'd been preoccupied with how she was to lead these people as those who had done so before her.

Captain Suph turned toward her, the lines around his mouth firmed. His eyes remained cold, filled with hatred. She stopped herself from taking a step back, from fleeing to her tent, and allowed a smile to curve her lips. She would show him courage, lest he find her weak and incapable of ruling Judah.

"I have a gift for you, Abigail."

She tilted her chin and waited. Suph stepped aside, revealing a rather muscular man in nothing but a loincloth and a gem the color of amber hanging from a leather cord around his neck. She drew in a shallow breath and forced calm into her limbs. Her practiced reserve kept her from blushing at the man's near nakedness, kept her from flinching at the grotesque swelling of his face and the open cuts decorating the rest of his body. She knew her mother had been cruel at times, but had she been this vicious? Would the captain expect the same from her? Abigail hoped not.

"This is the brother of Ari, former Commander of the Temple Guard. This man's brother is responsible for placing that imposter on the throne, and I've no doubt our prisoner took part in the rebellion as well. He'll fetch a handsome price. Perhaps even the return of your throne, Abigail."

She stepped forward and bent closer. The scent of his wounds hung in the air. The whites of his eyes glowed from the bloodied mess of his face. "Is this true?"

The man's nostrils flared. His jaw clamped tight. Suph yanked his sword from his sheath and swung wide.

Anger surged through her blood, thundered in her heart. How dare the captain threaten a man who couldn't even stand on his own? "Enough."

Spears of fire sparked in Suph's gaze. "You cannot think—"

"You will not dictate the thoughts of your future queen. Is that understood?"

Suph's chest expanded as he squinted his eyes to mere slits. The lines creasing the corners of his eyes twitched in tandem with the tick of his jaw. "Yes, Your Majesty."

"Good. Now, clean his wounds. We cannot negotiate using a dead man."

She twisted on the balls of her feet. Holding her shoulders straight and head high like she'd seen her mother do, she walked toward her tent. She ducked inside, fell to her knees and retched into an earthen jug. A gentle hand smoothed back her hair. Bilhah knelt beside her.

"What is it, child?" She pressed a cup into her hand.

Abigail swiped the back of her hand over her mouth and gave a nervous laugh. "You call me 'child,' yet we are the same age, you and I."

Bilhah scooted back to the furs and sank against a mound of decorated pillows, her eyes downcast. "We are. Come, what has upset you?"

Abigail curled beside her. "Was my mother so cruel?"

Sadly, Abigail had witnessed a few floggings, and from the way the servants spoke, her mother took pleasure in the beatings. Abigail had also heard them speak of others losing their heads. A part of Abigail had believed it was only to cause her fear so that perhaps she'd behave.

Bilhah's fingers stopped toying with the furs. "You've been sheltered."

Abigail sat up and looked into Bilhah's eyes. "You did not answer my question."

"I do not wish to speak ill of the dead, even your mother."

Abigail laid her palm against Bilhah's cheek. "I've always known she was cruel to you." She ran her hand over Bilhah's shiny head. "Forcing you to serve her gods when you should have married well."

Bilhah shook her head. "I was your father's niece—with my father dead I was nothing more than a servant. At the time it seemed a high honor. Or so your mother convinced me."

Abigail laid her head against Bilhah's chest. "Thanks to Jehoiada we are all that's left. I would see him pay."

Her words sounded hollow as the image of the bloodied prisoner invaded her mind. Her stomach churned. If treating a man like a mangy dog was what it would take, she did not know if she'd have it in her.

"Perhaps, not all has been as it seems, Abigail."

She ruminated on that for a few moments. She was about to ask Bilhah what she meant, but the rhythm of her heartbeat against Abigail's ear slowed. Rising up on her elbow, Abigail gazed at her cousin, so young yet hardened by the life chosen for her. She sat up and tucked her knees beneath her chin.

Had she truly been sheltered, or had she been forgotten? Bilhah was not the only one who'd experienced her mother's cruelty. Although she would miss her mother, Abigail would not miss the viperous tongue reminding her she was weak like her father and not the beauty her mother had hoped for. Her arms were too long, her hips too thin. She was lanky and awkward. With her limp hair, her lack of golden hues, her green eyes, a curse from the gods....she hadn't needed to see the disgust in her mother's eyes to know her she was a disappointment. Aye, she may miss her mother a little, but she would not miss the way she flogged the servants for their inability to make Abigail presentable.

A breeze blew from beneath the tent, carrying with it Suph's raised voice. Abigail rubbed her arms and rose. She pulled back the flap and peered at the group of men surrounding the prisoner. They had moved the man near the center of camp. To do her bidding and cleanse his wounds, she supposed. She had been unable to tell what sort of man he was. A warrior, if his sculpted chest and arms were any indication. He was taller than the captain, even slouched beneath the burden of the yoke around his neck. The captain tossed water into the man's face, causing him to straighten somewhat. The captain, a handsome man when he genuinely smiled, paled in comparison even with the cuts and bruises marring the prisoner's body. Especially knowing the man had been cruelly treated by Suph.

It had been a rare moment when she stood up to Suph. She'd never spoken with such boldness in her life, but something about the beaten man called to her sense of compassion. She would not allow Suph to kill him.

And how was she to stop him? She glanced down and dug the toe of her sandal into the ground. Her mother's beauty had commanded respect when she walked into a room. People near fell at her feet and begged to do her bidding, especially Suph. And though he'd shown her some tolerance since their flight from the palace, Abigail was certain it was a ruse. He held no great affection for her.

She was not so naive to believe she'd rule Suph, with or without great beauty, which meant she'd have to take care around him lest she found herself in a worse position than being locked in her chambers.

~

Cold water splashed against Jesse's face. His muscles refused to move away from the offensive attack. His arms were wrapped over a yoke, bound with leather straps. It seemed, by the grace of God, his captors intended to keep him alive. The least he could do was open his eyes and face the traitors.

His uncle Elam hovered before him. "Aye, nephew, you would do well to end your torment and join the captain's pursuit to recapture the throne."

"I am not a coward, Uncle. Nor will I betray God as you have done." Jesse still had difficulty believing his uncle had betrayed his family. If he'd not witnessed his uncle's insanity he would not have believed it.

Elam let out a low, harsh laugh. "You cannot think that the child you and your brother helped Jehoiada place on the throne is the rightful heir to the throne?"

"How can you believe otherwise, Uncle?" There were no doubts in Jesse's mind. Joash was the son of Ahaziah, descendant of King David. Grandchild to the deceased wicked Queen Athaliah. The Queen, in a jealous rage, had killed all her husband's descendants seven years before. All except the infant Joash, who had been rescued by his aunt.

"It is like Jehoiada to deceive the people to gain their cooperation. He's hungry for power."

Jesse drew in a breath and clenched his teeth against the pain throbbing in his head. "Is that what you believe? Jehoiada is a man of God, chosen to be God's high priest to intercede on behalf of God's people. He does not need to deceive the people, Uncle. He has the approval of God, unlike you and that queen you were loyal to."

A low growl emanated from his right. The captain shoved Elam aside and pressed the tip of the dagger beneath Jesse's chin. Eyes, red from too much wine and hatred, glared at him. "It is with great providence our future queen has a soft heart, else I'd leave little of you for the birds."

Queen?

Certainly the young woman with the pointy chin and high forehead wasn't a product of Athaliah. Although pretty with her waist-length chestnut hair and her strange green eyes, she wasn't the stunning beauty her mother had been; nor did she seem to carry the same abhorrent character. Her pale complexion at the sight of him said as much. No, the guard toyed with him. But if Suph thought to play games with the people of Judah, at least he could have chosen a more prominent woman, not one frightened of her own shadow.

Jesse straightened his shoulders, removing his flesh from the man's blade. "I killed your queen. And I'll kill her too, if need be."

The guard's fist slammed into Jesse's jaw. A flash of white light exploded in his head a moment before his feet were swept from beneath him. He landed on his back. Air stole from his lungs as the wooden yoke jammed against his shoulders.

The sun captured and glinted off the dagger held above his attacker's head. The captain's chest heaved with each breath. He meant to kill him.

Just as well. Although he did not relish passing from this earth, he hated being a pawn even more. With his eyes set on the captain, Jesse arched his neck. "Go on."

The captain inhaled as his blade rose higher.

"Enough!"

Jesse pressed his lips together at the sound of his uncle's voice. The old man's sanity returned at the oddest times. If Elam hadn't kidnapped Mira, Jesse's brother's betrothed, Jesse wouldn't have been taking him back to Jerusalem to face the elders, and he certainly wouldn't be facing death at the hands of a coward. Who killed a man when he was half-beaten and bound?

"Killing him will not achieve our goal, Suph."

The captain rolled his shoulders, leaned over Jesse and cut the leather strap holding the carbuncle from his neck before sheathing his dagger. "Stretch him out near the altar, but keep him alive."

Suph kicked Jesse before stalking away, his helmet tucked beneath his arm and Jesse's tribal identity loose in his fingers. Jesse narrowed his eyes. When he was free from his bindings, he wouldn't show such mercy. When he was done with the traitor, the captain would beg for the sun's hottest kiss.

Elam knelt beside him and smoothed a cool cloth to Jesse's lips. "You should not provoke his anger."

Jesse narrowed his eyes. "You should have let him kill me."

A nervous laugh rumbled through Elam's chest, trembling his fingers. "Your father would have my head if anything happened to you."

"Your loyalties confuse me, Uncle."

Elam tilted his head, his brows furrowed. "I've always been loyal to my family. Have done what I thought best."

"And God?"

"Has abandoned us in our greatest time of need." Elam braced his arms beneath Jesse's shoulders and helped him to sit. "We must fend for ourselves, stand with those who are strong and bound to rule like Suph's pawn, Queen Athaliah's disgraceful daughter. Whether we agree with their beliefs or not."

Elam motioned for two soldiers to approach. "Stretch him between the postings erected, and then have a servant clean his wounds and feed him. My nephew needs his strength for what he is about to endure."

The soldiers lifted Jesse to his feet. He looked at his uncle. "I do not know how, or when, but God will reign. He did not restore Joash to the throne only to fail, of that I have no doubt."

They began to move forward, but Elam's hand held him still. He leaned close and whispered, "You've great potential, nephew. You are strong and with a bit of discipline you could be self-controlled. If you would only see to reason you could become what your brother Ari rejected. You'd make a much better captain of the guard than Suph. A much better husband to Judah's rightful queen. If you would only choose, I could make it happen. You could be King of Judah and I the high priest."

An image of unique green eyes, the color of olive leaves, flickered through his mind.

"So be it, Uncle, but I would not serve a god imagined in the mind of a fallible man. And you can be sure I would never marry a spawn of Athaliah."

Get it here

* * * * *

Dear Reader,
I hope you enjoyed reading Ari and Mira's story as much as I did writing it. I'm sure many of you are wondering about this fictional story. Let me start by saying that the only real people are Athaliah, Joash, Jehoiada and Jehosheba. All other characters are fictional.

If you are familiar with the Bible story about King Joash you're probably scratching your head. Believe me, it's not my intention to go against any passages of the Bible. My prayer, above all, is that you'll see the message of Ari and Sh'mira's story: God's love for us, even when we don't do things exactly right. His grace supersedes law. Always! As Jesus says in Matthew 5:17, "Think not that I am come to destroy the law, or the prophets: I am not come to destroy, but to fulfill."

Books by Christina Rich

Historical
Love at Twenty Paces (A Coaly Creek Novel)
Love in the Midst of Scandal (A Coaly Creek Novella)
Quinn McCall Gets His Bride
Dear Author (A Hopper Falls Novella)
Thread of Hope (A Hopper Falls Novella)
The Lady's Companion and the Detective
Saving Miss Ryan from the Bootleggers

Steampunk
An Unlikely Governess (A Harris-Spotchnet School of the Peculiar Kind)

Contemporary
Rekindling the Flame
Thank God for My Country Boy
Exposing Love
Perfectly Posed for Love
Dance with Me Where the Jellyfish Glow

www.ingramcontent.com/pod-product-compliance
Lightning Source LLC
LaVergne TN
LVHW012014060526
838201LV00061B/4299